BESTS

DIANA
PALMER

KASEY MICHAELS
CATHERINE MANN

More Than Words:
STORIES OF HOPE

Five bestselling authors.
Five real-life heroines.

**Don't miss a brand-new collection
of stories inspired by women who
have made a difference in their communities.**

NEW YORK TIMES AND USA TODAY BESTSELLING AUTHOR

JOAN JOHNSTON

ROBYN CARR
CHRISTINA SKYE
ROCHELLE ALERS
MAUREEN CHILD

Original stories inspired by real women
who've made a difference

MORE THAN WORDS
Volume 6

Coming soon!

Visit
www.HarlequinMoreThanWords.com
to find out more or to nominate
a real-life heroine
in your community.

ISBN-13:978-0-373-83670-3

50699

EAN

PHMTW670IFC

Dear Reader,

Within these pages you will find three remarkable tales of hope. The stories, written by some of Harlequin's most popular authors, are fiction, but the women who inspired them are real. They are women who have dedicated their lives to helping others, and all are recipients of a Harlequin More Than Words award.

The Harlequin More Than Words program, established in 2004, awards women for their extraordinary commitment to their communities and makes a $10,000 donation to each woman's chosen charity. In addition, some of Harlequin's most celebrated authors donate their time and creativity to writing fictional novellas inspired by the lives and work of our award recipients. The collected stories are published, with proceeds reinvested in the Harlequin More Than Words program.

Along with Diana Palmer, Kasey Michaels and Catherine Mann, I invite you to meet the Harlequin More Than Words award recipients highlighted in these pages. We hope their stories will inspire you to participate in charitable activities in your community, or perhaps even with the charities you read about here. In fact, just by purchasing this book, you are making a difference in the lives of many.

To learn more about the Harlequin More Than Words program or to nominate a woman you know for this very special award, please visit www.HarlequinMoreThanWords.com.

Sincerely,

Donna Hayes
Publisher and CEO
Harlequin Enterprises Ltd.

DIANA PALMER

KASEY MICHAELS
CATHERINE MANN

More Than Words:
STORIES OF HOPE

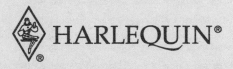

HARLEQUIN®

TORONTO • NEW YORK • LONDON
AMSTERDAM • PARIS • SYDNEY • HAMBURG
STOCKHOLM • ATHENS • TOKYO • MILAN • MADRID
PRAGUE • WARSAW • BUDAPEST • AUCKLAND

Recycling programs
for this product may
not exist in your area.

ISBN-13: 978-0-373-83670-3

MORE THAN WORDS: STORIES OF HOPE

Copyright © 2010 by Harlequin Books S.A.

Diana Palmer is acknowledged as the author of *The Greatest Gift*.
Kasey Michaels is acknowledged as the author of *Here Come the Heroes*.
Catherine Mann is acknowledged as the author of *Touched by Love*.

www.eHarlequin.com

Printed in U.S.A.

CONTENTS

SUE COBLEY

⊶ CHEFS TO THE RESCUE ⊶

Most people, if they think about it at all, just shake their heads at the food wasted in restaurants and grocery stores. Thirteen years ago, Sue Cobley decided to do something about it. That would be remarkable enough in itself, but Sue was no well-heeled suburbanite or high-placed executive with a mission statement and plenty of backing. In 1996, just divorced from an abusive husband, evicted from their rented property and living in a borrowed car with her five children, Sue embarked on a course of action that would literally move mountains of food—and change her community of Boise, Idaho.

To anyone else, just keeping body and soul—and the family—together would be challenge enough. But despite her own daily struggle for survival, Sue made what would turn out to be a life-changing decision: to be a link between surplus food and the many people who needed it. She didn't have to know the statistic—over 35 million Americans, 12.6 million of them children, living with hunger or on the edge of it, according to U.S. Department of Agriculture estimates, and a staggering 96 billion pounds of food wasted each year in the United States—to be aware that there were people going hungry in her own community. She began calling local grocery stores and restaurants for donations of surplus food to distribute to shelters and needy families. The response was encouraging. "Restaurants hate to throw away food they've prepared," Sue says. "They were happy to be able to help." From this humble yet bold beginning, Chefs to the Rescue was born, though it didn't yet have a name.

It started as a family project, one that Sue now sees as key in shaping her family's future. "I didn't want our experience to hurt my kids for the rest of their lives," she says. When the idea for redistributing food came to her, "it was like it was meant to be—helping other people empowered the kids. They have come out of the experience with a positive outlook, and I hope that when they have to go through hard times, they'll be able to draw on that."

Maintaining a routine was important in keeping the family together through these hard times. The two eldest children, then twelve and thirteen, were in school during the day; the other three, the youngest a baby, accompanied Sue when she cleaned houses, her only means of support. The older children elped with the younger ones, babysitting, reading to them and ssisting with homework, and all of them did chores. "They're wesome kids," Sue says.

Most nights the family stayed in motels when they could fford it, and Sue did her best to make it seem like camping ut, an adventure. Cole and Chase, then three and five, loved eing able to use the swimming pool, but for Sue, frightened nd at times on the edge of despair, keeping up a cheerful acade required all her resourcefulness. Sometimes after she as sure the children were asleep, she would cry, and she remembers all too clearly sitting in a park one day and coming o the realization that she might have to turn them over to velfare. "But we had a family meeting about it," she says, "and ney voted to stay together." During the two years it took to ave enough money to rent a house, they continued to deliver ood donations to soup kitchens, homeless centers and shelters. 'm so glad we were busy," Sue says. "It took our minds off our tuation."

What motivates such generosity of spirit? Sue's own partic-lar inspiration was her grandmother, the first female officer in ne Boise prison—dubbed "Feeder" by Sue's brother because of er habit of generously sharing food, even though she had little aoney. She also taught female prisoners how to sew. It was only ter, however, that Sue became fully aware of her grand-nother's influence. Though she'd studied social work in college,

Sue knew nothing about homelessness and says she probabl
shared most people's attitude of indifference. Her personal ex
perience taught her what it meant to be homeless, hungry an
abused, and during her time with Chefs to the Rescue and
statewide food bank, she says, "Every day I learned somethin
from somebody else. I met people who were priceless."

For more information about your local or statewide foo
bank, visit www.feedingamerica.org or write to Feedin
America, 35 East Wacker Drive, Suite 2000, Chicago, IL 60601

DIANA PALMER
~The Greatest Gift~

ᴐ— DIANA PALMER —ᴐ

A *New York Times* bestselling author of more than 100 novels, Diana Palmer is renowned as one of North America's top 10 romance writers. When she published her first novel in 1979, fans immediately fell in love with her sensual, charming romances. A die-hard romantic who married her husband five days after they met, Diana says that she wrote her first book at age 13—and has been hooked ever since.

Palmer lives in northeast Georgia with her husband, James Kyle, and a menagerie of animals that includes four dogs, four cats, assorted exotic lizards and an emu named George.

CHAPTER
ONE

The car lights passing by the side road kept Mary Crandall awake. She glanced into the backseat where her son, Bob, and her daughter, Ann, were finally asleep. Sandwiched between them, the toddler, John, was sound asleep in his little car seat. Mary pushed back a strand of dark hair and glanced worriedly out the window. She'd never in her life slept in a car. But she and her children had just been evicted from their rental home, by a worried young policewoman with a legal eviction notice. She hadn't wanted to enforce the order but had no choice since Mary hadn't paid the rent in full. The rent had gone up and Mary could no longer afford the monthly payments.

It was Mary who'd comforted her, assuring her that she and the children would manage somehow. The order hadn't mentioned the automobile, although Mary was sure that it would be taken, too. The thing was, it hadn't been taken today. By tomorrow, perhaps, the shock would wear off and she could function again. She was resourceful, and not afraid of hard work. She'd manage.

The fear of the unknown was the worst. But she knew that she and the children would be all right. They had to be! If only she didn't have to take the risk of having them in a parked car with her in the middle of the night. Like any big city, Phoenix was dangerous at night.

She didn't dare go to sleep. The car doors didn't even lock....

Just as she was worrying about that, car lights suddenly flashed in the rearview mirror. Blue lights. She groaned. It was a police car. Now they were in for it. What did they do to a woman for sleeping in a car with her kids? Was it against the law?

Mary had a sad picture of herself in mind as the police car stopped. She hadn't combed her dark, thick hair all day. There were circles under her big, light blue eyes. Her slender figure was all too thin and her jeans and cotton shirt were hopelessly wrinkled. She wasn't going to make a good impression.

She rolled the window down as a uniformed officer walked up to the driver's window with a pad in one hand, and the other hand on the butt of his service revolver. Mary swallowed. Hard.

The officer leaned down. He was clean-shaven, neat in appearance. "May I see your license and registration, please?" he asked politely.

With a pained sigh, she produced them from her tattered purse and handed them to him. "I guess you're going to arrest us," she said miserably as she turned on the inside lights.

He directed his gaze to the backseat, where Bob, Ann and John were still asleep, then looked back at Mary. He glanced at her license and registration and passed them back to her. "You can't sleep in a car," he said.

She smiled sadly. "Then it's on the ground, I'm afraid. We were just evicted from our home." Without knowing why, she added, "The divorce was final today and he left us high and dry. To add insult to injury, he wants the car for himself, but he can't find it tonight."

His face didn't betray anything, but she sensed anger in him. "I won't ask why the children have to be punished along with you," he replied. "I've been at this job for twenty years. There isn't much I haven't seen."

"I imagine so. Well, do we go in handcuffs…?"

"Don't be absurd. There's a shelter near here, a very well-run one. I know the lady who manages it. She'll give you a place to sleep and help you find the right resources to solve your situation."

Tears sprung to her light eyes. She couldn't believe he was willing to help them!

"Now, don't cry," he ground out. "If you cry, I'll cry, and just imagine how it will look to my superiors if it gets around? They'll call me a sissy!"

That amused her. She laughed, lighting up her thin face.

"That's better," he said, liking the way she looked when she smiled. "Okay. You follow me, and we'll get you situated."

"Yes, sir."

"Hey, I'm not that old," he murmured dryly. "Come on. Drive safely. I'll go slow."

She gave him a grateful smile. "Thanks. I mean it. I was scared to death to stay here, but I had no place I could go except to a friend, and she lives just two doors down from my ex-husband...."

"No need even to explain. Let's go."

He led her through downtown Phoenix to an old warehouse that had been converted into a homeless shelter.

She parked the car in the large parking lot and picked up the baby carrier, motioning to Bob and Ann to get out, too.

"Dad will probably have the police looking for the car by now," Bob said sadly.

"It doesn't matter," Mary said. "We'll manage, honey."

The police officer was out of his own car, having given his

location on the radio. He joined them at the entrance to the shelter, grimacing.

"I just got a call about the car…" he began.

"I told you Dad would be looking for it," Bob said on a sigh.

"It's all right," Mary told him. She forced a smile. "I can borrow one from one of the ladies I work for. She's offered before."

"She must have a big heart," the policeman mused.

She smiled. "She has that. I keep house for several rich ladies. She's very kind."

The policeman held the door open for them as they filed reluctantly into the entrance. As she passed, she noticed that his name tag read Matt Clark. Odd, she thought, they had the same initials, and then she chided herself for thinking such a stupid thing when she was at the end of her rope.

Many people were sitting around talking. Some were sleeping on cots, even on the floor, in the huge space. There were old tables and chairs that didn't match. There was a long table with a coffee urn and bags of paper plates and cups, where meals were apparently served. It was meant for a largely transient clientele. But the place felt welcoming, just the same. The big clock on the wall read 10:00 p.m. It wasn't nearly as late as she'd thought.

"Is Bev around?" the policeman asked a woman nearby.

"Yes. She's working in the office. I'll get her," she added, smiling warmly at Mary.

"She's nice people," the policeman said with a smile. "It's going to be all right."

A couple of minutes later, a tall, dignified woman in her forties came out of the office. She recognized the police officer and grinned. "Hi, Matt! What brings you here at this hour?"

"I brought you some more clients," he said easily. "They don't have anyplace to go tonight. Got room?"

"Always," the woman said, turning to smile at Mary and her kids. She was tall and her dark hair was sprinkled with gray. She was wearing jeans and a red sweater, and she looked honest and kind. "I'm Bev Tanner," she said, holding out her hand to shake Mary's. "I manage the homeless shelter."

"I'm Mary Crandall," she replied, noting the compassionate police officer's intent scrutiny. "These are my children. Bob's the oldest, he's in junior high, Ann is in her last year of grammar school, and John's just eighteen months."

"I'm very happy to have you here," Bev said. "And you're welcome to stay as long as you need to."

Mary's lips pressed together hard as she struggled not to cry. The events of the day were beginning to catch up with her.

"What you need is a good night's sleep," Bev said at once. "Come with me and I'll get you settled."

Mary turned to Officer Clark. "Thanks a million," she managed to say, trying to smile.

He shrugged. "All in a night's work." He hesitated. "Maybe I'll see you around."

She did smile, then. "Maybe you will."

Phoenix was an enormous city. It wasn't likely. But they continued smiling at each other as he waved to Bev and went out the door.

An hour later, Mary and the children were comfortably situated with borrowed blankets. She realized belatedly that she hadn't thought to take one single piece of clothing or even her spare cosmetics from the house. There had hardly been time to absorb the shock and surprise of being evicted.

Mary looked around, dazed. The homeless shelter was just a little frightening. She'd never been inside one before. Like many people, she'd passed them in her travels around Phoenix, but never paid them much attention. The people who frequented them had been only shadows to her, illusions she remembered from occasional stories on television around the holiday season. Helping the homeless was always a good story, during that season when people tried to behave better. Contributions were asked and acknowledged from sympathetic contributors. Then, like the tinsel and holly and wreaths, the homeless were put aside until the next holiday season.

But Mary was unable to put it aside. She had just sustained

a shock as her divorce became final. She and her three children were suddenly without a home, without clothes, furniture, anything except a small amount of money tucked away in Mary's tattered purse.

She was sure that when they woke up in the morning, the car would be gone, too. The policeman, Matt Clark, had already mentioned that there was a lookout for the car. She hoped she wouldn't be accused of stealing it. She'd made all the payments, but it was in her ex-husband's name, like all their assets and everything else. That hadn't been wise. However, she'd never expected to find herself in such a situation.

She'd told Bev that they were only going to be here for one night. She had a little money in her purse, enough to pay rent at a cheap motel for a week. Somehow she'd manage after that. She just wasn't sure how. She hardly slept. Early the next morning, she went to the serving table to pour herself a cup of coffee. The manager, Bev, was doing the same.

"It's okay," the manager told her gently. "There are a lot of nice people who ended up here. We've got a mother and child who came just two days before you did," she indicated a dark young woman with a nursing baby and a terrified look. "Her name's Meg. Her husband ran off with her best friend and took all their money. And that sweet old man over there—" she nodded toward a ragged old fellow "—had his house sold out from under him by a nephew he trusted. The boy cashed in everything and took off. Mr. Harlowe was left all on his own with nothing but the clothes on his back."

"No matter how bad off people are, there's always someone worse, isn't there?" Mary asked quietly.

"Always. But you see miracles here, every day. And you're welcome to stay as long as you need to."

Mary swallowed hard. "Thanks," she said huskily. "We'll find a place tomorrow. I may not have much money or property, but I've got plenty of friends."

Bev smiled. "I'd say you know what's most important in life." She followed Mary's quick glance toward her children.

With the morning came hope. They'd had breakfast and Mary was working on her second cup of coffee, trying to decide how to proceed. Mary watched her brood mingling with other children at a long table against the wall, sharing their school paper and pencils, because they'd had the foresight to grab their backpacks on the way out, smiling happily. She never ceased to be amazed at the ease with which they accepted the most extreme situations. Their father's addiction had terrorized them all from time to time, but they were still able to smile and take it in stride, even that last night when their very lives had been in danger.

One of the policemen who came to help them the last time there had been an incident at home, an older man with kind eyes, had taken them aside and tried to explain that the violence they saw was the drugs, not the man they'd once known. But that didn't help a lot. There had been too many episodes, too much tragedy. Mary's dreams of marriage and motherhood had turned to nightmares.

"You're Mary, right?" one of the shelter workers asked with a smile.

"Uh, yes," Mary said uneasily, pushing back her dark hair, uncomfortably aware that it needed washing. There hadn't been time in the rush to get out of the house.

"Those your kids?" the woman added, nodding toward the table.

"All three," Mary agreed, watching with pride as Bob held the toddler on his lap while he explained basic math to a younger boy.

"Your son already has a way with kids, doesn't he?" the worker asked. "I'll bet he's a smart boy."

"He is," Mary agreed, noting that Bob's glasses had the nosepiece taped again, and they would need replacing. She grimaced, thinking of the cost. She wouldn't be able to afford even the most basic things now, like dentist visits and glasses. She didn't even have health insurance because her husband had dropped Mary and the kids from his policy once the divorce was final. She'd have to try to get into a group policy, but it would be hard, because she was a freelance housekeeper who worked for several clients.

The worker recognized panic when she saw it. She touched Mary's arm gently. "Listen," she said, "there was a bank vice president here a month ago. At Christmas, we had a whole family from the high bend," she added, mentioning the most exclusive section of town. "They all looked as shell-shocked as you do right now. It's the way the world is today. You can lose everything with a job. Nobody will look down on you here because you're having a bit of bad luck."

Mary bit her lower lip and tried to stem tears. "I'm just a little off balance right now," she told the woman, forcing a smile. "It was so sudden. My husband and I just got divorced. I thought he might help us a little. He took away the only car I had and we were evicted from the house."

The woman's dark eyes were sympathetic. "Everybody here's got a story, honey," she said softly. "They'll all break your heart. Come on. One thing at a time. One step at a time. You'll get through it."

Mary hesitated and grasped the other woman's hand. "Thanks," she said, trying to put everything she felt, especially the gratitude, into a single word.

The worker smiled again. "People give thanks for their blessings, and they don't usually think about the one they take most for granted."

"What?"

"A warm, dry, safe place to sleep at night."

Mary blinked. "I see what you mean," she said after a minute.

The woman nodded, leading her through the other victims of brutal homes, overindulgence, bad luck and health problems that had brought them all to this safe refuge.

John curled up next to Mary while she sat at the long table with Bob and Ann to talk.

"Why can't we go back home and pack?" Ann asked, her blue eyes, so like her mother's, wide with misery. "All my clothes are still there."

"No, they aren't," Bob replied quietly, pushing his glasses up over his dark eyes. "Dad threw everything in the trash and called the men to pick it up before we were evicted. There's nothing left."

"Bob!" Mary groaned. She hadn't wanted Ann to know what her ex had done in his last drunken rage.

Tears streamed down Ann's face, but she brushed them away when she saw the misery on her mother's face. She put her arms around Mary's neck. "Don't cry, Mama," she said softly. "We're going to be all right. We'll get new clothes."

"There's no money," Mary choked.

"I'll get a job after school and help," Bob said stoutly.

The courage of her children gave Mary strength. She wiped away the tears. "That's so sweet! But you can't work, honey, you're too young," Mary said, smiling at him. "You need to get an education. But thank you, Bob."

"You can't take care of all of us," Bob said worriedly. "Maybe we could go in foster care like my friend Dan—"

"No," Mary cut him off, hugging him to soften the harsh word. "Listen, we're a family. We stick together, no matter what. We'll manage. Hear me? We'll manage. God won't desert us, even if the whole world does."

He looked up at her with renewed determination. "Right."

"Yes, we'll stick together," Ann said. "I'm sorry I was selfish." She looked around at the other occupants of the shelter. "Nobody else here is bawling, and a lot of them look worse off than us."

"I was thinking the same thing," Mary confided, trying not to let them all see how frightened she really was.

She left them near Bev, who promised to keep an eye on them while she went to make phone calls.

Fourteen years ago, she'd had such wonderful visions of her future life. She wanted children so badly. She'd loved her husband dearly. And until he got mixed up with the crowd down at the local bar, he'd been a good man. But one of his new "friends" had introduced him first to hard liquor, and then to drugs. It was amazing how a kind, gentle man could become a raging wild animal who not only lashed out without mercy, but who didn't even remember what he'd done the morning after he'd done it. Mary and the children all had scars, mental and physical, from their experiences.

Bob understood it best. He had a friend at middle school who used drugs. The boy could be a fine student one day, and setting fire to the school the next. He'd been in and out of the juvenile justice system for two years. His parents were both alcoholics. Bob knew too much about the effects of drugs to ever use them, he told his mother sadly, both at home and school. She hoped her other children would have the same stiff common sense later down the road.

First things first. She had a good job. She had clients who were good to her, often giving her bonuses and even clothing and other gifts for the children from their abundance. Now that they knew her situation, she knew this would increase. Nobody she worked for would let Mary and her children starve. The thought gave her hope and peace. A house was going to be impossible, because rents were high and she couldn't afford them yet. But there were small, decent motels where she could get a good weekly rate. It would be crowded, but they could manage. She could borrow a car to take them to and from school from one of her employers, who had a garage full and had often done this for her when her own car at home was in the shop. Clothing she could get from the local Salvation Army, or from the thrift shops run by the women's abuse shelter and the churches.

Her predicament, so terrifying at first, became slowly less frightening. She had strength and will and purpose. She looked around the shelter at the little old lady who was in a wheelchair and thin as a rail. She was leaning down on her side, curled up like a dried-up child, with one thin hand clutching the wheel, as if she were afraid someone would steal it. Nearby, there was a black woman with many fresh cuts on her face and arms, with a baby clutched to her breast. Her clothes looked as if they'd been slept in many a night. Against the far wall, there was an elderly man with strips of cloth bound around his feet. She found that she had more than the average guest here. She closed her eyes and thanked God for her children and her fortitude.

Her first phone calls were not productive. She'd forgotten in the terror of the moment that it was Sunday, and not one person she needed to speak to was at home or likely to be until the following day. She asked Bev if she and the children could have one more night at the shelter and was welcomed. Tomorrow, she promised herself, they would get everything together.

The next morning she was up long before the children. The shelter offered breakfast, although it was mostly cereal, watered down coffee and milk.

"The dairy lets us have their outdated milk," the woman at the counter said, smiling. "It's still good. We have a lot of trouble providing meals, though. People are good to help us with canned things, but we don't get a lot of fresh meats and vegetables." She nodded toward some of the elderly people working their way through small bowls of cereal. "Protein, that's what they need. That's what the children need, too." Her smile was weary. "We're the richest country in the world, aren't we?" she added, her glance toward the occupants of the shelter eloquent in its irony.

Mary agreed quietly, asking for only a cup of coffee. The young mother, Meg, sat down beside her with her baby asleep in her arms.

"Hi," Mary said.

The young woman managed a smile. "Hi. You got lots of kids."

Mary smiled. "I'm blessed with three."

"I just got this one," Meg said, sighing. "My people are all in Atlanta. I came out here with Bill, and they warned me he was no good. I wouldn't listen. Now here I am, just me and the tidbit here. Bev says she thinks she knows where I can get a job. I'm going later to look."

"Good luck," Mary said.

"Thanks. You got work?"

Mary nodded. "I'm a housekeeper. I work for several families, all nice ones."

"You're lucky."

Mary thought about it. "Yes," she agreed. "I think I am."

The elderly man, Mr. Harlowe, joined them at the table

with his cup of coffee, held in unsteady old hands. "Ladies." He greeted in a friendly tone. "I guess poverty's no respecter of mothers, is it?"

"You got that right," Meg said with a faint smile.

"At least we're in good company," Mary added, glancing around. "The people here are nice."

"Noticed that myself." He sipped his coffee. "I retired two years ago and had all my money in a corporation money market fund. Last year, the corporation went belly-up and it came out that we'd all lost every penny we had in our retirement accounts." He shrugged. "At least the top scalawags seem headed to prison. But it turned out that I was related to one. My nephew talked me into giving him power of attorney and he took it all. I lost my house, my car, everything I had, except a little check I get from the veterans' service. That isn't enough to buy me a week's groceries in today's markct. I was going to prosecute him, but he went overseas with his ill-got gains. No money left to use to pursue him now."

"Gee, that's tough," Meg said quietly.

The elderly man glanced at her, noting the cuts on her face and arms. He grimaced. "Looks like you've had a tough time of your own."

"My man got drunk and I made him mad by being jealous of his other girlfriend. He said he'd do what he pleased and I could get out. I argued and he came at me with a knife," Meg said simply. "I ran away with the baby." She looked away. "It wasn't the first time it happened. But it will be the last."

"Good for you, young lady," he said gently. "You'll be okay."

She smiled shyly.

"What about you?" the old man asked Mary. "Those kids yours?" he added, indicating her small brood.

"Yes, they are. We lost our house and our car when my divorce became final." She gave Meg a quick glance. "I know about men who drink, too," she said.

Meg smiled at her. "We'll all be all right, I expect."

"You bet we will," Mary replied.

The old man chuckled. "That's the spirit. You got a place to go after here?"

"Not just yet," Mary said. "But I will soon," she said with new confidence. "I hope both of you do well."

They thanked her and drifted off into their own problems. Mary finished her coffee and got up with new resolve.

It was Monday, and she had to get the kids to school. She used the shelter's pay phone and called one of her friends, Tammy, who had been a neighbor.

"I hate to ask," she said, "but the kids have to go to school and Jack took the car. I don't have a way to go."

There was an indrawn breath. "I'll be right over," she began.

"Tammy, I'm at the homeless shelter." It bruised her pride

to say that. It made her feel less decent, somehow, as if she'd failed her children. "It's just temporary," she added quickly.

"Oh, Mary," she groaned. "I noticed the For Rent sign on your place, but I didn't know what to think. I'm so sorry."

"The divorce became final Friday. Jack is failing to pay alimony or child support…and we were evicted." She sighed. "I'm so tired, so scared. I've got nothing and three kids…"

"You could stay with us," came the immediate reply.

Mary smiled, seeing the other woman's quiet, kind smile in her mind. "No, thank you," she added gently. "We have to make it on our own. Jack might track us down at your house, you know. I don't want the children close to him. We'll find a place. I'll get the loan of a car later, but right now, I have to have the kids in school before I go to work. I can take John with me, but the others must be in school."

"I'll come and get you," Tammy said. "Be five minutes."

"Thanks," Mary choked.

"You'd do it for me in a heartbeat," she replied. "And you know it."

"I would." It was no lie.

"Five minutes." She hung up.

Sure enough, five minutes later, Tammy was sitting in front of the shelter, waiting. Mary put the kids in the back of the station wagon, with John strapped securely in his car seat.

"I can't thank you enough," she told the woman.

"It's not a problem. Here. Give this to the kids." It was two little brown envelopes, the sort mothers put lunch money in. Mary almost broke down as she distributed the priceless little packets to the children.

First stop was grammar school, where Mary went in with Ann and explained the situation, adding that nobody was to take Ann from school except herself or her friend Tammy. Then they went to middle school, where Mary dropped off Bob and met with the vice principal to explain their situation again.

Finally they were down just to John.

"Where do you go now?" she asked Mary.

"To Debbie Shultz's house," she said. "She and Mark have about eight cars," she said fondly. "They'll loan me one if I ask. They've been clients of mine for ten years. They're good people. They don't even mind if John comes with me—they have a playpen and a high chair and a baby bed, just for him."

"You know, you may not have money and means, but you sure have plenty of people who care about you," Tammy remarked with a grin.

"I do. I'm lucky in my friends. Especially you. Thanks."

Tammy shrugged. "I'm having a nice ride around town, my-self," she said with twinkling eyes. "Before you go to work, want to try that motel you mentioned?"

"Yes, if you don't mind."

"If I did, I'd still be at home putting on a pot roast for supper," Tammy said blandly. "Where is it?"

Mary gave her directions. Tammy was dubious, but Mary wasn't.

"One of my friends had to leave home. She went to the women's shelter first, and then she came here until she got a job. She said the manager looks out for people, and it's a good decent place. Best of all, it's not expensive. If you'll watch John for a minute..."

"You bet!"

Mary walked into the small office. The manager, an elderly man with long hair in a ponytail and a young smile, greeted her.

"What do you rent rooms for on a weekly basis?" she asked after she'd told him her name. "I have three children, ranging in age from thirteen to a toddler."

He noted the look on her face. He'd seen it far too often. "Fifty dollars a week," he said, "but it's negotiable. Forty's plenty if that's what you can manage comfortably," he added with a grin. "You can use the phone whenever you like, and there's a hot plate in the room where you can heat up stuff. We have a restaurant next door," he added, "when you want something a little hotter."

"I couldn't afford the restaurant," she said matter-of-factly, but she smiled. "I'll have the money tonight, if I can come after work with the kids."

"They in school?"

"Two are."

"Is one old enough to look after the others?"

"Bob's thirteen, almost fourteen. He's very responsible," she added.

"Bring them here after school and pay me when you can," he said kindly. "I'll check on them for you and make sure they stay in the room and nobody bothers them."

She was astonished at the offer.

"I ran away from home when I was twelve," he said coldly. "My old man drank and beat me. I had to live on the streets until an old woman felt sorry for me and let me have a room in her motel. I'm retired military. I don't need the money I make here, but it keeps me from going stale, and I can do a little good in the world." He smiled at her. "You can pass the help on to someone less fortunate, when you're in better economic times."

Her face brightened. "Thank you."

He shrugged. "We all live in the world. It's easier to get along if we help each other out in rough times. The room will be ready when you come back, Mrs. Crandall."

She nodded, smiling. "I'll have the money this afternoon, when I get off work. But I'll bring the children first."

"I'll be expecting them."

She got back into the car with Tammy, feeling as if a great weight had been lifted from her. "They said he was a kind man, not the sort who asked for favors or was dangerous around kids. But I had no idea just *how* kind he really is until now." She looked at Tammy. "I never knew how it was before. If you could see the homeless people, the things they don't have...I never knew," she emphasized.

Tammy patted her hand. "Not a lot of people do. I'm sorry you have to find out this way."

"Me, too," Mary said. She glanced back at the motel. "I wish I could do something," she added. "I wish I could help."

Tammy only smiled, and drove her to her job.

Debbie was aghast when she learned what had happened to Mary in the past twenty-four hours.

"Of course you can borrow a car," she said firmly. "You can drive the Ford until the tires go bald," she added. "And I'll let you off in time to pick up the kids at school."

Debbie's kids were in grammar school now, so the nursery was empty during the morning. Mary had made a habit of taking John to work with her, because Jack had never been in any condition to look after him.

Mary had to stop and wipe away tears. "I'm sorry," she choked. "It's just that so many people have been kind to me. Total strangers, and now you...I never expected it, that's all."

"People are mostly kind, when you need them to be," Debbie said, smiling. "Everything's going to be fine. You're a terrific housekeeper, you always keep me organized and going strong. You're always smiling and cheerful, even when I know you're the most miserable. I think a lot of you. So does Mark."

"Thanks. Not only for the loan of the car, but for everything."

Debbie waved a hand. "It's nothing. If I were starving and in rags, then it might be, but I can afford to be generous. I'll get you up some things for the kids, too. Please take them," she added plaintively. "You of all people know how choked my closets are with things I bought that the kids won't even wear!"

Mary laughed, because she did know. "All right then. I'll take them, and thanks very much."

"Have you got a place to stay?" was the next question.

"I have," Mary said brightly. "That was unexpected, too. It's a nice place."

"Good. Very good. Okay. I'll leave you to it. Just let me know when you're going after the kids and I'll watch John for you."

"Thanks."

Debbie just smiled. She was the sort of person who made the most outlandish difficulties seem simple and easily solved. She was a comfort to Mary.

The end of the first day of their forced exile ended on a happy note. From utter devastation, Mary and the kids emerged with plenty of clothing—thanks to Debbie and some of her friends—sheets and blankets and pillows, toiletries, makeup, and even a bucket of chicken. Not to mention the loaned car, which was a generous thing in itself.

"I can't believe it," Bob said when she picked him up at school, putting him in the back with John while Ann sat beside her. "We've got a home and a car? Mom, you're amazing!"

"Yes, you are," Ann said, grinning, "and I'm sorry I whined last night."

"You always whine," Bob teased, "but then you're a rock when you need to be."

"And you're an angel with ragged wings, you are, Mama," Ann said.

"We all have ragged wings, but I'll have a surprise for you at the motel," she added.

"What is it?" they chorused.

She chuckled. "You'll have to wait and see. The manager is Mr. Smith. He'll look out for you while I'm away. If you need to get in touch with me, he'll let you use the phone. I'll always leave you the name and number where I'll be, so you can reach me if there's an emergency."

"I think we've had enough emergencies for a while," Bob said drolly.

Mary sighed. "Oh, my, I hope we have!"

She loaded up the car with all the nice things Debbie had given her, and put the children in the car. Debbie had a brand-new baby car seat for John that she'd donated to the life-rebuilding effort as well. When he was strapped into it, Mary impulsively hugged Debbie, hiding tears, before she drove away. The old seat was coming apart at the seams and it couldn't have been very safe, but there had been no money for a new one. Something Debbie knew.

Bob and Ann met her at the door with dropped jaws as she started lugging in plastic bags.

"It's clothes! It's new clothes!" Ann exclaimed. "We haven't had new clothes since…" Her voice fell. "Well, not for a long time," she added, obviously feeling guilty for the outburst. They all knew how hard their mother worked, trying to keep them clothed at all. She went to her mother and hugged her tight. "I'm sorry. That sounded awful, didn't it?"

Mary hugged her back. "No, it just sounded honest, honey," she said softly.

The other two children crowded around her, and she gathered them in close, giving way to tears.

"What's wrong?" Bob asked worriedly. "Is there anything else you're not telling us?"

She shook her head. "No. It's just that people have been so good to us. Total strangers. It was such a surprise."

"My friend Timmy says we meet angels unawares when we don't expect to," Ann said in her quiet, sensible way.

"Perhaps that's true, baby," Mary agreed, wiping her eyes. "We've met quite a few today." She looked around at her children. "We're so fortunate to have each other."

They agreed that this was the best thing of all.

"*And* chicken," Bob exclaimed suddenly, withdrawing a huge bucket of it from the plastic bag.

"Chicken…!"

Little hands dived into the sack, which also contained biscuits and individual servings of mashed potatoes and gravy and green beans. Conversation abruptly ended.

* * *

Life slowly settled into a sort of pattern for the next couple of days as the memory of the terrifying first day and night slowly dimmed and became bearable.

The third night, Mary walked gingerly into the restaurant Mr. Smith had told her about, just at closing time.

"Excuse me," she said hesitantly.

A tall, balding man at the counter lifted his head and his eyebrows. "Yes, ma'am?" he asked politely.

"I was wondering..." She swallowed hard. She dug into her pocket and brought out a five dollar bill left over from the weekly rent she'd paid in advance. "I was wondering if you might have some chicken strips I could buy. Not with anything else," she added hastily, and tried to smile. "It's so far to the grocery store, and I'd have to take all three children with me..." She didn't want to add that they had hardly any money to buy groceries with, anyway, and that Mr. Smith was at his poker game tonight and couldn't watch the children for Mary while she drove to the store.

The man sized up her callused hands and worn appearance. Three kids, she'd said, and judging by the way her shoes and sweater looked, it wasn't easy buying much, especially food.

"Sure, we have them," he said kindly. "And we're running a special," he lied. "I'll be just a minute."

She stood there in her sensible clothes feeling uncomfortable, but it only took a minute for the man to come back smiling, with a plastic bag.

"That will be exactly five dollars," he said gently.

She grinned, handing him the bill. "Thanks a million!"

He nodded. "You're very welcome."

She took the chicken strips back to the motel and shared them around. There were so many that they all had seconds. She was over the moon. But there was always tomorrow, she worried.

She needn't have. The next afternoon, when she dragged in after work, she found the man from the restaurant on her doorstep.

"Look, I don't want to insult you or anything," he said gently. "But I know from your manager here that you're having a rough time. We always have food left over at night at our restaurant," he said kindly. "You see, we can't carry it over until the next day, it has to be thrown out. I could let you have what there is. If it wouldn't insult you. If you'd like it?"

"I'd like it," she said at once, and smiled. "Oh, I'd like it so much! Thank you."

He flushed. "It's no problem. Really. If you don't mind coming over about ten o'clock, just as we're closing?"

She laughed. "I'll be there. And thank you!"

* * *

She went to the restaurant exactly at ten, feeling a little nervous, but everybody welcomed her. Nobody made her feel small.

The restaurant assistant manager went to the back and had the workers fill a huge bag full of vegetables and meats and fruits in neat disposable containers. He carried it to the front and presented it to Mary with a flourish. "I hope you and the children enjoy it," he added with a smile.

She started to open her purse.

"No," he said. "You don't need to offer to pay anything. This would only go into the garbage," he said gently. "That's the truth. I'd much rather see it used and enjoyed."

"I'm Mary Crandall," she said. "My children and I thank you," she added proudly.

"I'm Cecil Baker," he replied. "I'm the assistant manager here. It's nice to meet you."

"Thank you," she said huskily. "Thank you so much."

"It's my pleasure. I hate waste. So much food goes into the trash, when there are people everywhere starving. It's ironic, isn't it?"

"Yes, it is," she agreed.

"Here. I'll get the door for you."

She grinned up at him as she went out. "I can't wait to see

the children's faces. They were only hoping for a chicken finger apiece," she added, chuckling.

He smiled, but pity was foremost in his mind. He watched her walk back the way she'd come, to the small motel.

Mary walked into the motel with her bag. Bob and Ann looked up expectantly from the board game they were playing. The toddler, John, was lying between them on the floor, playing with his toes.

"More chicken strips?" Bob asked hopefully.

"I think we have something just a little better than that," she said, and put her bag down on the table by the window. "Bob, get those paper plates and forks that we got at the store, would you?"

Bob ran to fetch them as Ann lifted John in her arms.

Mary opened the bag and put out container after container of vegetables, fruits and meats. There were not only chicken strips, but steak and fish as well. The small refrigerator in the room would keep the meats at a safe temperature, which meant that this meager fare would last for two days at least. It would mean that Mary could save a little more money for rent. It was a windfall.

She held hands with the children and she said grace before they ate. Life was being very good to her, despite the trials of the past week.

CHAPTER
~TWO~

Mary took the children with her to the grocery store on Friday afternoon. It was raining and cold. Trying to juggle John, who was squirming, and the paper bag containing the heaviest of their purchases, milk and canned goods, she dropped it.

"Oh, for heaven's sake!" she groaned. "Here, Ann, honey, take John while I run down the cans of tuna fish…!"

"I'll get them," came a deep voice from behind her. "I'm a fair fisherman, actually, but catching cans of tuna is more my style."

Mary turned and saw a police officer grinning at her. She recognized him at once. "Officer Clark!" she exclaimed. "How can I ever thank you enough for what you did for us?" she exclaimed. "Bev has been wonderful. We have a place to stay, now, too!"

He held up a hand, smiling. "You don't need to thank me, Mrs. Crandall. It was my pleasure."

In the clear daylight, without the mental torment that had possessed her at their first meeting, she saw him in a different way. He was several years older than she was, tall and a little heavy, but not enough to matter. He was good-looking. "You seem to have your hands full as it is," he added, scooping up the cans and milk jug. "I'll carry them for you."

"Thank you," she said, flustered.

He shrugged. "It isn't as if I'm overwhelmed with crime in this neighborhood," he said, tongue-in-cheek. "Jaywalking and petty theft are about it."

"Our car's over here. Well, it's not really our car," she added, and then could have bitten her tongue.

"You stole it, I guess," the policeman sighed. "And here I thought I was going to end my shift without an hour's paperwork."

"I didn't steal it!" she exclaimed, and then laughed. "My employer let me borrow it..."

"On account of Dad taking our car away after he left us," Bob muttered.

The policeman pursed his lips. "That's a pretty raw way to treat someone."

"Alcohol and drugs," she said, tight-lipped.

He sighed. "I have seen my share of that curse," he told her. "Are all these really yours?" he added, nodding toward the kids. "You didn't shoplift these fine children in the store?" he added with mock suspicion.

The children were laughing, now, too. "We shoplifted her," Bob chuckled. "She's a great mom!"

"She keeps house for people," Ann added quietly.

"She works real hard," Bob agreed.

"Have you got a house?" the policeman asked.

"Well, we're living in a motel. Just temporarily," Mary said at once, flushing. "Just until we find something else."

The policeman waited for Mary to unlock the trunk and he put the groceries he was carrying into it gingerly. Bob and Ann added their packages.

"Thanks again, Officer Clark," Mary said, trying not to let him see how attractive she found him. It was much too soon for that.

"Do you have any kids?" Ann asked him, looking up with her big eyes.

"No kids, no family," he replied with a sad smile. "Not by choice, either."

He looked as if he'd had a hard life. "Well, if you haven't stolen the car, and you need no further assistance, I've no choice but to go back to my car and try to catch a speeder or two before my shift ends. I hope I'll see you around again, Mrs. Crandall.... Mary."

"Are you married?" she blurted out.

He chuckled. "Not hardly. I entered the divorced state ten years ago, and I heartily recommend it. Much better than verbal combat over burned potatoes every single night."

"Your wife couldn't cook?" Mary asked involuntarily.

"She wouldn't cook and I couldn't cook, which led to a lot of the combat," he told her with a chuckle. "Drive safely, now."

"I will. You, too."

He walked off jauntily, with a wave of his hand.

"And I used to think policemen were scary," Bob commented. "He's really nice."

"He is, isn't he?" Mary murmured, and she watched him as he got into his squad car and pulled out of the parking lot. She found herself thinking that she had a very odd sort of guardian angel in that police uniform.

Mary went to her jobs with increasing lack of strength and vigor. She knew that some of the problem had to be stress and worry. Despite the safe haven she'd found, she knew that all her children had only her to depend on. Her parents were dead and there were no siblings. She had to stay healthy and keep working just to keep food on the table and a roof over their heads. In the middle of the night, she lay awake, worrying about what would happen if she should fail. The children would be split up and placed into foster homes. She knew that, and it terrified her. She'd always been healthy, but she'd never had quite so much responsibility placed on her, with so few resources to depend on. Somehow, she knew, God would find a way to keep her and the children safe. She had to believe that, to have faith, to keep going.

Somehow, she promised herself, she would. After all, there were so many people who needed even more assistance than she did. She remembered the elderly gentleman at the homeless shelter, the mother with her new baby. The shelter had a small budget and trouble getting food.

Food. Restaurants couldn't save food. They had to throw it out. If the restaurant near Mary's motel room had to throw theirs out, it was logical to assume that all the other restaurants had to throw theirs out, too.

What a shame, she thought, that there were so many hungry people with no food, where there were also restaurants with enough leftover food to feed them. All people had to do was ask for it. But she knew that they never would. She never would have, in her worst circumstances. People were too proud to ask for charity.

She put the thought into the back of her mind, but it refused to stay there. Over the next few days, she was haunted by the idea. Surely there were other people who knew about the restaurant leftovers, but when she began checking around, she couldn't find any single charity that was taking advantage of the fact. She called Bev at the homeless shelter and asked her about it.

"Well, I did know," Bev confessed, "but it would entail a lot of work, coordinating an effort like that. I've sort of got my hands full with the shelter. And everybody I know is over-worked and understaffed. There's just nobody to do it, Mary. It's a shame, too."

"Yes, it is," Mary agreed.

But it was an idea Mary couldn't shake. Maybe nobody else was doing it because it was *her* job to do it, she thought suddenly. She'd always believed that people had purposes in life, things that they were put here on earth to do. But she'd thought hers was to be a wife and mother—and it was, for a time. But she had more to give than that. So perhaps here was her new purpose, looking her in the face.

When she got off from work, she went to the restaurant where the assistant manager had given her the leftovers, and she spoke to him in private.

"It's just an idea," she said quickly. "But with all the restaurants in the city, and all the hungry people who need it, there should be some way to distribute it."

"It's a wonderful idea," Cecil replied with a smile. "But

there's just no way to distribute it, you see. There's no program in place to administrate it."

"Perhaps it could start with just one person," she said. "If you'd be willing to give me your leftovers, I'll find people to give them to, and I'll distribute them myself. It would be a beginning."

He found her enthusiasm contagious. "You know, it would be a beginning. I'll speak with the manager, and the owner, and you can check back with me on Monday. How would that be?"

"That would be wonderful. Meanwhile, I'll look for places to carry the food. I already have at least one in mind. And I'll get recommendations for some others."

"Do you think you can manage all alone?" he wondered.

"I have three children, two of whom are old enough to help me," she replied. "I'm sure they'll be enthusiastic as well."

They were. She was amazed and delighted at her children's response to the opportunity.

"We could help people like that old man at the shelter," Bob remarked. "He was much worse off than us."

"And that lady with the little baby. She was crying when nobody was looking," Ann told them.

"Then we'll do what we can to help," Mary said. She smiled at her children with pride. "The most precious gift we have is the ability to give to others less fortunate."

"That's just what our teacher said at Christmas," Bob said,

"when he had us make up little packages for kids at the battered women's shelter."

"That's one place we could check out, to see if they could use some of the restaurant food," Mary thought aloud. "I'm sure we'll find other places, too," she added. "It will mean giving up some things ourselves, though," she told them. "We'll be doing this after school and after work every day, even on weekends."

Bob and Ann grinned. "We won't mind."

Mary gathered them all close, including little John, and hugged them. "You three are my greatest treasures," she said. "I'm so proud of you!"

Monday when she went back to the restaurant, Cecil was grinning from ear to ear. "They went for it," he told her. "The manager and the owner agreed that it would be a wonderful civic contribution. I want to do my bit, as well, so I'll pay for your gas."

She caught her breath. "That's wonderful of you. Of all of you!"

"Sometimes all it takes is one person to start a revolution, of sorts," he told her. "You're doing something wonderful and unselfish. It shames people who have more and do less."

She chuckled. "I'm no saint," she told him. "I just want to make a little difference in the world and help a few people along the way."

"Same here. So when do you start?"

"Tomorrow night. I'm already getting referrals."

"I'll expect you at closing time."

"I'll be here."

Mary was enthusiastic about her project, and it wasn't difficult to find people who needed the food. One of the women she cleaned for mentioned a neighbor who was in hiding with her two children, trying to escape a dangerously abusive husband who'd threatened to kill her. She was afraid to go to a shelter, and she had no way to buy food. Mary took food to her in the basement of a church, along with toys and clothes for the children that had been provided by her employer. The woman cried like a baby. Mary felt wonderful.

The next night, she took her box of food to the homeless shelter where the elderly man was staying. The residents were surprised and thrilled with the unexpected bonanza, and Bev, who ran the shelter, hugged her and thanked her profusely for the help. Mary made sure that Meg, the young woman with the baby, also had milk, which the restaurant had included two bottles of in the box. The elderly man, whom Bev had told her was called Sam Harlowe, delved into the food to fetch a chicken leg. He ate it with poignant delight and gave Mary a big smile of thanks.

On her third night of delivering food, after the children had helped her divide it into individual packages, Mary decided that there might be enough time to add another restaurant or two to her clientele.

She wrote down the names and numbers of several other restaurants in the city and phoned them on her lunch hour. The problem was that she had no way for them to contact her. She didn't have a phone and she didn't want to alienate her motel manager by having the restaurants call him. She had to call back four of them, and two weren't at all interested in participating in Mary's giveaway program. It was disappointing, and Mary felt morose. But she did at least have the one restaurant to donate food. Surely there would be one or two others eventually.

She phoned the remaining four restaurants the next night after work and got a surprise. They were all enthusiastic about the project and more than willing to donate their leftovers.

Mary was delighted, but it meant more work. Now, instead of going next door to get food and parcel it up, she had to drive halfway across town to four more restaurants and wait until the kitchen workers got the leftovers together for her. This meant more work at the motel, too, making packages to take to the various shelters and families Mary was giving food to.

It was a fortunate turn of events, but Mary was beginning to feel the stress. She was up late, and she was tired all the time. She worked hard at her jobs, but she had no time for herself.

The children were losing ground on homework, because they had less time to do it.

What Mary needed very much were a couple of volunteers with time on their hands and a willingness to work. Where to find them was going to be a very big problem.

She stopped by the homeless shelter to talk with the manager and see if they could use more food, now that Mary was gaining new resources. Bev was on the phone. She signaled that she'd be through in a minute. While she waited, Mary went to talk to Mr. Harlowe, who was sitting morosely in the corner with a cup of cold coffee.

"You still here?" Mary asked with a gentle smile.

He looked up and forced an answering smile. "Still here," he replied. "How are you doing?"

She sat down. "I've got a place to live, clothes for the children and this new project of distributing donated food in my spare time."

He chuckled. "With three kids, I don't imagine you've got much of that!"

"Actually, I was hoping to find a volunteer to help me."

He lifted an eyebrow and took a sip of coffee. "What sort of volunteer?"

"Somebody to help me pick up and deliver the food."

He perked up with interest. "The last time you delivered

food here, Bev said something about what you've been doing. But she didn't go into specifics about how all this came about. Tell me more."

"I've discovered that restaurants throw out their leftover food at the end of the day because they can't resell it the next day," she explained. "I found five restaurants that are willing to let me have what they don't sell." Her eyes brightened as she warmed to her subject. "And now I'm looking for places to donate the food and people to help me carry it and sort it into parcels."

"You're almost homeless yourself, and you're spending your free time feeding other people?" He was astounded.

She grinned. "It helps me to stop worrying about my own problems if I'm busy helping others with theirs. Feeding the hungry is a nice way to spend my spare time."

"I'm amazed," he said, and meant it. "I don't have a way to go..."

"I'll come by and pick you up in the afternoons before I make my rounds," she promised, "if you're willing to help."

"I've got nothing else to do," he replied gently. "I don't have anything of my own, or any other place to go except here," he added, glancing around. "They haven't tried to throw me out, so I suppose I can stay."

"Don't be silly," Bev laughed as she joined them. "Of course you can stay, Mr. Harlowe!"

"Sam," he corrected. "Call me Sam. Do you know about Mrs. Crandall's new project?"

"Mary," she corrected. "If you get to be Sam, I get to be just Mary."

"And I'm Bev," the older woman laughed. "Now that we've settled that, what's this project, Mary?"

"Remember I told you I discovered that restaurants throw away their food at the end of the day," Mary said.

"And they don't save the leftovers. . . ." Bev said with a frown.

"They can't. It's against the law. So all that food goes into the garbage."

"While people go hungry," Bev mused.

"Not anymore. I've talked five restaurants into giving me their leftover food," Mary said. "I'm carrying some to a lady who's in hiding from her husband."

"Doesn't she know about the battered women's shelter?" Bev asked at once.

"She does, but she can't go there, because her husband threatened to kill her, and she doesn't want to endanger anyone else," Mary said. "She's trying to get in touch with a cousin who'll send her bus fare home to Virginia, before her husband catches up with her. She's got two kids. So I'm taking her food. There's an elderly lady staying in the motel where we are, and I take some to her. But there's still so much food left over. I thought you might like some for the shelter," she added hopefully.

Bev smiled from ear to ear. "Would I!" she exclaimed. "Have you thought of the men's mission and the food bank?" she added.

"Men's mission?" Mary asked blankly.

"It's another shelter, but just for men," Bev said. "And the food bank provides emergency food for families in crisis—where one or both parents are sick or out of work and there's no money for food. Or disabled people who can't get out to shop, and elderly people who have no transportation and no money."

Mary started to feel a warmth of spirit that she'd never had before. Her own problems suddenly seemed very small. "I've heard of the food bank, but I never knew much about it. And I didn't know we had a men's mission."

"There's a women's mission, too," Bev told her. "We have a Meals-On-Wheels program with its own volunteers who take hot meals to elderly shut-ins. There's quite an outreach program, but you wouldn't know unless you'd been homeless or badly down on your luck."

"I'm ashamed to say I never knew much about those programs, and never noticed them until I got into this situation," Mary confessed. "But now I'm wondering if there wasn't a purpose behind what happened to me. Otherwise, I'd never have been looking into the restaurant food rescue."

"It's nice, isn't it, how God finds uses for us and nudges us into them?" Bev teased.

Mary's eyes shimmered. "I don't think I've ever thought of

that before, either," she said. "But whole new avenues of opportunity are opening up in front of me. You know, I never knew how kind people could be until I lost everything."

"That's another way we fit into the scheme of things, isn't it?" Bev said. "Until we're caught up in a particular situation, we never think of how it is with people in need. I was homeless myself," she said surprisingly, "and I ended up in a women's mission. That opened my eyes to a whole world that I'd never seen. When I got involved trying to better the situation of other people in trouble, my own life changed and I found a purpose I didn't know I had. I became useful."

Mary grinned. "That's what I'm trying to become. And so far, so good!" She glanced at Mr. Harlowe. "I've just found a willing volunteer to help me parcel up and pass out food."

Bev's eyebrows lifted. "You, Sam?"

He nodded. "I do think I've just become useful, myself," he said with a chuckle. "I can't lift a lot of heavy things," he added hesitantly. "I had a back injury from service in Vietnam, and it left me unable to do a lot of lifting."

"The food parcels the children and I have been making up aren't heavy at all," Mary was quick to point out. "We try to make sure we have bread, vegetables, fruit and meat in each one. And dessert, too. But that was only from the one restaurant. With the four new ones added, we can make up larger ones."

"You'll need containers," Bev said. "I know a woman at one

of the dollar stores who's a good citizen. She contributes paper plates and cups to our shelter, and if you go and see her, I'll bet she'd contribute those plastic containers for your project."

Mary, who'd been buying such things herself, was surprised and delighted at the suggestion.

Bev had a pen and paper. "Here. I'll write down her name and address for you. And I'll see if I can find you one more volunteer with a car and some free time."

"That's great!" Mary exclaimed.

"You borrowed a car, didn't you?" Bev asked. "Does the person who loaned it mind if you use it for this?"

That was something Mary hadn't asked about. She bit her lower lip. "I don't know," she confessed. "I'll have to go and see her and ask if it's all right."

"That may not be necessary. We have a patron who has an old truck that he's offered to donate to us," Bev volunteered. "I'll ask him if he's still willing to do that. You might talk to one of the independent gas stations and see if they'd donate gas."

"Bev, you're a wonder!" Mary exclaimed.

"I've learned the ropes," Bev said simply, "and learned how to get people to follow their most generous instincts. After you've been in the business for a while, you'll be able to do that, too."

"I never knew how many people went to bed hungry in this country," Mary commented. "I've learned a lot in a few days."

"Welcome to the real world."

Sam sighed. "Well, then, when do we begin?"

"Tonight," Mary said enthusiastically.

"Wait just a minute," Bev said, and went to the phone. "I want to see if I can get in touch with our patron before you go."

Amazingly she did, and he promised to have the truck at the shelter promptly at 6:00 p.m. that evening.

"Thanks a million, Bev," Mary said.

"We're all working toward the same goal," Bev reminded her. "Go see that guy about the gas, okay?"

"I'll do it on my way back to the motel."

Mary stopped by the gas station, introduced herself, mentioned Bev, and outlined her new project. "I know it's a lot to ask," she said, "and if you don't want to do this, it's okay. I've been paying for the gas myself..."

"Hey, it doesn't hurt me to donate a little gas to a good cause," he told Mary with a chuckle. "You bring your truck by here before you start out tonight, and I'll fill it up for you. We'll set up a schedule. If I'm not here, I'll make sure my employees know what to do."

"Thanks so much," Mary told him.

He shrugged. "Anybody can end up homeless," he commented, "through no fault of his or her own. It's the times we live in."

"I couldn't agree more!"

* * *

Mary told the children what was going on, and how much work it was going to be. "But we do have a volunteer who's going to help us with the deliveries," she remarked. "It will mean getting up very early in the mornings to get your homework done, or doing it at school while you're waiting for me to pick you up."

"We could stay at the homework center until you get off work, instead of you coming to get us as soon as school's out," Bob suggested.

"Sure," Ann agreed. "We wouldn't mind. There's a boy I like who's explaining Spanish verbs to me," she added shyly.

"This will work, I think, until we get some more volunteers," Mary said with a smile.

"We want to help," Ann said. "It's not going to be that much work."

"It's sort of nice, helping other people. No matter how bad it is for us, it's worse for many other people," Bob agreed. "I like what we're doing."

Mary hugged them all. "When they say it's better to give than to receive, they're not kidding. It really is. I feel wonderful when we take these packages out to people who need them."

"Me, too," Ann said. "I'm going to do a paper on it for my English class."

"Good for you!" Mary said.

"We're doing okay, aren't we, Mom?" Bob asked gently. He smiled at her. "Dad didn't think we could, I'll bet."

The mention of her ex-husband made Mary uneasy. She'd been afraid at first that he might try to get custody of the children, just for spite. But perhaps he didn't want the aggravation of trying to take care of three of them. Mary had never minded the responsibility. She loved her children, she enjoyed their company. As she looked at them, she felt so fortunate. Things got better every day.

That evening, she and the children went to the homeless shelter to pick up the donated truck.

"Can you drive it?" Bev asked worriedly, when she noted petite Mary climbing up into the high cab of the big, long bed, double-cabbed vehicle. It was red and a little dented, but the engine sounded good when it was started.

"I grew up on a farm," Mary said with a grin. "I can drive most anything, I expect. I'll bring it back, but it will be late, is that okay?"

"If I'm not here, George will be," Bev assured her. "You keep the doors locked and be careful."

"Don't you worry," Sam Harlowe said as he climbed up into the passenger seat. "I may be old, but I'm not helpless. Mary will have help if she needs it."

"Sure she will," Bob added, chuckling. "I play tackle on the B-team football squad."

"Good luck, then," Bev called to them as Mary put the truck in gear and pulled out into the street.

Mary stopped by the gas station. True to his word, the manager filled up the tank and even checked under the hood to make sure the truck was in good running shape. He checked the tires as well.

"Thanks," she told him.

He grinned. "My pleasure. Drive carefully."

"I will," she promised.

She pulled out into the sparse traffic and headed toward the first of the five restaurants. "We'll probably have to wait a while at first, until we get into some sort of routine."

"No problem," Bob said. "We all brought books to read."

Sam laughed. "Great minds run in the same direction." He pulled out a well-worn copy of Herodotus, the Histories, and displayed it.

"I've got my piecework, as well," Mary said, indicating a small canvas bag with knitting needles and a ball of yarn. "I'm making hats for people in the shelters. I can only knit in a straight line, but hats are simple."

"I wouldn't call knitting simple," Sam assured her.

She laughed. "It keeps my hands busy. Okay, here we are," she added, pulling into the parking lot of the first restaurant.

The waiting was the only bad part. They had to arrive at or near closing time in order to gather the leftovers. On the first night, the last restaurant was already closed by the time they got to it.

"We'll have to do better than this," Mary murmured worriedly. "I hadn't realized how long it would take to do this."

"First times are notoriously hard," Sam said. "We'll get better at it. But perhaps we can find one more volunteer to go to the last two restaurants for us and pick up the leftovers."

"There aren't a lot of volunteers who can work at night," Mary fretted.

"Listen, if things are meant to happen, the details take care of themselves," Sam said. "You wait and see. Everything's going to fall into place like clockwork, and you'll wonder why you ever worried in the first place."

Mary glanced at him and was reassured by his smile. She smiled back. "Okay. I'll go along with that optimism and see what happens."

Sam glanced out his window confidently. "I think you'll be surprised."

CHAPTER
~THREE~

As the days passed, Mary and her helpers got more efficient at picking up the food and parceling it out. The truck ran perfectly, and Mary got better at managing her finances. She picked up two more cleaning jobs, which was the maximum she could fit into the week.

Debbie, who'd loaned her the car, also suggested that a slight raise in her hourly rate would provide her with more money. Mary was hesitant to do that, for fear of losing customers.

"You just tell them that I raised you two dollars an hour and they'll be ashamed not to follow suit," Debbie said firmly.

"What if they let me go?" Mary worried.

"You've come a long way in a short time," Debbie said.

"You're much more confident, more poised, and you're a whiz at organization. I'm amazed at the change in you."

"I've changed?" Mary asked hesitantly.

"You've taken charge of your own life, and the lives of your children. You've organized a food rescue program to benefit needy people, you've kept the children in school and up with their homework, you've found a decent place to live and you're on your way to financial independence." Debbie grinned. "I'm proud of you."

Mary smiled. "Really?"

"Really. You just keep going the way you've been going. You're going to make it, Mary. I'm sure of it."

That confidence made Mary feel on top of the world. "You're sure you don't want the car back now?"

"When you can afford one of your own," Debbie said, "you can give mine back. Listen, honey, it sits in the garage all day and hardly ever gets driven. You're actually doing us a favor by keeping it on the road, so that it doesn't gum up and stop working."

"You make things seem so easy," Mary said. "You've done so much for us. I don't know how to repay you."

"I'm doing it for selfish motives," Debbie whispered conspiratorially. "If you leave, my husband will divorce me when the dishes and the laundry pile up and start to mold."

Mary knew that wasn't true. Debbie did, too. But they both smiled.

* * *

The food rescue program was growing. Mary now had ten restaurants on her list, and two more volunteers who helped to gather the food and make it up into packages. One of the new volunteers had a car. And his identity was a shock.

It was Matt Clark, the policeman they'd met their first night in the car. He was wearing a neat new sports shirt and khaki slacks with a brown leather bomber jacket. He'd had a haircut and he looked younger.

"I've never seen him look so neat off duty," Bev whispered wickedly as Mary entered the shelter with armloads of packaged food. "I think he's dressing up for somebody. Three guesses who."

"Hush!" Mary exclaimed, blushing.

"Well, hello," Matt greeted her, taking some of the containers from her arms. "I had some free time and I heard you were looking for help. So here I am."

"We're happy to have you here," Mary replied breathlessly. "There's so much food to pick up and deliver, and it takes a lot of time."

"I don't see how you managed, when you were doing it alone," Matt remarked as they put the food parcels on the long table.

"I'm beginning to wonder that, myself," Mary had to admit. She smiled shyly at him. "This is just the first load. There are two more in the truck, at least, and the other volunteers will be along soon with even more."

"Where do all these go?" Matt asked.

"There's a list," Sam volunteered as he joined them, grinning, with an armload of food. "How's it going, Matt?"

"Fair to middling, Sam," came the reply. The two men smiled and shook hands, and then Sam went back to collect some more food packs.

"You know each other?" Mary asked Matt curiously, in a low voice.

"Before he retired, Sam worked for the city as a building inspector," Matt told her. "I had to rescue him from an irate client once. We had a beer together and discovered we had a lot in common. We were having lunch once a month until Sam's bad luck." Matt shook his head. "Pity about what happened to him. I remember a time when ethics were the most important part of business. Now it seems to be that only the corrupt prosper."

"I know what you mean," Mary agreed. "It's nice of you. Helping us make the deliveries, I mean."

He smiled at her. "It isn't as if I have a hectic social life. Mostly I work."

"Same here!" she laughed.

He hesitated, his dark eyes quiet and searching. "You're an amazing person," he commented quietly. "Most people would be thinking about themselves in your position, not about helping others."

"I wasn't always like this," she said. "I can remember a time when I was afraid of street people. It makes me a little ashamed."

"All of us have to learn about the world, Mary," he said gently. "We're not born knowing how hard life can be for unfortunate people. For instance, Sam there—" he nodded toward the elderly man "—was a decorated hero in Vietnam. He's had a bad shake all the way around. His wife left him while he was overseas and took their daughter with her. They were both killed in a car wreck the week after Sam got home from the war. He remarried, and his second wife died of cancer. Now, his retirement's gone with his thieving nephew, after he worked like a dog to become self-sufficient. The nephew was only related to him by marriage, which makes it even worse." He shook his head. "Some people get a bad shake all around. And Sam's a good man."

"I noticed that," she said. "He's proud, too."

"That's the problem that keeps so many people out of the very social programs that would help them," he said philosophically. "Pride. Some people are too proud to even ask for help. Those are the ones who fall into the cracks. People like Sam. He could get assistance, God knows he'd qualify. But he's too proud to admit that he needs relief."

She smoothed over a food package. "Is there any way we could help him?"

He grinned. "I'm working on something. Let you know when I have any good ideas, okay?"

She grinned back. "Okay."

Sam returned with four more big containers of food. "Been talking about me behind my back, I guess?" he asked them.

"We don't know that many interesting people, Sam," Matt pointed out.

Sam shrugged, shook his head and went back inside with the packages.

Matt drove the truck, giving Mary a brief rest. It had been an especially long day, because one of her employers wanted to take down and wash and press all the heavy curtains in the house. It had been a backbreaking job, although the house certainly looked better afterward. Bob and Ann had stayed after school for their individual sports programs. The extracurricular activities were important to them and Mary was going to make sure that they had as normal a life as possible, even with all the complications of the moment.

"Where are the kids?" Matt asked, as if he'd sensed her thoughts.

"At sports and band practice," she said. "I arranged rides for them back to the motel, and the manager's promised to keep an eye on them."

"And the youngest?"

She grinned. "My friend, Tammy, is keeping John tonight until we get through. I have to pick him up at her house."

"I'll drive you," Matt offered. "Don't argue, Mary," he added gently. "I wouldn't offer if it was going to be an imposition. Okay?"

Sam glanced at her. "I'd give in, if I were you. He's the most persistent man I ever met."

She laughed. "All right, then. Thank you," she told Matt.

Their first stop was at the men's mission. Mary had passed by the building many times in the past, and never paid it much attention. She'd had a vague idea of the sort of people who stayed there, and not a very flattering one.

But now she took time to look, to really look, at them. There were several sitting in the lobby watching a single television. Two were paraplegics. One was blind. Five were elderly. Two were amputees. She could understand without asking a single question why they were here.

"We brought you some food," Mary told the shelter's manager, a portly gentleman named Larry who had a beard and long hair.

"This is a treasure trove!" Larry exclaimed. "Where did you get this?"

"From restaurants in town," Mary said simply as Matt and Sam started bringing in the parcels. "They have to throw away their leftovers, so I've asked for them. Now I'm finding more places to donate them."

"You can put us on your list, and many thanks!" Larry exclaimed, lifting the lid on one of the plastic containers. "Good Lord, this is beef Stroganoff! I haven't had it in six years!"

Mary grinned. "There's a price," she told him. "You have to wash the containers so that I can pick them up when I bring your next delivery. I thought maybe Monday, Wednesday and Friday?"

"That would be great," Larry said enthusiastically. "Thanks. What's your name?"

"Mary Crandall," she said, shaking hands.

"I'm Larry Blake," he said, "and I'm very happy to meet you. Thanks a million!"

One of the men, a paraplegic, wheeled over to ask what was going on. He took a sniff. "Is that lasagna?" he queried hopefully.

"It is," Mary said. "And there's tiramisu and cake and all sorts of pastries for dessert, too."

"I think I have died and gone to heaven," the man in the wheelchair said with a sad smile. "Thank you."

She noticed that his wheelchair had no footrests and that it squeaked terribly. One of the tires was missing part of its rubber tread. She wished with all her heart she had a little extra money so that she could offer it to him for a newer chair.

He saw her sad glance and he smiled. "I can see what you're thinking, but I don't want a new chair. This is my lucky one. That sticky wheel kept me from going off the edge of a building when I got lost. I wouldn't trade it for the world."

She smiled. "So much for women's intuition," she said.

He chuckled. "Never you mind. Thanks for the food!"

"My pleasure," she replied.

Their second stop was a small village of tents and boxes that moved from time to time when the authorities made half-hearted efforts to clear away the homeless people. It was a temporary measure at best, because the homeless had no place to go except shelters, and most of the people in the moveable village didn't like being shut up inside.

"These are the real hard cases," Matt said quietly as they stopped. "They don't want to be subject to rules of any kind. Periodically the police are asked to break up these camps, but they just set up across town all over again."

"Why are so many people homeless?" Mary asked absently.

"Thousands of reasons," Matt told her. "Some are mentally ill and have no family and no place to go. Some are alcoholics. Some are drug users. A few have relatives who are trying to forget all about them. Society today is so mobile that extended families just don't exist in one town anymore. This never happened a century ago, because families stayed put and were required by morality to take care of their own and be responsible for them. These days, morality is very widely interpreted."

"In other words, everybody's looking out for number one," Sam murmured.

Matt nodded. "In a nutshell, yes."

"I think the old way of taking care of one's own was better," Sam said with a sigh.

Several people from the camp came close, hesitantly, looking around suspiciously. "What do you want?" a man asked.

"We brought you some food," Mary said, indicating the boxes in the bed of the pickup truck.

"That don't look like cans," the man commented.

"It isn't." Mary took down one of the bags, opened it, took out a plastic container and opened it. "Smell."

The man sniffed, stood very still, then sniffed again. "That's beef. That's beef!"

"It is," Mary said. "In fact, it's beef Stroganoff, and you should eat it while it's still warm. Do you have something to put it in?"

The man went running back to the others. They came back with a motley assortment of plates and cups and bent utensils. Mary and the men filled all the plates and cups to capacity, adding a bag of bread and another with containers of fruit and vegetables.

A ragged old woman came shyly up to Mary and took her hand. "'Ank oo," she managed to say.

"That's old Bess," the man introduced the little woman,

who took her plate and waddled away. "She's deaf, so she don't speak plain. She said thank you."

Mary had to bite back tears. "She's very welcome. All of you are. I'll come back Friday with more, about this same time."

The man hesitated. "They're making us move tomorrow," he said dully. "We never get to stay noplace long."

"Where will you go?" Mary asked.

He shrugged.

"When you have another place, get in touch with the shelter on Blair Street, can you do that? They'll get word to me," Mary said.

He nodded slowly, then smiled. "Thanks."

She sighed. "We're all victims of circumstance, in one way or another," she told him. "We have to help each other."

"Good!" An unshaven man with overlarge eyes was tugging on Mary's sleeve. "Good, lady, good!" he said, pointing his spoon at the food in his cup. "Good!"

He turned away, eating hungrily.

"That's Billy," the man said. "He's not quite right in the head. Nobody wanted him, so he lives with us. My name's Art."

"I'm Mary," she said. "Nice to meet you."

"I'll get word to you," he said after a minute, nodding politely at Matt and Sam. He went back with the others into the darkness of the camp.

The three companions were very quiet as they drove toward the nearby women's mission.

"That hurts," Sam spoke for all of them.

"Yes," Mary agreed. "But we're doing something to help."

"And every little bit does help," Matt added quietly. He glanced at Mary. "I'm glad I came tonight."

"Me, too," Sam said. "I'll never feel sorry for myself again."

Mary smiled tiredly. "That's exactly how I feel."

The women's mission was very much like the men's mission, but the women seemed a little livelier and more receptive to the visitors.

Three of them were doing handwork in the lobby, where an old movie was playing on a black-and-white television. Two others were filling out forms.

The mission was run by a Catholic nun, Sister Martha, who welcomed them, surprised by the food and its quality.

"I would never have thought of asking restaurants for leftover food!" she exclaimed, grinning at Mary. "How resourceful of you!"

Mary laughed. "It was a happy accident, the way it came about," she said. "But I feel as if I have a new lease on life, just from learning how to give away food."

"Giving is a gift in itself, isn't it?" the sister asked with a secretive smile. "I've learned that myself. No matter how hard my life is, when I can help someone else, I feel as if I've helped myself, too."

"That's very true," Mary said.

She introduced Sam and Matt, and they unloaded the last of the food. The women gathered around, impressed by the fancy food and anxious to taste it. When Mary and the men left, the women were already dishing it up in the small kitchen.

"That's all I have tonight," Mary said. "I'll call some more restaurants, and maybe Bev can suggest another volunteer or two."

"You know there's a food bank around here, too," Matt suggested. "They might like to have some of this restaurant chow."

"Already got that covered," Mary murmured. "I'm planning on giving them a call tomorrow."

"If you'll give me some names," Matt said, "I'll make some calls for you."

"So will I," Sam volunteered. "I'm sure Bev won't mind letting me use the phone."

"But how are we going to manage this?" Mary wondered aloud worriedly. "It's taken us two hours to give away what we had, and that's just from five restaurants. Besides that, the truck was full when we started."

"We'll need another truck," Matt said. "Maybe a van."

"Where are we going to get one?" Mary asked.

"I'll make some arrangements," Matt said.

She smiled at him. "You're a wonder."

"Oh, I'm in good company," he replied, glancing from Mary to Sam with a grin.

When they dropped Sam off at the shelter, along with the truck, Matt put Mary into his sedan and drove her to Tammy's house. Mary was uneasy until they were back in the car with John strapped in his car seat in the back of Matt's car, and on their way out of the neighborhood.

As they passed Mary's old house, she noticed that there were two cars in the driveway and that the For Rent sign had been removed.

"What is it?" Matt asked, sensing that something was wrong.

"I used to live there before I was evicted," she commented sadly as they passed the old house. "Those must be the new tenants."

"I don't know how you're handling all these changes," he said with admiration. "You have three kids to support, a full-time profession and spending all your nights handing out food to people." He shook his head. "You're an inspiration."

"I'm getting an education in the subject of people," she told him. "It's a very interesting subject, too."

He smiled in the rearview mirror at the baby. "You have great kids," he commented.

"Thanks," she said shyly. "I think they're pretty terrific. I could be prejudiced," she added with a grin.

He laughed. "No, I don't think so. Where are we going?" he added.

She realized that he didn't know where they lived. "It's that old motel next to the new Wal-Mart superstore," she told him.

He glanced at her. "Al Smith's motel?"

She laughed. "You know Mr. Smith?"

"Do I," he laughed. "We were in the military together, back when the Marines were stationed in Lebanon and the barracks were car-bombed. Remember that, in the eighties?"

"Yes, I do," she said.

"Two of my friends died in the explosion," he said. "Smith was in my unit, too. He's good people."

"I noticed," she said, and explained how kind he'd been to her family while they were adjusting to the new uncertainties of their lives.

"He's that sort of person," he agreed. "He's done a lot of good with that motel, taking in people who had nowhere else to go and trusting them for the rent. I don't know of one single person who's skipped without paying, either."

"He's been great to us," she said.

"So it would seem."

He pulled up at the door of their room and got out, opening Mary's door for her with an old-world sort of courtesy. He helped her get John out of his car, and carried the car seat into the room for her as well.

"Hi!" Bob called, bouncing off the bed to greet Matt. "Did you bring Mom home?"

"I did," he told the boy with a smile. "We've been handing out food all over town. How was football practice?"

"Pretty good, if we could teach Pat Bartley how to tackle," he said with a wistful smile. "He won't wear his glasses and he can't see two feet in front of him. But the coach is working on him."

"Good for him. Who's in band?"

"Me," Ann said, grinning. "I play clarinet. I'm good, too."

"I used to play trombone in band," Matt volunteered.

"You did?" Ann exclaimed. "That's neat!" She looked up at Matt curiously. "You look different when you aren't wearing a uniform."

"I'm shorter, right?" he teased.

She smiled shyly. "No. You look taller, really."

"We've got leftover pizza. Want some?" Bob offered. "Mr. Smith brought it to us. It's got pepperoni."

"Thanks, but I had egg salad for supper. I'm sort of watching my weight." His dark eyes twinkled at the boy. "New uniforms are expensive."

"Tell me about it," Mary sighed. "I'm trying to keep my own weight down so mine will fit."

"You wear a uniform?" Matt asked.

"Just for one lady I work for," she said. "She's very rich and very old, and traditional. When I work for everybody else, I just wear jeans and a T-shirt."

"Amazing," he mused.

"Look, Mom, there's that movie Bob wants to see!" Ann enthused, pointing at the small television screen.

It was a promo for a fantasy film with elves and other fascinating creatures.

"I want to see that one, myself," Matt commented. "Say, you don't work Sunday, do you?" he asked Mary.

"Well, no, but there's still food to pick up and deliver—"

"There are matinees," he interrupted. "Suppose we all go?"

Mouths dropped open. None of them had been to a movie in years.

"I guess I could ask Tammy to keep John…" Mary thought out loud.

"Wowee!" Bob exclaimed. "That would be radical!"

"Sweet!" Ann echoed.

"I need a dictionary of modern slang," Matt groaned.

"We mean, it would be very nice," Ann translated. "We'd like very much to go, if it wouldn't be an imposition."

Matt glanced at her and then at Mary. "We don't need a translator," he pointed out.

They all laughed.

"Then, that's settled. I'll find out what time the matinee is and call Al and have him tell you when I'll be here. Okay?"

"Okay," Mary said breathlessly.

Matt winked at her and she felt suddenly lighter than air. Worse, she blushed.

"She likes him!" Bob said in a stage whisper.

"Think he likes her, too?" Ann whispered back, gleefully.

"Yes, he likes her, too," Matt answered for them. "See you all Sunday."

"I'll walk you out," Mary said quickly, with a warning look at her kids, who suddenly assumed angelic expressions.

On the sidewalk, Mary wrapped her arms around her chest. It was cold. "Matt, thanks so much, for everything. Especially tonight."

He paused at the door of his car and looked back at her. "I like your kids," he said. "I really like them. They're smart and kindhearted and they're real troopers. Under the circumstances, I wouldn't be surprised if they were sad and miserable. But they're so cheerful. Like you."

She smiled. "We've been very lucky, the way things have worked out for us," she explained. "But the kids have always been like this. They get depressed sometimes. Everybody does. But they're mostly upbeat. I'm crazy about them."

"I can see why." He gave her a long, quiet look. "You're one special lady."

She stared back at him with a racing heart and breathlessness that she hadn't felt since her teens.

He bent, hesitantly, giving her plenty of time to back away if she wanted to. But she didn't. He brushed his mouth tenderly across her lips and heard her soft sigh. He lifted his head, smiling. He felt as if he could float. "Dessert," he whispered wickedly.

She laughed and blushed, again. He touched her cheek with just the tips of his fingers, and the smile was still there.

"I'll look forward to Sunday," he said after a minute, and grinned as he got into his car. "Don't forget," he called before he started the engine.

"As if I could," she murmured to herself.

She stood and watched him drive away. He waved when he got to the street.

Mary walked back into the room. Three pair of curious eyes were staring at her.

"He's just my friend," she said defensively.

"He's nice," Bob said. "And we like him. So it's okay if you like him, too. Right?" he asked Ann.

"Right!" she echoed enthusiastically.

Mary laughed as she took little John from Ann, who was holding him. She cuddled the little boy and kissed his chubby little cheek.

"I'm glad you like him," was all she said. "Now, let's see if we can get our things ready for tomorrow, okay?"

CHAPTER
~FOUR~

Mary felt like a new woman as she went to her job the next day. It was too soon to become romantically involved with any man, at the moment. But Matt was a wonderful person and she was drawn to him. Her children seemed to feel a connection to him as well, which was terrific.

One of her employers, a middle-aged society hostess named Billie West, was married to old money and dripping diamonds. She was particularly interested in Mary's project.

"You mean these restaurants are actually willing to just *give* you food?" she exclaimed.

"At the end of the business day," Mary replied with a smile. "It's only the leftovers, not the full meals."

"Oh. I see." The woman shook her head. "And you call them up and they give it to you."

"Well, I do have to pick it up and deliver it to people."

"Deliver it? Hmm. Is Chez Bob one of your clients?" she persisted.

"No, ma'am. I asked, but they weren't interested."

The older woman smiled. "Suppose I ask the owner for you?"

Mary was surprised. The elderly woman wasn't usually talkative. Often, she wasn't at home when Mary cleaned for her, using a key that was kept in a secret place. "You would do that?" Mary asked.

"There are two others whose owners I know, Mary's Porch and the Bobwhite Grill. I could ask them, too."

Mary just stared at her.

"You're suspicious," the blonde replied, nodding. "Yes, I don't blame you. I'm filthy rich. Why should I care if a lot of society's dropouts starve. That's what you're wondering, isn't it?"

Mary perceived that only honesty would do in this situation. "Yes, ma'am, that's what I'm wondering," she said quietly.

Billie burst out laughing. "Honey, I grew up on the back streets of Chicago," she said surprisingly. "My old man was drunk more than he was sober, and my mother worked three jobs just so my brothers and I could have one meal a day. She could barely pay the rent. When I was sixteen, she died. It was up to me to take care of Dad, who had liver cancer by then, along with three young boys and get them and myself through school." She sat down on the sofa and crossed her long legs. "I wasn't smart, but I had a nice figure and good skin. I had a friend who was a photographer. He shot a portfolio for me and showed it to a magazine editor he did layouts for. I was hired to be a model."

That was news. Mary had never heard the woman speak of her background at all.

"Overnight, I was rolling in money," her employer recalled. "I got the boys through school and never looked back. Dad died the second year I was modeling. The third, I married Jack West, who had even more money than I did. But I never forgot how I grew up, either. I donate to the less fortunate on a regular basis." She stared at Mary curiously. "Your other client Debbie and I are friends. She said that after your divorce was final, you were on the streets with three kids to raise. And despite that, you were out begging food from restaurants and delivering it to people in shelters. I must admit, it didn't seem possible."

Mary smiled. "You mean, because we were in such bad shape ourselves?"

"Yes."

"I never learned how kind people could be until I hit rock bottom," Mary explained patiently. "Or how much poverty and need there is out there, on the streets. There are disabled people, handicapped people, paraplegics and diabetics and people dying of cancer who have nothing." Mary took a long breath. "You know, handing out a little good food might not seem like much to do for people in those situations. But it gives them hope. It shows them that they're important, that they're valuable to someone. It helps them to see that everyone doesn't turn away and avoid looking at them."

"I know what you mean," the woman said quietly as she got to her feet. "I'll make those calls. Have you got a way to pick up the food? What am I saying? You must have, or you wouldn't be adding restaurants to your list."

"The shelter where I started out was given a pickup truck. We use that."

"We?"

"I have a few volunteers who help me," Mary said. "And my children, of course."

"How do you manage to do that and keep your children in school?"

"Oh, not just in school," Mary assured her. "One of them plays football and one is in band. I think it's important for them to learn teamwork."

The other woman smiled. "Smart. I've always said that baseball kept my younger brothers out of jail. One of them plays for the Mets," she added, "and the other two are assistant managers on different ball teams."

"You must be proud of them," Mary commented.

"Yes, I am. I helped keep them out of trouble. Could you use another volunteer? I don't just have sports cars in the garage. I've got that huge SUV out back. It will hold a heck of a lot of food."

"You mean it?"

"I'm bored to death, alone with my fancy house and my fast cars and my money," Billie said blandly. "I don't have any kids and my husband is working himself to death trying to enlarge a company that's already too big. If I don't find some sort of useful purpose, I'll sit here alone long enough to become an alcoholic. I saw my Dad go out that way. I'm not going to."

Mary grinned, feeling a kinship with the woman for the first time. "We all meet at the Twelfth Street shelter about five in the afternoon."

"Then I'll see you at five at the shelter," Billie said, smiling back.

"Thanks," Mary said huskily.

"We all live on the same planet. I guess that makes us family, despite the ticky little details that separate us."

"I'm beginning to feel the same way."

The two women shared a smile before Mary got back to work. It was so incredible, she thought, how you could work for somebody and not know anything about them at all. So often, people seemed as obvious as editorial cartoons. Then you got to know them, and they were really complex novels with endless plot twists.

* * *

Not only did Billie show up with her SUV at the shelter, but one of Matt's colleagues from the police force, a tall, young man named Chad, drove up in another SUV and offered to help the group transport the food.

It was getting complicated, because there were now so many restaurants contributing to the program. Mary had been jotting down everything in a small notebook, so that she could refer back to it, but the notebook was filling up fast.

"We've got a small laptop computer with a printer that was donated last week," Bev mentioned. "We really should get all this information into the computer, so that you can keep up with pickup and delivery locations and the time frames."

Mary agreed. "That would be nice. But I don't know how to use a computer," she added with a grimace. "We were never able to afford one."

"I work with them all the time," Matt said with a lazy smile. "Suppose I come over an hour before we start tomorrow and key in the data?"

"That would be great, Matt!" Mary exclaimed.

"It shouldn't be too difficult," he added. "If I can read your handwriting, that is," he mused.

"Well," Mary began worriedly.

"Could you get off an hour early and have Smith watch the kids for you?" Matt persisted.

"She works for me tomorrow, and sure she can get off early," Billie volunteered, stepping forward. "Hi. I'm Billie West. Don't let the glitter fool you," she added when the others gave her odd looks. "I came up in Chicago, on the wrong side of the tracks."

The odd looks relaxed into smiles.

"I'm Bev, I run the shelter. Welcome aboard," Bev said, shaking hands. "That's Sam Harlowe over there, and this is Matt Clark. Matt's a police officer."

"Nice to meet you," Billie said. "Thanks for letting me and my SUV join up."

"You and your SUV are most welcome," Mary replied. "And thanks in advance for the hour off."

"Where do we start?" Billie asked.

Now that they'd added three restaurants to the ten they already had, Mary realized the waiting time and the packaging of the donated food once it was picked up was going to pose a problem.

"This isn't going to work," she told Matt while they were briefly alone in the shelter's kitchen, finishing up filling the last containers of food. "We really need one more vehicle so that we can split the list three ways and each truck will have a third of the restaurants to pick up from."

"Bev said that she's already had calls from six more restaurants that heard about your project and want to contribute," Matt told her. "Your little project is turning into a business."

"But there aren't enough people," Mary said worriedly. "Not nearly enough."

"You need to talk to someone about the future of this project," Matt pointed out. "You can do a great job if you just have more volunteers. It's a wonderful thing you're doing. You can't let it overwhelm you."

"It already has," she said with a husky laugh.

"It shows," Matt said with some concern. "You look worn-out, Mary, and I know you can't be getting much rest at night. Not with a toddler."

"John's a good boy, and the kids are great about helping look after him," Mary said defensively.

"Yes, but you still have to be responsible for all of them. That includes getting them to and from practice and games, overseeing homework, listening to problems they have at school," he said gently. "That's a heck of a responsibility for one woman, all by itself. But you've got a full-time job, and you're spending every night running around Phoenix to restaurants and then distributing food until late. Even with your energy and strength of will, you must see that you can't keep this up indefinitely."

Until he said it, she hadn't realized how thin she was spreading herself. She was beginning to have some chest pain that was unexpected and alarming. She hadn't mentioned it, thinking that perhaps if she ignored it, it would go away. But that wasn't happening.

"I can do it as long as I need to," she said firmly.

"You're like me, aren't you?" he mused, smiling. "You're stubborn."

"Yes, I think I am," she agreed, smiling back. He made her feel young. He was like a sip of cold water on a hot day. He was invigorating.

"I have ulterior motives, you know," he commented. "I'm fond of you. I don't want you to keel over from stress."

She was touched. "I promise not to keel over," she told him.

He signed. "Okay. That will have to do for now. But you really should think about delegating more. And eventually, you're going to need some agency to help you oversee the project. It's outgrowing you by the day."

"I don't even know where to begin," she said.

"Talk to Bev," he told her. "She's been in this sort of work for a long time, and she knows everybody else who's involved in it. She may have some ideas."

"I'll do that," Mary promised.

"Meanwhile," he drawled, "don't forget Sunday."

She had forgotten. Her wide-eyed stare made him burst out laughing.

"Well, that puts me in my place," he said with a grin. "I'll have to stop strutting and thinking I'm God's gift to over-worked womanhood."

She smiled at him. "You're a nice guy, Matt. I'd only forgotten today. I'd have remembered when I went home, because it's all the kids talk about."

"So I made an impression, did I?"

"A big one," she agreed. "They like you."

"I'm glad. I like them. A lot."

"Speaking of the movies, it turns out Tammy has a prior commitment and can't watch the baby after all. Looks like he'd be joining us. Hope that's okay."

"No problem," Matt reassured her.

"Hey, are you guys coming, or what?" Sam called from the parking lot. "We're running behind schedule."

"Sorry, Sam," Mary said at once, preceding Matt out the door. "Let's go!"

They had a routine of sorts by now, through the various shelters and homeless camps. People came out to meet them when they saw the headlights, and there were beaming faces when the smell of food wafted out of the containers that were presented to the staff for their residents.

"We never had stuff like this to eat before," one disabled young woman commented to Mary at the women's shelter. "You sure are nice to do this for us."

"You're very welcome," Mary said, searching for the right words.

The young woman smiled and walked away to the kitchen as quickly as she could with her crutches.

"That's Anna. She has multiple sclerosis," the shelter manager told Mary quietly. "Usually she's in a wheelchair, but it got stolen two days ago when she left it outside the stall in a rest room a block away." She shook her head. "Imagine, somebody stealing a woman's wheelchair and nobody noticing!"

"How did she get here?" Mary wondered.

"One of our regulars saw her holding on to walls trying to walk. She came back here and borrowed our spare crutches that I keep in the office for Anna. She's been using them ever since, but it's hard for her to walk with wasted muscles."

"Is there some sort of program that could get her a wheelchair?"

The woman grimaced. "She'd probably qualify if she could get into the system. That's the problem. We have to have a caseworker come here and fill out forms, then there's a waiting period, and she might or might not get accepted on the first try. Bureaucracy is slow."

Mary sighed. "If I had the money, I'd buy her a wheelchair," she said.

"Me, too," the shelter manager said quietly.

They exchanged glances.

"No matter how much we do, it's like filling up a barrel with a teaspoon, isn't it?" Mary asked. "There's so much need, and so few people trying to meet it. Federal and state and local programs do what they can. But there are limits to any budget, and so many people fall through the cracks."

"That's true."

"I found that out the hard way," Mary said.

"You?" the manager exclaimed.

"I'm living in a motel room with three kids, holding down a full-time job, six days a week, sometimes seven, and I do this after I get off, every day," Mary told her. "Because no matter how bad things are for me, everybody I meet in these shelters is so much worse off."

"My dear," the manager said, lost for words.

"It's been a learning experience for all of us," Mary told her. "We've learned so much about human nature since we began this project. And despite our own circumstances, people have just been so kind to us," she emphasized. "I never knew how kind total strangers could be until we ended up like this."

"I like the feeling I get when I know I've helped someone out of a particularly bad spot, given them hope," the manager said with a warm smile.

"I do, too. It makes it all worthwhile."

"And you have three kids." She shook her head. "I only had

one, and he's got a wife and three kids of his own. We had a good home and a comfortable income." She glanced at Mary. "You're unbelievable."

Mary laughed. "Maybe I'm just out of my mind," she suggested.

The other woman laughed, too. "If you are, I wish we had a hundred more just like you. Thanks, Mary. Thanks a million."

"It's my pleasure. And I mean that." Mary smiled.

The next day Billie let Mary off an hour early with no argument at all. "And I'll see you at the shelter in an hour," she added. "You know, this has given me a new lease on life. I've been so depressed lately. It was time I stopped feeling sorry for myself and started being useful for a change. I'm very grateful to you for helping me."

"We're all grateful to you for helping us," Mary replied. "And I'll see you at the shelter at five."

She was still driving the car that Debbie had loaned her, and Tammy had demanded that Mary let her keep John during the day.

"I have all this room and only two kids," Tammy had argued. "And both of them love having John around to play with. Besides, I heard from a reliable source that Jack left town so there's no danger that he's going to track the kids down anytime soon. It's only for a couple of weeks, until you get some sort of system worked out. So humor me!"

Mary had, with more gratitude than she could express.

She picked up John at Tammy's and went with him to the shelter where Matt was ready to feed information into the computer.

Two of the shelter workers came right up to take John.

"Let them," Bev coaxed when Mary started to protest. "We all love kids, you know that. You just help Matt get that schedule on a disk and we'll take care of John."

"Thanks," Mary said, smiling.

She sat down beside Matt at the long table. The computer was an old one, but it seemed to be workable.

"The one I have in my squad car is older than this," he pointed out as he opened a file in a word processor. "It's going to be a piece of cake, getting your schedule fed into this thing. Okay. I'm ready. Let's see that notebook."

She produced it and opened it to the appropriate page.

He glanced down and his eyes widened. "Good Lord, woman, you call this handwriting? I'm amazed you didn't fail first grade!"

She burst out laughing. "You listen here, I got awards for my penmanship in high school!"

"From doctors, no doubt," he drawled.

She gave him a restrained glare. "So I was in a little bit of a hurry when I scribbled these things down," she confessed finally.

He chuckled. "Actually, I had a partner whose handwriting was even worse than yours. Every time he wrote out a traffic citation, we got a call from the clerk of court's office asking us to translate for them."

"That makes me feel a little better," she replied with a laugh.

It was incredible how often she did that with him. Her blue eyes swept over his rugged, lined face. He put on a good front, but she could see the inner scars he carried. His whole life was there, in those deep lines.

"Have you ever had to shoot anybody?" she asked involuntarily.

"Not yet," he replied. "But I've threatened to shoot a few people who robbed banks or abused helpless people."

"Good for you," she said.

His hands paused over the keyboard and he glanced up at her. "Could you ever date a cop?"

She was suddenly flustered. "Well…well, I never thought about it."

He pursed his lips. "Wow. That puts me in my place."

"It does not," she retorted. "You're a terrific person. The job wouldn't bother me, really. I mean, I don't think it would matter so much if you cared about somebody." She ground her teeth together. "I can't put it into words."

"Oh, I think you did a pretty good job of expressing yourself," he drawled, and wiggled his eyebrows.

She chuckled. "You're a character, you are."

"Takes one to know one. I think you'd better read me that

list along with addresses and phone numbers. It will save hours of time trying to read your handwriting."

"Hold your breath until you ever get a letter from me," she teased.

"I like cards. Funny cards. My birthday is next month," he hinted. "You could send me one, and I'd put it on my mantel beside the pictures of my mother and father."

"I'll consider it seriously," she promised.

"You do that."

They joked back and forth as they went through the list and put all the necessary information into the computer. It wasn't as time-consuming as Mary had thought it would be. She had to admit, she enjoyed Matt's company. He was a complex person. She really wanted to get to know him. But it was much too soon for anything serious.

By the time Sunday arrived, Mary was so tired that she almost thought of backing out of Matt's generous offer to take them all to the movies.

She had some uncomfortable palpitations, and she felt sick in her stomach. It was frightening. She knew it probably had something to do with the stress, but for the moment, she had no idea how to get out from under it.

More importantly, she didn't want to frighten the children. Bob and Ann were already giving her curious looks. They began to notice that her mother was pale and listless when she wasn't working.

"Don't even think about trying to back out," Matt told Mary when he was standing in the motel room, comfortable in jeans and a long-sleeved blue checked shirt with a leather jacket. "You're going to enjoy today. I promise. Won't she, kids?" he asked the others.

"You bet!" they chorused.

"A movie and a few hours of being away from work, from any work at all, will rejuvenate you," Matt promised as he smiled down at her. "We're going to have a ball!"

Mary wasn't so sure, but she got her old coat on, put the kids in theirs, and all of them went out the door to pile into Matt's sedan.

CHAPTER
~FIVE~

The theater was crowded, even at the matinee, but most of the audience was made up of children. Bob met one of his friends, and went to sit with him. Ann sat on one side of Matt, and the baby, John, curled into Mary's shoulder and promptly went to sleep.

"He really is a good baby," Matt whispered, watching the little boy with a tender smile.

"He always has been," she whispered back.

Matt glanced toward the other kids, who were engrossed in the movie. "Were the others like this?"

She shook her head. "Bob was a live wire, always in trouble for being mischievous. Ann refuses to show her work in math

which gets her into
ntelligent."

"I noticed," Matt agreed.

People in the seats ahead we
exchanged wry glances and paid a

"That was just great!" Bob enthuse
over and they were back in the car, hea od
restaurant that served chili dogs—the childre e food.
"Thanks a lot, Mr. Clark."

"Matt," the older man corrected lazily. "I'm glad you enjoyed
t, Bob. So did I. I think the last movie I went to see was the
second of the new Star Wars films."

"That was ages ago," Ann exclaimed.

Matt shrugged, smiling. "My social life is mostly work."

"Join the club," Mary had to agree.

"We need to do this more often," Matt said. "At least a
movie a month. If you guys would like to do that," he added.

There was a loud chorus of assents and excited smiles all
around.

"You're terrific, Matt," Ann said. "Thanks."

"My pleasure," he replied, with a smile in Mary's direction.
"Now, for chili dogs!" he added as he pulled into the fast-food
restaurant.

Mary and Matt had shared the cost of the outing, because
she insisted. It had made a hole in her meager savings, but as

...ant faces of her children, she couldn'...

...ht. Sometimes in the struggle just to survive, sh...

...ot that the children needed more than school and work i...

order to thrive. They needed a little breathing space from th...

problems of everyday life. In fact, so did she.

"That was really great, Matt," Mary told him as he deposite...

her and the children at the motel. "I enjoyed it. So did they,...

she added, nodding toward the children filing into the roo...

with Ann carrying little John carefully in her arms.

He smiled. "That was obvious. I'm glad, because I had a goo...

time, too. I haven't been out on a date since my wife left me...

She gave him a wry glance. "Some date," she mused. "Me an...

three kids."

He chuckled. "I was an only child. It was sort of a dream o...

mine to have a big family." He shrugged. "My wife hated kids...

She didn't like my job, either. She wanted to party all the time...

and I came home dead tired at night. We were doomed t...

failure, I guess. Neither of us was any good at looking ahead...

We married on an impulse. It was a really bad impulse."

She sighed. "I had those same ideals myself. I did, at least...

get the big family," she said with a smile. "But I never expecte...

that I'd have to raise it all by myself. It's a big responsibility."

He touched her hair gently, just a gesture without any de...

mands or insistence. "Listen, if you ever need somebody to loo...

after your brood in an emergency, I've got a big-screen televi...

sion and lots of G-rated movies. They'd be company for me."

Her face became radiant. "Wouldn't you faint if I said yes?"

"Try me."

She hesitated. "I might do that one day, if you mean it."

His dark eyes swept over her face. "You've got guts. You never complain, no matter how hard your life is. You love those kids and it sticks out like a neon light. You've got a good sense of humor and you don't back away from trouble. I think you're an exceptional woman. Having got that out of the way," he continued when she tried to speak, "I'll add that I think your sons and daughter are the nicest children I've ever met, and some of the most unselfish. It wouldn't be any chore to look after them, as long as I'm not on duty. I don't think you'd like having me take them on a high-speed chase or to make a drug bust."

She laughed. "No, really I wouldn't. But if I get in a tight spot, I'll remember you. I will."

"Good. I'll see you at the shelter tomorrow afternoon."

"Thanks again, Matt."

"I'm lonely," he said simply. "It was fun."

She watched him walk away. Her heart felt warm and safe. She sighed like a girl. Perhaps, someday, she thought to herself.

The routine was more fulfilling than Mary had ever dreamed it might be. She really enjoyed her trips to the restaurants and then to the shelters and homeless camps. It was the first time in her life that she'd ever felt she was making a difference. It was more than just feeding the hungry. She felt a sense of self worth, of responsibility and pride, that she hadn't ever known.

To her surprise, her work was sparking comment in the community, to the extent that the shelter Bev ran got a call from a daily newspaper reporter. She wanted to do a feature article on Mary.

At first, Mary thought about refusing. She didn't want people to think she was doing the work just for publicity. But Bev assured her that this wasn't going to be the case. The reporter was a vivacious young lady who sat down with Mary for half an hour and wrote a story that sounded as if she'd known Mary her whole life. Best of all, people called the shelter and volunteered their time, and money, to help the needy.

Mary's kids were also learning a lot about the world through helping their mother with the project. Their own generosity in helping with their mother's routine without complaint said a lot for their unselfish natures.

"You know," Bob commented one evening when they'd just dropped off several containers of food at the women's mission, "I didn't understand how people could lose their homes and end up in places like this. I mean, not until we started taking them food." He frowned. "There are a lot of desperate people in the world, aren't there, Mom?" he added. "I guess what mean is, when we're doing this stuff for other people, it kind of helps me forget how scared and uncertain I feel myself."

Mary reached over and hugged him. "That's a good feeling, too, isn't it?"

"It is," Ann joined in.

But despite the pleasure it gave Mary to pursue her project, she was feeling the pressure of trying to hold down several physically demanding jobs and look after the children's needs, as well as drive around most of the night picking up and delivering food. She had several volunteers, and she was grateful for every one of them. But her list was growing longer and the demands were increasing.

"You really are going to have to have help," Bev told her firmly. "You need someone to help you coordinate all this."

"Matt made a computer program," Mary began.

"You need an organization to sponsor what you're doing, Mary," came the quiet reply. "You're going to fold up if you keep trying to do it all by yourself."

"But I don't know any organizations," she said heavily.

"I do," Bev replied. "The head of the local food bank has been in touch with me. That article they did about you in the morning paper has gained some interest from some important people around the city. I've been asked to introduce you to the food bank manager tomorrow. Can you get off an hour early and meet me here?"

Mary was dumbfounded. "He wants to meet...me?"

Bev smiled. "You're an inspiration to all of us, a woman in your circumstances who's willing to give time and money she doesn't have to help people less fortunate than she is."

She shook her head. "Anybody else would have done the same thing."

"Not in a million years," Bev said quietly. "Will you come?"

Mary sighed. "Okay. I'll be here at four, is that all right?"

Bev grinned. "Just right!"

The manager of the City Food Bank, Tom Harvey, was tall and elegant, a soft-spoken gentleman with a warm smile and kind dark eyes.

"I'm very pleased to meet you, Mrs. Crandall," he said when he shook Mary's hand. "I must say, you've come as a surprise to all of us. I didn't really believe the story in the paper until I talked to Bev. So many times, reporters exaggerate the truth. But in your case, I think the story was actually an understatement. I'm amazed at what you've done on your own initiative."

"It's tiring, but it's the most rewarding thing I've done in my life," Mary told him. "I enjoy every minute of it."

"So I've been told." He frowned. "But your list of participating restaurants is growing bigger by the day, and even with your volunteers, you're not going to be able to keep up this pace."

"I'm beginning to realize that," Mary had to admit. She looked up at him curiously. "Do you have any suggestions?"

"Yes, I do. I'd like to consider adding your project under our program and putting you in charge of it. You'd work part-time, but it would be a paid job."

Mary felt the blood drain out of her face. It seemed almost too good to be true. "You're joking."

He shook his head. "I assure you, I'm not. Your program is unique, and it's doing a lot of good. I want to see it continue. I want to see you continue," he emphasized with a smile. "With three children to support and your full-time cleaning job, and this, I feel that you must be stretched pretty thin."

"I'm almost transparent," she confessed with a smile. "But that wouldn't stop me from doing it."

He nodded. "I thought you were that sort of person. There's a pilot program in California which does much the same manner of food rescue that you're doing. I'd really like to fly you out there and take a look at it, and see what you think. If you like it, we can expand your project and put it in place here."

Mary was thinking. Her mind was whirling. She could do this with professional help on the organizational level. She could do it part-time as a salaried employee and cut her cleaning jobs in half. She'd be able to spend more time with the children. They might be able to afford to rent a house, even buy a car. It was overwhelming.

"You haven't answered," Tom Harvey said gently.

She smiled from ear to ear. "I'm speechless," she admitted. "I'd like very much to see the California program and make my decision afterward."

"Great!" he exclaimed. "Then we'll get the ball rolling!"

Mary took Matt up on his offer to keep the children over a weekend, while she flew to San Diego. Although money wasn't an issue since the City Food Bank covered all her travel expenditures, she was nervous about the trip. However, Matt assured her that she was going to do just fine. The kids kissed her goodbye and told her not to worry. Matt gave her a speaking look, because he knew she'd worry anyway. He'd given her both his home and cell phone numbers, to make sure she could reach him whenever she wanted to check on the children. It made her feel better.

When she got to San Diego, she checked into the nice motel they'd put her up in and took a cab to the food bank office. There, she met a live wire of a woman named Lorinda who ran the food rescue program for the food bank there. It was similar to Mary's, except that it was much more efficient. There was a special unit of volunteers who made the rounds of the restaurants to pick up food, and a separate unit that had panel trucks with which to make the deliveries. It worked like clockwork, and served many shelters.

"We're adding to our suppliers all the time," Lorinda said with a contagious smile. "It's time-consuming and we spend a lot for gas, but the program is very successful. It's lucky that we have plenty of volunteers. I'm amazed at what you're able to do with so few people."

"Yes," Mary agreed. "Imagine what I could do with a setup like yours!"

The other woman just smiled. "We have the advantage of a comfortable budget and people with great organizational skills."

"I've been offered both," Mary said thoughtfully. "And I believe I'm going to accept them."

Two weeks later, Mary was officially on the staff of the food bank as a part-time employee in charge of food rescue.

She sat at a desk in the shelter and used the phone excessively in the first week on the job, setting up even more restaurants to be clients of the food bank. She was also trying to keep the cleaning jobs she'd had for so many years. The stress of it all suddenly caught up with her early one morning after she'd dropped the kids off at school and John at a nearby day-care center with a woman she trusted.

She was walking into the food bank office when she felt

something like a blow to her chest. She saw the floor coming up to meet her. Everything went black.

She came to in a hospital bed with Matt sitting beside her in full uniform, except for his hat, which was on the floor beside him. He looked worn and worried.

Her eyes opened slowly and she blinked. "What happened?" she asked weakly. She looked around. "Where am I?"

His eyebrows lifted above wide dark eyes. "Apparently you decided to take a sudden nap on the floor of your office."

She smiled weakly. "Bad decision."

"Very bad." He reached over and stroked her cheek. "How do you feel?"

"Odd. Floaty. Disconnected."

"That would be the sedative kicking in," he assessed.

"Have I had a heart attack? Has a doctor been in?"

"A few minutes ago," he said. "But it wasn't a heart attack. The palpitations were induced by stress and you collapsed from exhaustion. I told him what you'd been doing, and he asked if you had a death wish."

She laughed softly. "I guess I need a vacation."

"You're having one," he pointed out. "All meals included."

"This is much too expensive a vacation," she argued. "I have minimal insurance coverage and it's brand-new."

"It's quite enough, as you'll find out," he replied. "I checked."

"The children...!"

"I picked them up from school, and John from day care and brought them here with me. They're with your friend, Tammy. I phoned her and she came straight over to pick them up. I would have been glad to keep them," he added at once, "but I'm on duty and I can't get anybody to cover for me. I took my lunch hour early to come and see about you."

"Thanks, Matt."

"No problem," he said gently. "I don't mind looking after people I lo...people I care about," he corrected abruptly, afraid that he'd gone too far too fast. She was fragile enough already without having to carry the burden of his feelings for her.

But Mary had caught his slip of the tongue, and even through the fog of the sedatives, she felt exhilarated. "You're a wonder, Matt. I don't know how to thank you..."

"I don't need thanking," he replied gently. "I'm glad to do it. Thank your friend, Tammy. She didn't even have to be coaxed into baby-sitting—if that's the right word to use."

"Are my babies all right?" she whispered.

They were terrified and half out of their collective minds with worry, he thought, but he wasn't about to tell her that. He smiled convincingly. "They're doing great. I'm going to bring them to see you when I get off duty tonight."

"I'll try to look better so that I don't scare them."

He reached out and took her hand gently in his. Her fingers

were like ice. "Listen, you're going to have to make some hard decisions, and soon. The doctor said you'll make a speedy recovery—provided that you slow down. If not for your own sake, then for the children's. What are they going to do without you, Mary?"

She winced. "I've tried so hard to give them everything I could. Life is so hard sometimes, Matt."

"I may not look as if I know that, but I do," he said, curling her small hand into his big one. "Nevertheless, you're going to have to slow down."

"Where do I start?" she worried. "I can't give up my cleaning jobs, they're all I have to support me."

"You have a part-time job at the food bank that will help a lot. That should allow you the luxury of cutting down on your cleaning jobs, at least. And you'll have more volunteers to help with the pickups and deliveries of your program. Who knows, Mary, it might someday work into a full-time job. All you have to do is hang in there for the time being. But the pace is going to kill you if you don't put on the brakes." His eyes lowered to her hand. He brought it gently to his lips and kissed the palm hungrily. "I've suddenly got a family of my own," he added huskily, and without looking at her. "I don't want to be left alone."

Her heart skipped wildly. "Matt!" she whispered huskily.

His dark eyes lifted to hers. He searched them slowly, and her face began to grow radiant with faint color.

"I know," he murmured. "It's too soon after your divorce for this. You don't really know me yet, or trust me. But I'm going to be around for a long time, and I can wait until you're comfortable with me."

She laughed a little shyly. "I don't think I'll ever be that, exactly. You're…sort of an electrifying personality. You make me feel as if I could do anything."

"Same here," he replied, his lips tugging into a tender smile. "So don't skip out on me, okay? You have to get better. A lot of us can't go on without you."

She smiled up at him with her heart in her eyes. She drew the back of his big hand to her cheek and held it there. "I'm not going anywhere. Honest."

He stood up, bending over her with his heart in his eyes. "I'll hold you to that," he whispered, and, bending, he touched his lips tenderly to her forehead.

She sighed with pure bliss.

He lifted his head, dropped his eyes to her mouth, and bent down to give her a real kiss that took her breath away. When the door opened and a young nurse came into the room, she noted how quickly the policeman stood up, and how flushed he and the patient looked.

"Uh-huh," she murmured dryly. "I can see that I'll have to keep a closer eye on you two!" she teased.

The tension broke and they both started laughing.

"He's the one you have to watch," Mary said with a possessive smile in Matt's direction. "But not too closely, if you don't mind," she added with a wink at the pretty nurse. "I can't stand the competition."

"That's what you think," Matt drawled.

Mary sat up in bed. "Oh, my goodness," she exclaimed. "Who'll do my pickups and deliveries tonight? You can't do it all, not even with the children helping."

He held up a hand. "Already taken care of," he said easily. "I phoned Bev and she phoned a few people. Tonight, even if you could get out of that bed, you'd be superfluous. So you just concentrate on getting your strength back. Okay?"

Mary felt as if she had a new lease on life, as if tomorrow and all the tomorrows to come would be worth waking up for. The look in Matt's eyes made her tingle like an adolescent with her first crush.

He seemed to understand how she felt, because his eyes darkened and a faint ruddy flush darkened the skin on his high cheekbones.

"I really have to go," he bit off.

Mary was watching him hungrily while the nurse checked

her blood pressure, and then her temperature, with her high-tech arsenal of diagnostic tools.

"You'll be back tonight, with the kids?" Mary added.

He nodded, and smiled. "Around seven."

"I'll expect you," Mary said huskily. "I'm going to phone Tammy and thank her."

"Good idea." He winked again. "Stay out of trouble."

"Look who's talking!" Mary exclaimed, and smiled back at him.

"See you." He went out with a quick wave of his hand. Mary stared after him until the door closed.

"Handsome guy," the nurse murmured dryly. "I gather he's spoken for?" she asked.

"Oh, yes, indeed, he is," Mary replied with a becoming blush.

"No wonder you're improving so much," the nurse laughed. "If you need me, just buzz. You're doing great."

"Thanks," she said.

The nurse smiled and went to her next patient down the hall.

Her family doctor, Mack Barker, stopped by just at supper-time to check her over. He dropped into a chair by her bedside after he'd checked her chart and taken her vitals himself.

"I suppose you know now that you can't go on burning the

candle at both ends," he told her. "You were pushing yourself too hard. Something had to give."

"I suppose I just went on from day to day without thinking about how much stress I was under," she had to admit.

"You're going to have to learn how to delegate more," he warned her. "Or this may not be the last trip you make to the hospital."

She drew in a lazy breath. "It's just that I've got three kids to look after, and now I'm doing this food rescue program..."

"Which is a very worthwhile thing," the doctor admitted. "But if you don't slow down, somebody else is going to be doing it instead of you. Or maybe nobody else will be able to do it at all, and it will fold. Either way, you're going to destroy your health if you don't find a way to curtail your work. I'm sorry. I know how much it means to you. But you can't possibly keep it up any longer."

"I can't give up what I do at the food bank," she said miserably. "You can't imagine how many people depend on those food deliveries—"

"Yes, I can imagine," he interrupted. "It's a tremendously worthwhile and unselfish thing you've been doing." He smiled quietly. "It's just that I'd like you to be able to continue it. This is going to require some compromise. But you can salvage some of your charity work and keep your job at the food bank as well. You only need to cut your housekeeping duties in half. Believe me, your clients will understand."

"It's the money," Mary argued. "I have to be able to keep the kids in clothes and food and pay my bills. We're living in a motel room, we can't even afford to rent a house!"

"Do you believe in miracles?"

Mary looked up as Bev stepped into the room with a big smile on her face.

She blinked. "Well, yes. Of course."

"Your hard work hasn't gone unnoticed. I know someone who has a house for rent, at a price you can afford."

"You're kidding!" she exclaimed.

"I'm not. And my friend knows where you can get some good used furniture and appliances to go in it."

"I can't believe it," she exclaimed.

When the doctor left the room a few minutes later, Bev filled her in on the details. "It gets better. The house is half a block from the shelter, so that you could walk to work."

She just stared at Bev, dumbfounded.

"I know you can afford the utilities on your salary. You could probably even afford to make payments on a good used car, since you won't have rent to worry about."

Tears stung her eyes and rolled down her pale cheeks. "I just can't believe it!"

When Matt returned that evening with the kids, she filled him in on her wonderful news.

He smiled. "It's amazing how kind people can be," he remarked. "I see a lot of cruelty in my line of work. Sometimes it really gets me down, seeing the dark side of human nature. But then, somebody like you comes along and renews my faith in mankind. Womankind, too. People who give always get repaid for it, Mary."

She wiped away the tears. "Bev went out of her way looking for that house, didn't she?"

He nodded.

"What a kind thing for her to do."

"I'll tell her," he said with a laugh. "For now, you just concentrate on getting better, and out of here."

She let out a long breath, thinking what an odyssey her life had become. It was a journey, an adventure, an obstacle course. But she'd become strong and self-sufficient and independent because of the hardships and challenges.

"Deep thoughts?" Matt probed.

She looked at him. "I was thinking that it's not the destination, it's the journey. I've heard that all my life. I never really understood it until I ended up in a shelter with my kids."

He nodded. "The journey is the thing. Not to mention the exciting and interesting people you meet along the way." He gave her a devilish wink and brought her hand to his lips.

Warmth flooded through her. "I never expected that people would be so kind to me, when I was about as low on the social ladder as a person could get. Even the people I work for have been supportive and generous. And you were the best surprise of all," she said softly.

"Right back at you," he said gruffly.

She laid back on the pillows. "Thank you, Matt, for everything. And you'll be happy to know I'm listening to the doctor. I'll speak with my employers when I get out of here. And I will slow down."

"That's a really good idea," he mused. "I'll be back with the kids first thing tomorrow."

After Mary kissed the kids good-night and exchanged a highly charged look with Matt that was ripe with possibilities of what the future could hold, she was left alone to rest. Closing her eyes, she thought about the changes she was going to have to make. Perhaps it wouldn't be so bad after all, slowing down. Well, slowing down just a little, she amended.

CHAPTER
∽ SIX ∽

Mary had a long talk with three of her employers about giving up her work. They were nice, but she knew they didn't really understand why Mary had to quit working for them.

One asked if the money wasn't enough, and offered a substantial raise if Mary would stay on.

That was just too hard to turn down. Mary agreed to stay, but she was adamant about the other two jobs. She explained that if she had another stress attack, it could be much worse, and she had her kids to think about. She had to stay healthy so that she could get them all through school. Her doctor had insisted that she had to give up some work. In the end, they accepted her decision and even gave her severance pay.

Matt was delighted that she was following doctor's orders. "We get to keep you around for a while, right, kids?" he asked them when they were all enjoying hamburgers after a particularly great fantasy movie on their Saturday out.

"Right!" they chorused.

"It's been a super evening, Matt. Thanks again."

He smiled warmly at her. "It's only the second of many," he said easily, finishing his hamburger. "I see a pleasant future for us."

"Us?" she teased lightly.

"Us," he agreed. "We'll be best friends for a couple of years and then I'll follow you around Phoenix on one knee with a ring in my hand until you say yes."

She laughed delightedly. "I just might hold you to that," she murmured.

"We can carry your bouquet," Ann enthused.

"And tie tin cans to the bumper of the car we haven't got yet," Bob added, tongue-in-cheek.

"We can take care of him when he's sick," Ann added in her sensible way.

Matt gave Ann a beaming smile. "And I can take care of all of you, when you need it."

"I might be a policeman one day myself," Bob mused.

It was nice to see that the children liked Matt as much as she did. It wasn't wise to look too far down unknown roads.

But she felt comfortable and secure with Matt. So did the children. He was truly one of a kind. She had a feeling that it would all work out just perfectly one day.

"Deep thoughts?" Matt mused.

"Very nice ones, too," she replied, and she smiled at him.

Her new job was more fulfilling than anything she'd done in her life. She felt a sense of accomplishment when she and her volunteers—many of them, now—carried food to the legions of hungry people around town.

More newspaper interviews had followed, including stories about her co-workers, which made her feel like part of a large, generous family. Which, in effect, the food bank was.

"You know," she told Tom one afternoon, "I never dreamed that I'd be doing this sort of job. It's like a dream come true."

"I understand how you feel," he replied, smiling. "All of us who became involved in this work are better people for having been able to do it. The more we give, the more we receive. And not just in material ways."

"Yes," she said. "There's no greater gift than that of giving to other people."

He nodded.

She glanced at her watch and gasped. "Goodness, I have to get on the road! Mr. Harvey, did I ever tell you how grateful I am to have this job?"

"Only about six times a day," he murmured dryly. "We're happy to have you working for us, Mary."

"I'll get on my rounds. Good night, Mr. Harvey."

He smiled. "Good night, Mary."

She went out the door with a list of her pickups and deliveries in one hand, her mind already on the evening's work. Matt was on duty tonight, Bob and Ann were at sports competitions, John was with Tammy, who'd agreed to pick up Bob and Ann at the games—her kids were playing, as well. Mary could pick them up on the way home.

Home. She thought of the neat little house she was now living in with her kids, rent free, and of the nice used compact car she'd been able to afford. It didn't seem very far away that she and the children had been living on the streets, with no money, no home, no car and no prospects. Life had looked very sad back then.

But now she was rich, in so many ways that had little to do with money. She waved to the volunteer staff standing by their own vehicles, waiting for her to lead the way. How far she'd come, from taking a little leftover food from a restaurant and delivering it to one or two clients.

Her heart raced as she climbed in behind the wheel. She started the car and drove off, leading the others out to the highway. There would be a lot of deliveries tonight, a lot of people to help. She felt as if she could float on air. She'd not only survived life at the bottom, she'd bounced back like a happy rubber ball to an even better place.

The future looked very bright. Life was good.

Dear Reader,

One of the greatest pleasures of my life was doing this story for Harlequin, especially in the company of other such gifted authors. My contribution, "The Greatest Gift," tells the story of Sue Cobley, a big-hearted, generous, compassionate woman who put her own troubles aside to do something for people she considered in worse straits than she was herself. It lifts the heart to see how one person can make such a huge difference in the world, just by putting other people first.

In our busy and hectic lives, sometimes we fail to think about people who need help. It is more than an obligation to help people in need, it is one of the greatest joys in life. Sue Cobley inspired me to get more involved with programs that do good in our communities. I hope that her story will inspire you, too. You don't have to be a millionaire to change the world. You just have to have the desire. Thanks, Sue Cobley, for the wonderful things you have done for others. And the example you have set for us all.

Diana Palmer

DEB FRUEND
⚬— TEAM ACTIVITIES FOR —⚬
SPECIAL KIDS

F
ew would deny that Deb Fruend is busy. When she's not putting in eight-hour days as an adaptive physical education instructor for the Special School District of St. Louis County, she's spending evenings on the basketball court, soccer field and even the bowling alley running TASK—Team Activities for Special Kids.

But ask Deb what drives her to burn the midnight oil and she barely misses a beat.

"The kids," she says simply. "It's the look in kids' eyes when they accomplish something they haven't been able to do before. It's the look in their eyes when they know someone believes in them."

Yet when Deb first launched TASK back in 1996, she was also thinking of the parents. Sitting in on education meetings with parents of special needs kids, she kept hearing the same refrain.

"My child doesn't have anywhere to play a sport," the clearly frustrated parents would say.

Finally Deb decided to do something about it. She formed an instructional T-ball league specifically for special needs kids who were itching to be athletes like their brothers, sisters and friends.

"When we started we had one little sport. It was just a bunch of kids on a church field. We've come a long way," she says.

That's no exaggeration. Today TASK offers twelve sports to special needs kids in the St. Louis area—basketball, bowling, coach-pitch softball, dance, floor hockey, golf, soccer, softball, swimming, T-ball, tennis and volleyball. More than 200 volunteers, from teachers to physical therapists and speech and language pathologists, work with over 800 kids to help them with anything from how to do the butterfly stroke to learning how to play as a team. Each sport focuses on learning and practicing athletic and interpersonal skills, with an emphasis on teamwork and good sportsmanship.

Sports are often tailored to match the abilities of players. For instance, in modified softball, batters are allowed five strikes instead of three. Swimming classes include one called "terrified of water" for children who have an extreme reaction to water and do not like to swim.

The kids' needs run the gamut from visual impairment to learning disabilities, mental disabilities, Down syndrome, behavioral concerns and autism. No child is ever turned away.

With such a wide range of abilities, not to mention ages, it's no wonder Deb has her work cut out for her, matching the right kids with each team. But, says Deb, playing a sport is more about developing self-worth and accepting others than it is about playing to win.

"I wanted to create a league atmosphere so the kids could feel good about themselves. I wanted them to say, 'My sister has a game this weekend. Well, I've got a game this Saturday, too,'" she says.

Building esteem

TASK is about helping kids feel they belong. Before Deb's work with the organization, parents often complained that their children were struggling out on the field or on the court. Other parents were yelling at the child because he didn't seem to be listening to the coach. The other kids yelled at him because he wasn't running fast enough.

TASK has a motto: we build self-esteem, self-esteem builds confidence, confidence builds skill.

And that is exactly what seems to happen, says Deb, a firm believer in the benefits gained from team activities, including the development of self-esteem, physical coordination, cooperation skills and other critical life skills.

"If the kids feel good about themselves they're going to try harder. If they try harder they're going to do better," she maintains.

Kids who are part of TASK also build esteem by developing relationship skills. Many become close friends away from the league, sometimes driving an hour to visit each other at home or watch a movie together. These children probably never would have met if it had not been for TASK.

To help these relationships grow, TASK has branched out to create a Kids' Club and Social Club so the children can find new buddies and socialize. Then there's also TASK Summer Camp, a week-long program offered to kids with special physical and mental concerns. The campers enjoy what other camp kids have always taken for granted: assembling crafts, taking a dip, bike riding and making new friends.

"It's amazing to me how excited a child can get whenever they've accomplished something and they feel they are part of a team. What does belonging mean to a special needs child?" Deb asks. "Everything. Absolutely everything."

The parents also become good friends while watching their kids score goals or learn to bowl.

Off the field

While TASK athletes certainly learn skills that come in handy while dribbling a ball or passing the puck to a teammate, Deb says many of the more important skills are transferred to everyday life.

One of her favorite stories revolves around a boy who is adamant that he call her "Miss Fruend" while in school and "Deb" during TASK events. One afternoon he ran up to her in the school's hallway. He was beaming.

"Miss Fruend! I just came in from recess and I scored three soccer goals," he said.

"You did?" Deb asked.

"Yes, and I was picked fourth," the boy answered. "Last year they didn't pick me at all."

Then her student turned, looked up at Deb and simply said, "Thanks."

Deb says she's lucky to be a teacher to some of her TASK kids. She can see the benefits of the program spilling out into recess, during phys-ed classes and even at home. Some parents claim that since joining TASK, their kids have become more responsible, doing their chores more often because they know they can accomplish a goal if they try. When kids believe in themselves, their confidence blooms, and Deb couldn't be happier.

"That's what we stand to do—help these kids be the best that they can be. They get knocked down a lot, but this is a way for them to shine. That's what keeps me going," says Deb.

Not surprisingly, it all comes back to the kids.

For more information visit www.tasksports.org or write to Team Activities for Special Kids, 11139 South Towne Square, Suite D, St. Louis, MO 63123.

KASEY MICHAELS
‑ HERE COME THE HEROES ‑

∾ KASEY MICHAELS ∾

The hallmarks of *New York Times* and *USA TODAY* best-selling author Kasey Michaels' writing are humor, romance and happy endings. She is the author of over 100 books and has received a trio of coveted starred reviews from *Publishers Weekly*. She is also a recipient of a RITA® Award from Romance Writers of America, a Waldenbooks and BookRak Bestseller Award, and many awards from *RT Book Reviews* magazine, including a Career Achievement Award for her Regency-era historical romances. Kasey and her husband live in Pennsylvania. Each summer her entire family volunteers with the golf tournament her son founded to benefit the Gift of Life Donor Program of Philadelphia. Monies raised contribute to the costs of transporting the youngest members of Team Philadelphia to the annual Transplant Olympics.

CHAPTER
~ONE~

The fourth house down from the corner and on the east side of Redbud Lane looked very much like the other houses in the small, rural Pennsylvania development, except that maybe the cars in the driveway were a few years older than those of the neighbors, and the trim around the windows could probably use a fresh coat of paint. Otherwise, there were no real outward signs that for the past several years life had been a financial struggle for the Finnegans.

Inside the three-bedroom ranch house, the television set might be older, the couches in the family room more broken than broken-in, the second mortgage a little larger, but the Finnegans didn't care. They'd been in a battle—a rough one and a long one—and they'd come out winners. Charlie was still with them.

Unfortunately, tension was also in residence in the white brick house on Redbud Lane; it had moved in when Charlie got sick, seemed to like the place, and now was reluctant to leave.

"Charlie, please slow down," Laura Finnegan said as her son shoved another forkful of roast beef into his mouth. The family was sitting around the kitchen table, the afternoon sun streaming in through the large window overlooking a fenced backyard that sported its own home plate and makeshift baseball diamond. "We've still got plenty of time."

"Do I have to go, Mom? I don't understand why I have to go." Nine-year-old Sarah Finnegan, with her father's sandy hair and his stubborn streak, too, had strong opinions on the subject of being dragged along to baseball practice every night for the past two weeks, none of them good. "I'll bet I could stay at Brenda's house. Her mom won't mind. She almost never minds."

"Oh, honey, I know. But not tonight." Laura tried to pretend she wasn't planning to use her own daughter as a buffer if things got too bad—Jake was always careful not to go ballistic around the kids. Then again, she also was less likely to let her emotions control her mouth and, yes, her tears, if she knew the kids were within earshot. After all, in the past couple of years she and Jake had both had a lot of practice in hiding their emotions, their fears, their anger when the terror had threatened to devour them.

To some, they'd survived their ordeal and should just be

grateful and move on. But the Finnegan family couldn't do that. Nothing was the same now, and they had changed, too. They could only move on, carrying all the baggage that had been heaped on them, do their best to learn to live with that baggage. Memories. Fears. Uncertainty. And, yes, tension. Always, always that tension that hung around, refusing to leave, that feeling of waiting for the other shoe to drop.

Like tonight. Tonight wasn't going to be pretty. Tonight both she and Jake knew what was coming, even if one didn't want to admit it and the other didn't want to have to watch it. When was enough enough? When did it become too much? And, damn it all anyway, why wouldn't it just, please, *stop?*

"Ah, come on, Mom. *Please?*"

"Sarah, honey, I said no. We're all going to be there tonight to root Charlie on, right?"

"Can't I root now, and stay home and play video games with Brenda?" Sarah pulled a face, looking very much like her father, which was usually a good thing for her. That look tended to wrap Laura around her little finger. But not tonight.

"We're all going, Sarah. For moral support." As she spoke, Laura looked across the dinner table at her husband, trying to signal him with her raised eyebrows: *This isn't going to be good. You know it, I know it. Say something!*

Jake didn't seem to be getting the message or, if he had gotten it, was ignoring it. "You've got second base cold, Charlie, don't sweat it. If not first team, then second. I know the bat's been a bit of a problem, but we'll work on that."

Laura shut her eyes. Why did she always have to be the bad guy? When did Dad and Mom turn into Good Cop, Bad Cop? "Charlie, you do realize that the coach is going to cut at least six players tonight, right? I want you to be prepared...just in case everything doesn't go the way we hope." *Life isn't always fair, my sweet baby boy. Sometimes you win and sometimes you lose. The luck of the draw is just that and, oh yeah, Coach Billig is a card-carrying jerk.* She didn't say any of that as she looked at her earnest fourteen-year-old son. But she thought it.

Charlie lived for baseball. He also lived because he'd had a kidney transplant six months ago. He was healthy now, after years of not being so healthy, but a kidney transplant wasn't a magic bullet. It didn't make everything all right again, turn back the clock so Charlie could start over and be on an equal footing with the world.

He was small because children without kidney function don't grow, and Charlie had a lot of catching up to do. He was fourteen, but he looked ten. He'd begun to grow now, sure, but he was already fourteen, and he was running out of "growing time." Soon Sarah would be taller than her older brother. He was smart, eager, and had more guts than almost anyone else on the planet...but he could not stand toe to toe, physically, with other boys his age, especially other boys his age trying out for the local summer baseball team.

But that was the way the deal worked; teams were divided into age groups. Not ability groups. Not common-sense groups. Age groups. So what if two of the kids already topped six feet and her kid still hadn't hit five feet? So what if Charlie could stand behind the wide-body catcher and disappear?

What had Coach Billig said the first time he saw Charlie? As if Laura would ever forget: "Second base, huh? Does the kid want to play second base, or *be* it?"

And then he'd laughed at his own joke. The bastard.

No, Laura wasn't holding out much hope that Charlie would make the team.

But not Jake. Not the optimist. He thought it was great that Charlie walked nearly every time he was up at bat during practices because the pitchers couldn't locate his small strike zone. He thought Billig would see the advantage there, put Charlie in when the bases were loaded and assure the team of a run. Jake would take any crumb, cling to any hope, so that his boy could be on the team. Good old Jake, always the cheerleader, the optimist who never saw the blow coming until he was flat on his back with another disappointment.

It was enough to make Laura hide out in the shower so nobody would hear her when she cried. Or cursed. Why could she watch, dry-eyed and resolute, as Charlie was put through painful tests, then fall apart now, when he was healthy again, just because some thoughtless moron decided it would be fun to get a laugh at her son's expense?

The world was upside down...she was upside down...

"Laura, are you going to finish that, or what?" Jake asked, and Laura realized she'd been holding a forkful of salad halfway between her plate and her mouth, probably for a full minute or more.

"Oh, sorry," she said, putting down the fork, her appetite gone. "Just let me rinse the dishes and put them in the dishwasher, and I'll be ready to go. Sarah, finish your broccoli. What time is practice? Six?"

"I'll take care of the dishes, hon." Jake was already on his way to the sink with his plate, pausing only to rub Charlie's mop of dark red curls. "And it's five-thirty, Laura, not six, so we've really got to move. *Women,*" he added in that special husband voice men acquire the moment they say *I do.* "Right, Slugger?"

"Right, Dad," Charlie said, shoveling one last bite of mashed potatoes into his mouth, then following his father to the sink. "I have to be early, maybe get in a little more batting practice before the last tryout. I think you're right, Dad. If I just step up a little in the box, I can..."

Laura tuned them both out and left them to rinse the dishes as she ran upstairs to change her sneakers. Maybe, if she was extremely lucky, she'd trip on the stairs, sprain her ankle and not have to go to the ball field at all. But that would be chickening out, and Charlie never chickened out, so neither could she.

In ten minutes they were in Jake's car, heading for the Harley Memorial Playground, named after a young boy who had lost his battle with leukemia twenty years earlier, a young boy who had loved baseball. *You'd think people would take a hint and remember that,* Laura always thought when she sat on the grassy hill during practice, watching Charlie do his best to impress Coach Billig.

"I don't need this, Mom," Charlie complained once they arrived at the field. He was dancing in place as Laura strapped the homemade protector around his waist and let the Velcro secure it. Charlie's new kidney was in the front of his body, not shielded by his skeletal structure, and a fastball to the gut could be real trouble. Laura tried to be upbeat, but there was a part of her that still wanted Charlie protected at all times...even if he did look as if he was hiding a pillow under his T-shirt.

"Humor me," Laura said, as she always did, then resisted the urge to grab her son close, beg him to duck if he saw a ball coming his way.

Once Charlie had his bat and glove and was running down the grassy slope to the ball field, and Sarah had found a playmate to run up and down the hill with her, Laura turned on Jake. She'd planned to be tactful, but plans like that rarely worked out. Not when they'd been left to simmer too long. "You have to stop building him up for a fall, Jake. Billig doesn't want him. He wants to win. That's all he cares about, winning. Not the kids. Not our kid."

Jake smiled at her, that dumb, melting smile that still had the power to weaken her knees. "I pulled Billig aside and talked to him, Laura, after last night's practice, after you and Sarah left for the mall. I explained to him about Charlie, why he's shorter than the other kids, and maybe not quite as fast. But I told him what Charlie lacks in size, he makes up for in heart, in determination, and he'll get better as the season moves on. Billig understood, he really did."

"Oh, Jake." Laura rolled her eyes. "I don't know who's going to be more disappointed tonight, Charlie, or you."

Jake wasn't smiling now. "Why do you always have to be such a damn pessimist, Laura?"

"I don't know, Jake. Why do you always have to be such a damn optimist? Charlie's different. He's ours, we love him, but he can't compete with other kids his age, not on the ball field. It's just not possible." She lowered her eyes for a moment, and then said what she didn't want to say. "He could get hurt."

"Ah! And now we have it, don't we? Charlie could get hurt. Laura, we can't wrap the kid in cotton wool. We didn't work this hard to get him well and then only allow him to live half a life. It's not fair, damn it!"

Quick tears stung behind Laura's eyes, and she just as quickly blinked them away. "I wish it had never happened, too, Jake. I wish he were still our perfect little boy. But he's not. He's special. That doesn't mean we can't be proud of him."

"I *am* proud of him, Laura. He's my son. I couldn't have done what he did, fight the way he fought. And I'm not going to let him down now, you understand? He's going to play baseball, and if this is the only team in town, *this* is damn well where he's going to play baseball." He shoved his fists into his pants pockets. "I'm going to go get a soda. You want one?"

Laura shook her head and watched as Jake walked away, putting a little space between them, which was probably a good thing. It was all so hard for Jake, and always had been. His own son, and Jake couldn't help him, couldn't stop bad things from happening to him. Laura couldn't either, but at least she was the one who'd stayed with Charlie at the hospital, had performed dialysis on him three times a week. Jake hadn't had that hands-on involvement in his care, so he'd stepped into the role of cheerleader, always doing something to take Charlie's mind off the pain, the problems, the fears.

And all the while screaming silently inside, angry with the world and God and himself, because he couldn't do more to help his son. Jake just wanted them to be a normal family again. He wanted to forget the scary years, and she didn't blame him. But if every family taking care of a chronically ill or disabled child needed an optimist, it probably also needed a pessimist, someone who worried, someone who planned ahead, someone who kept them all grounded.

Or at least that's what she'd read in one of those ridiculous self-help books that are so great in theory but not always so terrific in practice.

She'd read so many books, tried so many things, and couldn't beat out of her head the worst thing she'd read...that the majority of parents who have a seriously ill or impaired child are divorced; the deck is stacked against them.

Laura and Jake had, she believed, pretty much avoided the more obvious pitfalls while Charlie was so sick. They'd been too busy fighting the problem, solving the problem. But now? Now that Charlie was okay? Now they had to learn to live with something that was so much better—so very much better—but was still not the life or the dreams they'd had before Charlie got sick.

And it wasn't easy.

"I figured you really did want one," Jake said, holding out a soda for her, and then bending to kiss her cheek. "Sorry, I was being a jerk."

"I love you, too," Laura said, going up on tiptoe to return his kiss. "And I will think positive on this. I promise."

"No, you won't," Jake teased, ruffling her dark copper curls just as he'd done earlier to Charlie. "You worry better than anyone I know, and you're really good at it. But just ease off this one time, okay? Charlie's going to get some bumps and bruises, but he'll be fine. He'll prove himself."

"Does that mean I have your permission to close my eyes when he comes up to bat and Richie the Giant Killer tries to—what did you call it last night?—back him up with his curveball?" Laura asked, smiling.

"Permission granted...you wuss." Jake hugged her close against his side. "Uh-oh, here comes Billig, and he's carrying a piece of paper." He dropped his arm to his side. "What the hell? He's going to make the cuts *before* practice? How can he do that? He has to give Charlie another chance to—damn it!"

Laura felt as old as time as she watched Charlie and five other boys walk away from the group gathered around Billig, pick up their bats and gloves from the bench and slowly head back up the hill. *Oh, God.* She hadn't wished this on him, had she? She was heartbroken for Charlie, but was she also relieved that he wouldn't have to compete physically with boys twice his size? Would that make her an unnatural mother?

Charlie reached them, dragging the barrel of his aluminum bat along the ground. He didn't stop, he just kept walking, his steps plodding, his head down. "Let's go. I'm done."

Jake grabbed his son's arm. "Whoa, wait a second, son. What happened? What did he say?"

"Later, Jake, please," Laura pleaded. Charlie wasn't crying. He wouldn't cry, not in front of the other kids, but he was on the brink. The best thing to do would be to get him out of here before the dam broke. "Let's go get some ice cream. Take Charlie to the car. I'll round up Sarah and be right behind you."

Charlie looked up at his mother. "Mom? Coach said I should come back when I grow some more." Then he dropped the bat he was so proud of and the mitt he'd worked a good pocket into with linseed oil every night for the past month, and ran for the parking lot.

"Why, that no good son of a—"

"Jake. Jake—*stop*. It won't change anything if you hit him."

"Oh yeah? It would make me feel a whole hell of a lot better."

"I know," Laura said in sympathy, because she'd like to pop the tactless guy herself. "But that won't help Charlie, will it? Just let it go."

"Let it go. That's your answer for everything, isn't it? You know what, Laura? I'm tired of letting it go. Here," he said, taking the car keys from his pocket and tossing them at her. "Take the kids for ice cream. I'm going to walk home."

Laura couldn't keep her own anger and hurt out of her voice. "And just how does that help Charlie?"

"I don't know, Laura, I honestly don't. But I can't face that kid right now."

"Because he's disappointed? Or because you are? Because you helped set him up for this fall?" She quickly put a hand on his arm. "Oh, Jake, I'm sorry. I didn't mean that..."

"Don't wait up," Jake said, glaring at her for a moment before he turned and walked away.

Laura looked toward the parking lot and could see that Charlie was already in the backseat of the car, watching as his father strode off. So now she'd have to go to Charlie, tell him how sorry she was that he didn't make the team, that maybe next year would be better, even though she knew that wasn't true...and then explain to her son how much his father loved him.

Because that was how it had to be, how she and Jake had learned to operate. They tried their best to present a strong, united front, but when one couldn't do it anymore and fell down, the other had to pick up the ball. They'd been taking turns like this for years. Tonight was her turn to pick up the ball.

She signaled to Sarah to follow her and began the slow walk to the car, hoping her daughter didn't climb into the backseat beside Charlie and say something typically nine-year-old, like, "Hooray! Now I can go play with Brenda!"

Yeah. Life was just one long carnival...

"Excuse me! You forgot these."

Laura stopped and turned around to see a petite, blond woman she'd noticed at a few of the other practices. She was holding up Charlie's bat and glove. "Thank you," Laura said, taking the equipment. "I don't know where my head is tonight."

"If it's anywhere near where mine is, you're plotting to go

home and stick pins in a Billig doll. I'm thinking a bad knee first, then on to his gallbladder, maybe a migraine."

Laura smiled at the woman. "Only if I get to stick in the pin that gives him a raging case of hemorrhoids." She tucked Charlie's mitt under her arm and held out her hand. "Hi, I'm Laura Finnegan. You're Bobby's mother, right?"

"When he acknowledges me, yeah, I am. I have this tendency to cheer a little too loud, you understand, and fourteen-year-old boys don't like that." She extended her own hand. "Jayne Ann Maitz. Bobby also got cut, but I'm guessing you know that."

"Oh, I'm sorry, I didn't realize—" Laura stopped, shook her head. "I was so wrapped up in watching Charlie that I didn't even notice who else was cut. How's Bobby taking it?"

Jayne Ann shrugged. "He's used to it. This is his third year in a row. I think Billig figures he's going to give up, not come back, but he doesn't know my Bobby. He's afraid of him, but he doesn't know him."

"Afraid of him? I don't understand."

"Bobby has a seizure disorder," Jayne Ann told her as both mothers proceeded toward the parking lot. Bobby had run ahead, and Laura saw that Charlie had rolled down the window in the backseat and the two boys were talking. "We've got the seizures pretty well under control, but we still have our...well, we still have our moments. Unfortunately, two years ago Billig witnessed one of those moments. Bobby hasn't had a chance since then."

Laura rested the bat on her shoulder as she and Bobby's mother stopped just at the edge of the parking lot. "Did you ever hear the monologue where Bill Cosby goes on and on about the problems with having kids, raising kids, and says he doesn't know what happened—all he and his wife wanted was to have some kids to send to college? And that was years before his only son was murdered. Life doesn't always work out the way we think it's supposed to, does it?"

"No. Not even close. And definitely not the way my ex thought it was supposed to. He took a hike a year after Bobby had his first seizure. Just couldn't take it that his son wasn't perfect, so whatever was wrong with Bobby had to have come from my side of the family. He's got a new wife and three perfect kids now. Maybe, while you're at it, you could give him a dose of hemorrhoids, too? I'd even pay you."

"You saw my husband stomp off, right?" Laura asked, smiling weakly as she came to Jake's defense. "He's not ashamed of Charlie. He just remembered that when we married I promised to love and honor him—possibly even obey him from time to time if I'm in the mood—but did not agree to bail him out of jail after an assault-and-battery charge."

"Well, damn, you should think about putting that in the marriage contract," Jayne Ann said, grinning. "I would have loved to see Billig go down on his skinny, sanctimonious backside. I mean, I don't know what's going to happen in your house tonight, but there's going to be a lot of crying and throwing things and feeling sorry for ourselves going on in ours. And that's just me. Bobby will be worse."

"Yeah, sounds like we'll be running the same program at our house. Look, Jayne Ann, if we can't change what's going to happen, maybe we can at least delay the inevitable. How about we all go for ice cream?"

"Sounds like a plan to me. Ripley's? I'll follow you in my van."

"Okay, good," Laura said, looking back toward the ball field one last time as the kids who'd made the team began their practice session. "Jayne Ann? How about the other kids who were cut? Why did he cut them?"

"Well, let's see. There were six, and we're two of those six. The other four kids? Marvin Bailey couldn't hit a barn door with a cannon. Someday his father is going to figure out that the poor kid plays a mean game of chess, but that's it. As for the other three, two of them are about as good in the field as Marvin is with the bat—which leaves Bruce Lee Pak."

"Bruce Lee was cut? I thought he was fairly good, not that I know much about baseball. Why him?"

"Bruce Lee's just a little slow, God love him. Not a lot, but just enough that his reactions are not always as fast as they should be. Billig could have cut him a little slack—let kids like

Charlie and Bobby and Bruce Lee warm the bench and come in when the score is already out of reach, or something. That's all they want, to be part of the team. Marvin Bailey was relieved to be cut, and the other two are only thirteen, and can try again next year. But our kids? Next year they'd have to move up again, to the fifteen- and sixteen-year-old bracket, and we already know that's not going to work. Sorry, I got on my soapbox there for a minute. Why do you ask?"

"Nothing. No reason." Laura hefted the bat a time or two. "But...don't you think a kid should be able to play baseball if a kid wants to play baseball?"

"Well, it is America's pastime," Jayne Ann said. "But America likes winners, remember?"

Laura knew she was close to tears, which she hated, because that meant a loss of control, and she needed to be in control, Charlie needed her to be in control. "Charlie *is* a winner. Your Bobby is a winner. The fact that they're still both *here* makes them winners, damn it! So is Bruce, because he won't stop trying. This is wrong, Jayne Ann, just plain wrong."

"Hey, hand me the petition and I'll sign it. Baseball for all kids! Then what? We work on that world peace thing?"

"I don't know," Laura said, feeling her blood pump through her veins. She was making sense, she knew she was—baseball is for *all* kids. "But there has to be something, doesn't there? Something we can do? I mean, hell, these are our *kids*. We've climbed other mountains for them. They've climbed a lot of mountains. Are we really going to just...just take our bats and mitts and go home?"

"I think I really like you, Laura Finnegan." Jayne Ann flipped a fistful of keys in her palm. "Let's talk about this some more over butter brickle, okay?"

CHAPTER
~TWO~

Once upon a time, Laura and Jake Finnegan refused to go to bed angry. Once upon a time, their arguments didn't go much deeper than who forgot to record a check in the checkbook. But somewhere along the way the arguments stopped, because the problems they'd had back then didn't mean a whole hell of a lot when compared with the possibility of losing their son.

Also along the way, they'd lost the power to communicate on one very important emotional level. Maybe Laura was trying to hide her fears from Jake so as not to worry him; maybe Jake was trying to keep a positive attitude. Or maybe they were both so afraid that if they let themselves go, let themselves feel too much, the resulting explosion would flatten them all.

So when Jake came wandering home just before ten o'clock that night, Laura greeted him from the couch with a quick whisper as she pointed to the television set. "Two minutes left, and I'm still not sure why he killed her."

Jake wearily sank down into the worn-out cushions beside her. "Probably because she forgot she had his keys and locked the front door so he had to come in through the garage, which she did forget to lock. But that's just a wild guess."

"Uh-huh," Laura said, only vaguely listening. Moments later she slapped a hand down hard on his leg. "I *knew* it! She didn't know he was the one—he only *thought* she knew. If he had just let it alone, not killed her, he would have gotten away with the whole thing." She hit the mute button and looked at Jake. "Do you want something to eat? There's still plenty of roast beef. I could make you a cold sandwich?"

"Would you mind?" Jake asked as she handed the remote to him, because she knew she only ever had the thing on loan— remotes were the property of men. Women couldn't be trusted not to turn on some shopping network or, worse, Martha Stewart, and then, next thing the poor guy knew, he was sitting on flowered slipcovers.

Laura got to her feet and smiled down at him. "So you built up an appetite on your walk?" She'd keep it light, because otherwise she'd have to ask him where he'd been for the past three hours.

"I stopped down the street to talk to Gary about the transmission of that old car he bought, and he's set up a TV in his garage, so I stayed to have a friendly beer and watch the game with him. The Phillies won, by the way, and if Gary puts one more dime into that transmission, Julia has threatened to have him committed. And I'm sorry, Laura, sorry I left you to deal with all the fallout. I just...I don't know. I just couldn't take it tonight."

She sat down once more and laid her head on his shoulder. "I know. And Charlie's fine, honest. He cried a little, and I'm afraid his Jim Thome bobblehead doll bit the big one, but he'll be all right."

"His Thome bobblehead? Damn. That thing could be worth something some day." Jake dropped a kiss on the top of her head. "Might have put Charlie through one full day of college. Okay, come on. Let's make the sandwiches together. You're hungry, too, aren't you?"

And so they paved over another bump in the road, all mention of the way Jake had left her at the ball field shelved, supposedly forgotten. But both knew it was just a temporary fix, and the pothole would open up again some other time, and be even bigger, large enough to fall in and trap them both.

"I met someone tonight," Laura said as she watched Jake slice the beef.

Jake grinned at her. "Really? Is he going to sweep you up and take you away from all this? Don't believe him, Laura. Men are animals. We all make the same empty promises, but we're really only trying to get in your pants."

"Funny," Laura said, leaning against the kitchen counter. "And it was a woman…is a woman. Jayne Ann Maitz. Her son is Bobby, one of the kids Billig cut."

The knife hovered over the hunk of rump roast. "He cut Bobby Maitz? That kid's got a good arm. Damn. Why'd he cut him?"

"Epilepsy," Laura said, her jaw tight. "I guess he didn't want to take the chance Bobby might have a seizure on the field. Jayne Ann said he cuts him every year."

Jake finished slathering slices of bread with mayonnaise, nodding his head. "Laura, Gary made a good point tonight. As a lawyer, he says he can understand why kids like Charlie and Bobby can't make the team. You know. Insurance. Liability. Whatever." He handed one sandwich to Laura, waggling his eyebrows at her with pure devilishness. "But he's still willing to toilet-paper Billig's house with me if I'm game."

Laura tried not to laugh. "Really? Tell me, just how many friendly beers did you two boys have?"

"Two each, and they were small bottles. Come on, you want to watch the early news?"

"Not especially, no," Laura said, following him back to the family room. "But I would like to talk to you about something."

"You backed my beautiful seven-year-old four-door into a telephone pole?"

"Jake, be serious," Laura said as she sat down on the couch, bending one leg beneath her and balancing the paper plate in her lap. "You said something just now—about insurance. And what else? Liability? What did you mean?"

He spoke around his first bite of sandwich. "Oh, this is good. I love cold roast beef sandwiches. Why would you want to know that?"

"I don't know. Why not? I'm...I'm interested, that's all. And it's easier than finding a pagan priestess to put a curse on Billig, I guess."

"There's a story there that I don't want to know, right?" Jake asked, taking a drink straight from the soda can he'd popped in the kitchen. "Okay, this is what Gary told me. The township owns the ball field, and if anyone's hurt, coaches, players, spectators— bam! The township could get hit with a lawsuit. Same for the Summer League, of which Coach Billig has been president for the past two thousand years, give or take a century. So, having a kid like Charlie—and, yeah, a kid like Bobby—on one of the teams just ups the ante for them, I suppose."

"But when we signed up Charlie—and there's thirty-five bucks we'll never see again, I suppose—we had to show proof of health insurance or else he couldn't even go on the field. You're saying that's not enough?"

"Apparently not, at least not according to Gary. Both the league and the township are taking a risk every time those kids are on the field. Add a Charlie or a Bobby to the mix, and I guess it could all get pretty dicey. I still want to take the guy apart, but that's because of what he said to Charlie. I mean, why didn't he just tell him the truth up front? Tell us the truth? Why'd he have to make that crack about going home and growing, then come back and try again?"

"Maybe he didn't want to give the boys a final no vote. Maybe he didn't want to completely dash their hopes." Laura shook her head. "Naw, never mind. It's Billig. If he could say what he said, make jokes at Charlie's expense, then he could have told the truth."

Jake nodded his agreement as he concentrated on his sandwich and Laura weighed the pros and cons of telling him what she and Jayne Ann had discussed over hot-fudge sundaes at Ripley's—butter brickle didn't have enough calories for their "weighty" discussion.

"Um, Jake, honey?"

He pushed back a thick lock of sandy hair and grinned at her. "No, you can't have my body. I'm in training."

"In training for what?" God, how she loved this man. He tried so hard…even if tonight he was trying too hard in his attempt to skate over what had happened at the ball field.

"Olympic pogo-sticking," he said, finishing off his sandwich in one large bite. "Oh, hell, go ahead. Ask your question. I can see you're dying to ask me something. You're wearing that earnest expression I've learned to fear."

Laura adjusted her leg beneath her and leaned closer to her husband. "Are you and Gary saying that Charlie, or Bobby—kids with special circumstances, I guess I'm saying—that they'll never be able to play ball on any township fields? Because of insurance and liability, I mean?"

Jake sat back, frowning. "I don't know. I guess so, but even Gary couldn't be sure. I remember seeing some news stories on towns putting a stop to sports teams because they didn't want to get sued someday. Maybe Gary's wrong. Maybe he was just throwing a possibility out there. You know, trying to make me feel better. Damn, it didn't work." Then he looked at her, and Laura attempted to put an "I'm only asking this in a clinical, objective way" look on her face. "Why did you ask?"

Okay. It was now or never. "Well, because Jayne Ann and I were talking tonight, and we were saying that every kid should be able to play baseball if he or she wants to play baseball and—"

"Bobby can come over here anytime, play in the backyard with us. I hope you told her that."

Laura nodded, biting her lip for a moment. Maybe that was enough for tonight. Maybe she needed to think this thing through, before she dumped it all in Jake's lap, even got his hopes up in time for another fall.

Then again, he *was* listening, wasn't he?

"That's nice," she said. "Of course he can. And Bruce Lee Pak, too, and anyone else who wants to play. But that's not the point. Put aside the possible insurance problem for a minute, and let's just think about the kids. Why shouldn't the kids get to play on a real team, on a real field? Why can't they play on the Harley Field?"

"Because Billig is more interested in filling the trophy case at the recreation hall than letting more kids play the game?" Jake sat up straighter. "What's going on, hon? You've got that gleam in your eyes."

Laura lowered her eyelids. "What gleam? There's no gleam. You didn't see a gleam."

"Oh, brother," Jake said, raking his fingers through his hair. "I should have been good. I should have gone for ice cream with everyone and just come home. Laura—there's nothing we can do. I wish there were, but there isn't."

"And that's it? You have a couple of beers with Gary the Attorney and it's all over? We're not going to fight this?"

"Laura, I don't get it. You should be doing flips here. No more pipe dreams for me—or disappointments for Charlie. You were right, I was wrong. Baseball just isn't in the cards for him, not since he got sick. And you know what? I'm tired of beating my head against stone walls. I'm tired of watching the legs kicked out from under our son. No matter what, Charlie's different now. We're different now, and we've all got the scars to prove it. We just can't beat the system. I get that now—finally, I get it."

She got to her feet. "Oh yeah? Well, you know what? If you can't beat the system, Jake Finnegan, then maybe it's time for a new system. Charlie is going to play baseball. This year. On a real field. I mean it, he will."

Jake also stood up. "Terrific—just as I see reason, you take a lap around the bend. Okay. Fine. Go swirl your cape and perform a miracle. But I have to go upstairs to apologize to Charlie. He's still awake, right?"

Laura rubbed at the back of her neck, where the muscles had gone all tight. "I'm sure he's been waiting up for you. Like I said, he had a rough time for a while, threw his bat and mitt in the garbage, but he's over it now. Oh, and remind him that even though there's no school—some teacher in-service thing—we still have his checkup and blood work at the hospital tomorrow. I want to leave by nine o'clock for the blood work so they have it back by the time we see the doctor."

"Another long day at the zoo, huh?" Jake put his arms around her. "I'm sorry I can't go along, hon. But this is just routine, right?"

Laura snuggled against his chest, wrapped her arms around

him. "Just routine. His tests will be fine, everything will be fine. And some fine day we might even be able to think of it that way, without our stomachs being tied in knots until we hear the results."

"I know," Jake said, giving her a squeeze, then gently pushing her away from him as he looked down into her face. "How do you think Charlie feels about it? About the tests, waiting for the results?"

"I never really asked him," Laura said as she picked up the paper plates and handed Jake his empty soda can. "Isn't that strange? I've never asked. He just *does,* doesn't he? But he's got to be tired of it all. He just wants to be fourteen, you know?" She blinked rapidly as tears once more stung behind her eyes. "Oh, damn it, Jake, we do so well, we've *been* doing so well. Why does the world think it has to keep raining on our parade?"

"The world rains on everybody, Laura. We just have to figure out a way to get a bigger umbrella than a lot of other people need, that's all. Look, I'm sure you and Jayne what's-her-face had a great time tonight, trashing Billig and dreaming up some scheme to get the kids onto the team, but—"

"It's Jayne Ann," Laura told him, wiping away her tears, "and we weren't just dreaming. We're going to do it, Jake. We're going to find a way. You weren't here tonight when Charlie finally had his meltdown, but I was."

She watched as Jake's face seemed to close in on itself, his features shuttered. "So it's my fault? Is that it, Laura? I couldn't take it, so I took a hike, left you to do all the dirty work?"

"No, I...*yes*. Yes, Jake, you did. What was Charlie supposed to think when he saw that, huh? I can tell you what he did think. He thought you were disappointed in him because he didn't make the team. While you were off having your pity party, your son was here thinking he's not good enough for you."

Jake pressed his palms against his head as if he was in real physical pain. "Oh, Christ. That's not—it wasn't like that. I just—what did you tell him?"

Laura shrugged, wishing she hadn't said anything, wishing she'd kept her mouth shut. "I...I told him you were really angry with Coach Billig and needed to take a walk to cool off, which is what grown-ups should do rather than yell or hit or—I told him you love him."

He scrubbed at his eyes. "I shouldn't have taken off like that, and you shouldn't have had to deal with Charlie on your own."

"It's okay, Jake. We pick up the slack for each other all the time. But I know how you can make it up to me. Maybe speak to Gary about ways around this liability thing he talked about."

Jake shook his head. "No, Laura, I can't do that. That's one decision I came to tonight on my walk home. I'm through fighting this. Charlie has his physical limits now, that's just the way it is, and we all have to acknowledge that, face it and move on—all that touchy-feely crap. I never want that kid to think I'm not proud of him, but I'm done helping set him up, giving him hope, when I know in my heart he's just going to get shot down. I'm hurting now, I admit it, but I can't be hurting half as bad as Charlie is. Now I'm going upstairs to talk to him. You haven't told him about this idea of yours, have you?"

She shook her head, unable to speak.

"Good. Don't, please, Laura. Charlie's been slammed to the floor enough, and a couple of hours ago you'd have been the first one to point that out, remember? Now I finally see the light, understand where you were coming from, and you do a one-eighty on me? I don't get it."

Laura tried to smile. "Maybe this pessimist is just coming late to the party?"

"Maybe. Shame this particular party is already over," Jake said, leaning down to kiss her.

Laura watched as her husband left the family room. She couldn't have been more surprised if Jake had set his own hair on fire. Jake, turning into the pessimist? No! That wasn't the division of labor they'd decided on. Sure, they'd never discussed it, but that's how it had shaken out—Jake the cheerleader, Laura the worrier. How dare he try to change the ground rules now?

"Except it's just what he said—*I'm* changing the ground rules, too," she muttered to herself. "Man, talk about lousy timing." She headed back to the family room with another can of soda, hoping Jake would be in bed and asleep by the time she went upstairs, because she was too chicken to see him right now. "Cluck," she said quietly as she collapsed onto the couch and picked up the TV remote. "Cluck, cluck, cluck…"

Oh yeah. Life was just one big carnival….

CHAPTER
THREE

By ten o'clock the next morning Laura, Charlie and Sarah were munching junk food in the cafeteria of the local hospital. It was too late for breakfast, too early for lunch, but Charlie hadn't been allowed to eat before his blood was drawn, so they all took what they could find. Laura had a slice of lemon meringue pie that had probably been on the shelf since the Kennedy administration. She'd never had to chew meringue before…

Laura was the proverbial bundle of nerves, which upset her because she liked to think she had gotten beyond that. And she had to stay cool, look relaxed, because the kids took their emotional cues from her, and she couldn't let them know she was nervous.

But waiting for Charlie's blood test results was pretty much like waiting for that last thread to snap and the two-ton safe hanging three stories above your head to fall. Your chances of moving, getting out of the way, were pretty good. But there was always the possibility you'd get your foot caught in a crack in the sidewalk and couldn't jump fast enough or far enough.

She stabbed at the slice of pie one more time and the entire wedge of lemon pulled away from the crust and hung on her fork. She'd always said that the best diet aid would be eating all your meals in a hospital cafeteria.

She wished Jake could have been here with them. He'd be laughing and telling jokes with the kids, making the time pass quickly instead of the way every second, every minute was dragging now. And he was going out of town on business again, leaving her to deal with everything on her own. She'd like to go out of town. Hell, she'd like to go to the supermarket alone. When was their last vacation? Too long ago, if she couldn't even remember it.

"I could have stayed home with Brenda, but she has an orthodontist appointment," Sarah whined, not for the first time.

"I know, honey," Laura said with all the sympathy she could muster as she leaned over and kissed her daughter's curls. "And I would have left you with any number of total strangers if I wasn't afraid they'd bring you back, so let's just make the best of it, okay? We'll be home by two."

"Here, Sarah," Charlie said, handing over his Game Boy. "You can play with this if you promise to do it over there where I don't have to watch. Oh, and don't erase my scores."

"Thanks, Charlie," Sarah said, grabbing the toy before her brother could change his mind and retreating to an empty table some distance away.

Laura looked at her son, amazed. "I thought you said you'd never let her play with that."

Charlie shrugged. "She was being a pain in the neck so I figured I'd shut her up," he told her with the infinite wisdom of a fourteen-year-old. "Dad says life is full of compromises."

Laura smiled across the table at her son. "Oh, he did, did he? And when was that?"

Charlie slid his arms forward on the tabletop, resting his chin on the worn Formica. He'd learned, over the years, how to make himself comfortable anywhere, especially during long waits in hospitals. "Last night. Compromises and trade-offs, he said. I can't play on a team with kids my own age and I can't play with younger kids who are more my size because those are the rules, so maybe I should think about writing about baseball, being the team statistician or maybe taking photographs of baseball. Whatever."

"But you still want to play?"

"Yeah, well, sure." Charlie made a face. "But it's not going to happen, Mom. I'm not good enough. It's not just the kidney. I'm just not good enough. Not tall enough, not fast enough, not strong enough. It's like Coach said—if I tried to block second base on a double play, I'd be buried alive under the guy sliding into the bag."

"Then nobody should be allowed to slide," Laura said, sifting through this information and mentally purchasing a baseball rule book online. A rule book and a highlighting pen.

Charlie sat back in the chair, sliding down on the base of his spine, and grinned rather condescendingly at his mother. "Mom, baseball players *slide*. It's part of the game, for crying out loud. I can't ask the other kids not to play the game the way it's supposed to be played."

"No, you can't," Laura agreed, the wheels turning in her head again. "But maybe there's a way for a team to play by different rules, rules that make more sense for the kids..."

With inimitable eloquence, Charlie said, "Huh?"

Laura mentally slapped herself. Jake had warned her not to say anything, not to do anything that got Charlie all excited, just so he could be knocked down again. "Oh, nothing, honey, I was just thinking out loud. Women do that, you know. Hey, there's Duane. You remember him, don't you? Duane Johnson. He was your roommate here for a few days last year."

Charlie swiveled around as Duane and his mother entered

the cafeteria. "Oh, yeah, sure. Duane. Wow, he's walking a lot better, isn't he?"

As the boy came closer, Laura could see the braces sticking out from beneath the cuffs of his slacks. "He is. No more crutches. Isn't that wonderful? Why don't you go say hi?"

As Charlie got to his feet, Laura waved to Cherise Johnson, motioning for her to come sit at the table with her. "Hi," she said as the other woman sat down. "We haven't seen you guys in a while. Duane looks great."

Cherise smiled widely. "He does, doesn't he? This last surgery really has worked a miracle. Charlie looks good."

For a few minutes, the two women caught up on their children's' medical histories, because that was what the mothers of kids like Charlie and Duane did. Sometimes, when things were really bad, that became their only topic of conversation, something that had always scared Laura.

So she did her usual "he's been fine since the transplant, knock wood," then actually did knock wood by tapping the seat of her chair, and Cherise did a little bragging about twelve-year-old Duane's progress with his guitar lessons and his expertise at model plane construction.

"Does Charlie have any hobbies?" Cherise asked.

"If you can count computer games, I guess so," Laura said, smiling. "Oh, and he loves baseball. My husband actually carved out some bases in the backyard. We like to make sure Charlie gets exercise, gets outside in the fresh air, you know?"

"Yeah, I hear you, girl. That's always been the tough part with Duane. You know, that old thing—an object at rest tends to stay at rest? He's starting to put on a few too many pounds, and that has to stop."

Laura spoke before she thought, or before she could think to keep her mouth shut. "Does Duane like baseball?"

Cherise frowned. "Baseball? Duane? I don't know. To tell you the truth, I think he tries to stay away from things that might make him upset because he can't do them very well. When did Charlie start playing?"

"He started on a rubber-ball team back before he got sick, but now he can't seem to make the hardball team. While the other kids were growing bigger and stronger and playing ball, Charlie was stuck attached to a machine three days a week and too sick to do much of anything for most of the rest of them."

"I'm still hearing you. For a lot of years, Duane was either waiting for an operation or recovering from an operation. We've had several minor miracles, but not without a fight. Baseball, you said? Tell me more."

Laura felt the excitement she'd experienced at Riley's with Jayne Ann coming back to her. "Another mom and I started thinking last night—why shouldn't kids who want to play on a team be allowed to play, you know? We could make up our own teams—oh, and our own rules, as my son just pointed out to me. All we need are the kids. And a field. And some coaches." Laura wrinkled her nose. "And some uniform shirts and caps from a sponsor, and some bats and balls and mitts, and—well, we were just brainstorming."

Cherise looked over at her son, and then back at Laura. "Brainstorming, huh? But you're really serious, aren't you? Who all could be on the team? I mean, Duane's two or three years younger than Charlie. Could he be on the team?"

Laura's enthusiasm ratcheted up another notch and she leaned her elbows on the table. She hadn't been this excited, this hopeful, in a long, long time. "Sure, why not? Everyone's welcome. I mean, that's the whole idea, Cherise—getting the kids to play baseball. Giving them a team, making them feel part of a larger whole, allowing them to recognize their abilities and not just dwell on what they can't do. And the moms and dads, too. Getting them together, giving them something hopeful, you know? Something to cheer about. Not like a support group where we all sit around and dwell on what's wrong in our lives and try to comfort each other, but a reason to feel *happy* and *hopeful*. A reason to *cheer*..." She swiped at her stinging eyes. "Sorry, Cherise. It seems I care more about this than I realized."

Cherise grinned. "I thought you were coming over the table for me for a minute there, sweetie. But you know what? I like it.

I like it a lot, and I know my husband will like it, too. Bert's always trying to get Duane up and off his butt. Now, tell me again what we need, because I think I can help on one thing at least."

"Really? Because I have to be honest, a friend and I just started talking about this last night. I mean, it's mostly a dream right now."

"If you can't dream, what's left?" Cherise said, spreading her arms, and suddenly Laura did want to "come over the table" and hug the woman. "So, if you can figure out a way to get enough people together to do it, we can loan you a couple of acres Bert's dad owns about five miles out of town. You know, our own field of dreams?"

"A field of dreams," Laura repeated, looking over at the kids in time to see Charlie helping Duane to steady himself on his feet before they headed toward their mothers. Sarah was bringing up the rear, still madly pushing buttons on the Game Boy. "And a team of heroes."

"Right. All we're missing is Kevin Costner, and while I have to tell you that's a damn pity, I think we can manage without him." Cherise hugged her son against her side and planted an embarrassing kiss on his chubby cheek. "Hey, hero, how'd you like to play baseball with Charlie?"

Laura bit her lip and looked at her son. It was too late to back down now, wasn't it? She'd opened her big mouth and stuck her foot right in it.

"You mean in our backyard, Mom?"

"Well, sure, to start," Laura said, trying to keep the excitement out of her voice. "But maybe, if we can get enough kids together to make up a team, we could play on a real field."

"What kind of kids?" Charlie asked, looking at his mother as if she'd suddenly grown another head. "Kids like me, you mean? Kids like Bobby, and Bruce Lee, and Duane here? That kind of kids?"

Oh no. Was Charlie going to reject the idea out of hand? They'd tried so hard to impress on him that he was as normal as the next kid, that his problems were over and he could go on with his life, and now here she was, classing him with kids with different problems from his, but problems that clearly weren't ever going to go completely away.

"A bad idea, Charlie?" she asked him as he sat down beside her.

"Heck no, Mom, it's a great idea. I could play *and* coach, don't you think? I mean, I know the game, right? But we'd need more than one team. You need two teams to play baseball, or else it's just practice. I bet Jacob Cohen would want to play. You remember him, Mom, right? He used to ride the special bus with me when nobody wanted me riding the regular bus that year."

"No, I'm sorry. I don't think I remember Jacob."

"Sure you do, Mom," Sarah piped up. "He's the kid with, like, only one and a half arms. How could you forget that?"

Laura closed her eyes in embarrassment. Children were so unfailingly blunt. "Thank you, Sarah," she said, hoping Cherise didn't think she was raising rude, insensitive children. "I do think I remember Jacob now."

"He'd be fine, Mom," Charlie said. "There was this guy, Jim Abbott, who was a lot like Jacob. He only had one hand, but he pitched in the big leagues for the Angels and the Yankees, even pitched a no-hitter one year. That's *big,* Mom. He only batted twenty-three times because he mostly played in the American League and didn't have to bat, but he got *two* hits. That's better than a lot of pitchers with two hands. Oh, and he got a gold medal in the Olympics. Not that Coach Billig ever would have let Jim Abbott play on one of *his* teams."

"How do you know all of this?" Laura asked. Her son's ability to remember baseball statistics still amazed her. Especially when he couldn't seem to remember where they kept the clothes hamper.

"Grandpa got me his rookie card for Christmas last year. Hey, Duane, do you collect baseball cards?"

Duane shook his head. "Hockey cards. Me and Dad love the Flyers."

"Dad and I," Cherise said singsong, rolling her eyes. "Duane loves the idea of being on ice skates," she explained to Laura.

"They move so fast, up and down the ice. It looks like they're flying." Duane's huge brown eyes were filled with dreams. "Hey, maybe if we can play baseball in the summer, we can play ice hockey in the winter."

"Oh, Mrs. Finnegan, just look what you have started," Cherise said, laughing. She turned to her son. "One bite of the apple at a time, hotshot, all right? Why don't you and Charlie take my notebook and pen and go over there and write down some names. You know, kids you think might want to play baseball."

"Do we have to have girls on the team?" Duane asked warily.

"Do we have to have boys with braces on their legs on the team?" his mother shot back just as quickly, raising her eyebrows at her son.

Duane rolled his eyes. "Okay, okay. Everybody plays. Even *girls*."

Laura watched, her chin in her hand, as the three children returned to the table across the room, and then she looked at Cherise. "What have we started here? We don't have a clue what we're doing, but those kids think we do. Plus, my husband is going to *kill* me because he made me promise I wouldn't get Charlie's hopes up about this until and unless I knew we could do it."

"Sweetie, that horse left the barn awhile ago," Cherise said, pulling a second small notebook from her enormous purse, then extracting a second pen and pushing both pen and notebook across the table to Laura. "Now, let's make a list. Oh, and how many kids are on a baseball team? We should know that, right?"

Laura looked at the empty page of the notebook for a few moments, and then sat back, grinning from ear to ear. "Cherise, I haven't the faintest idea how many kids are on a baseball team. There's nine on the field at one time, but there's also a bunch more on the bench. Tell you what. I'll call Jayne Ann Maitz—her son will be on the team—and maybe the three of us can get together tonight and talk about all of this some more. In the meantime, now that he knows what we're planning, I'll raid Charlie's room for a book on baseball. Oh, and I think I'll take a look around on the Internet. Somebody must have had this idea already, right? I mean, we're good, but I doubt we're original. Maybe I can pick up a few pointers for us somewhere. Does that sound like a plan?"

Cherise nodded, reaching into her purse yet again, this time coming out with her computerized planner. Laura got the feeling that if she'd asked for a kitchen sink, Cherise would have promptly pulled one from her purse. "How about after dinner? Seven o'clock? Oh, and where?"

"You like ice cream?"

"Riley's," Cherise said, rubbing her palms together. "I am a glutton for Riley's. What about this Cohen kid?"

"I think Charlie knows where he lives. We'll stop off there on our way home, ask his mom if she wants to join us. Because you know what, Cherise? No men. Not right now at least. They'll go all logical on us and point out all the problems, and I think we're safer going into this like wide-eyed optimists, not worrying about pitfalls because we don't know where to look for them. Plus, I think Jayne Ann is pretty good at baseball—she'll be our expert for now. And you can bring anyone you think of who might want to become eligible for a good mental health plan—because we're nuts, you know, Cherise. Certifiably crazy, if we think we can pull this off."

"I'll have to tell Bert, since it's his dad's land. He'll be fine with it. Bert learned a long time ago that, with me, it's easier to just go with the flow, because that way there's less chance of getting run over. But you don't want to tell your husband yet?"

"I should. I know I should. Jake's a wonderful husband, and a wonderful dad. Please don't think he's an ogre or something. But he's kind of tired of being knocked down, and watching Charlie get knocked down. It's a phase and he'll get over it. I'd just like to come to him with something already accomplished, something positive." She tried to smile. "We've been taking a few hits lately, you know?"

"Yeah, we all know that story, chapter and verse," Cherise said, reaching across the table to squeeze Laura's hand. "We'll get some good news for him, and then you can hit him with the uppercut."

The two women giggled like children, until their own children told them to stop.

It wasn't until she was driving home from Jacob Cohen's house after speaking with his grandmother that Laura realized she'd sailed—positively sailed—through Charlie's appointment with the nephrologist, happily accepting his good lab numbers as something to be expected and then forgetting them because she was in a hurry to get home and think more about the baseball team. When was the last time she'd done that? Never. That was the last time. Lab test days were hell, always had been. The waiting, the worrying. But not today. Not since she and Cherise had put their heads together with Charlie and Duane in the cafeteria and started making plans.

It was only when she saw Jake's car in the driveway that her smile finally left her, because she had just done what he'd warned her not to do, and now she had to tell him.

Did she have to tell him? Cherise thought so, and she was probably right. "Nothing good ever comes from secrets," she had warned, and then grinned. "Besides, girlfriend, it's too late for you to back out. We're already in this up to our necks now that the kids know."

Laura tried bargaining with herself. She could wait to tell Jake until after the meeting tonight, because maybe their dream would come to nothing, and then there'd be nothing to report.

But Charlie would tell him. She couldn't ask Charlie, or Sarah, to keep secrets from their father.

So she'd tell him.

After dinner. No, before dinner. Before Charlie got to him.

"Stop it," she told herself out loud when she realized she was dreading seeing her own husband.

"What, Mom?" Charlie asked from the front passenger seat as he undid his seat belt. "Stop what?"

"Nothing, Charlie. I was just talking to myself. Dad's home. Why don't you go tell him about your great lab results?"

"Yeah," Charlie said, opening the car door. "He'll like that."

"And that's probably just about all he's going to like tonight," Laura mumbled as she struggled with her own seat belt, then walked into the house, her feet dragging, all her enthusiasm gone.

Maybe if she went on the Internet, as she'd discussed with Cherise, she could find something she could use with Jake as a good argument on how to turn this dream into a reality....

CHAPTER
❧ FOUR ❧

"**I**s that it?"

"That's it."

The silence, except for a few snatches of birdsong and the sound of an eighteen-wheeler roaring down the highway to their left, was pretty deafening.

"Wow."

Laura tried to keep her expression neutral, even after Jayne Ann's rather awed *wow*. "Well, it's flat," she said, looking over the weed-choked ground that spread out in front of the three women and Jacob Cohen's father. Jacob's mother had died when Jacob was two. And Laura thought *she* had problems. "I mean, there is that, right?"

"Right! There is that," Jayne Ann said brightly, probably to make up for the less than enthusiastic *wow*. "And it's not as if anyone is going to run off a cliff into a quarry way out here, not with the highway bordering us on two sides and the—what is that over there?"

"The sewage-treatment plant," Laura said quietly. "It could be worse."

"How?" Jayne Ann whispered back. "Granted, I don't see any warning signs about this being a toxic-waste dump, but it's pretty terrible, Laura. It will take us years to get this place ready for a baseball court—diamond—whatever. I'm always getting them mixed up, which drives Bobby crazy."

"Diamond," Laura said as Cherise and Larry Cohen walked deeper into the weeds. "And, for your information, it's home plate, not home *base,* and baseball has umpires, not referees. So much for me thinking you'd be our resident baseball expert. Charlie gave me a crash course this morning, and my head is still reeling. I always went to Charlie's games before he got sick, but I was usually too busy chasing after Sarah to pay much attention to what was going on."

"You're lucky," Jayne Ann said. "Bobby doesn't share much, although, after I told him about our idea, I did notice that his mitt is back on his desk, not on the floor of the closet underneath his dirty clothes. The dirty clothes are still there, unfortunately. We're having a serious mental struggle to see who lasts longer, me, the neatnik—or him, the slob. I think he's winning. One more day, and I know I'm going to gather up his laundry—before the Health Department steps in and his *room* is declared a toxic-waste dump. So, how's Jake?"

Jayne Ann had slid in her question just as Laura was smiling at the battle of the dirty clothes, which sounded very familiar. Charlie's room had been the scene of more than one skirmish over the same problem. Her smile faded slowly. "Good, he's good," she said, nodding her head. "We're good."

"That bad, huh?" Jayne Ann said, wincing. "I guess you were right to keep him out of this for a while. Or am I wrong, and he would have taken one look at this field and said, 'Yippee, perfect, just what we need'?"

Laura sighed, remembering something she'd thought yesterday at the hospital. "I'm turning my own husband into an ogre. And he's not, Jayne Ann. He's just had enough. He doesn't want to see Charlie hurt again."

"Or himself," Jayne Ann said. "It's hard, this acceptance thing. And I think it's harder for men with their sons."

"Jake played baseball in college," Laura told her, sighing yet again. "Second base, just like Charlie. He brought a tiny glove to the hospital with us the day Charlie was born." She raised her hands in a helpless gesture, then let them drop to her sides once more. "He never wanted to live through Charlie, recapture old glory or anything like that. He just wanted Charlie to enjoy what he'd enjoyed, you know? Oh, and he did. Charlie, that is. Jake made up that little field out back, and I'd watch them every night after dinner, as I washed the dishes. Charlie and his daddy. I wanted rosebushes, a real garden, you know? But I wouldn't give back one moment of watching the two of them out there for the most beautiful garden in the world."

She turned away from Jayne Ann, swiped at a tear that had escaped, then turned back with a smile. "Sorry. Jake was pretty good when I told him last night, he really was."

"But he's not going to have anything to do with this, is he?"

Laura shook her head. "Not yet, no. But he can't seem to really give me a reason, and I didn't push. He just needs some time, Jayne Ann. It's only been six months. He thought when Charlie was better that everything else would be better, too, that everything would just sort of morph back to the way it was before Charlie got sick. I tried to tell him, more than once, that it wouldn't be like that, but he's always been the optimist. Somebody had to be, Charlie needed that. So now it's my turn to be the cheerleader, I guess, and Jake's turn to take a little time off, get his head back in gear. It only seems fair, since he's propped me up plenty over the years. He leaves for Boston tomorrow, on business, and won't be back for a week. That's probably a good thing."

Jayne Ann nodded. "If it keeps him from looking at this field? Yeah, I'd say it's a good thing. Okay, here come Cherise and Larry. Put on your cheerleader uniform, because sounding optimistic right now is going to take pom-poms and high kicks to pull off."

Cherise was busy pulling her electronic notebook and cell phone from her purse as Larry Cohen approached, rubbing his hands together in front of him. Larry was a small man, rather thin, and had a bald spot that actually made him look rather endearing, Laura thought.

"He's cute, isn't he?" Jayne Ann whispered, fluffing her hair. "I mean, I gave up on Hugh Grant years ago, after he was caught with that hooker."

"Down, girl," Laura said, trying to regain her good humor. "But, yes, he's cute. In a sort of 'take him home and feed him dinner' sort of way."

"Thanks, Laura. I'll have to dig out my lasagna recipe."

Larry had his endearing smile firmly in place as he stopped in front of Laura and Jayne Ann. "Wrong sports analogy, ladies, but I think we're going to have to go back ten and punt. There's just too much work to do here to have a baseball field ready before the first snowfall."

"That's what I was afraid of," Laura said, her shoulders sagging. "And, you know, it's not just the field. Charlie said we need—wait, I've got a list." She dug into her own purse and came out with a folded sheet of pink paper with kittens stamped all over it that she'd commandeered from Sarah.

"You really should get one of these, Laura," Cherise said, holding up her electronic organizer. "Not that the kittens don't look professional, or anything," she added, winking at Jayne Ann.

"Hey, in my house, you get what you find, even if that means ripping off a nine-year-old," Laura said, grinning. Cherise was good for her, she really was. "Okay, here we go. Benches—the team has to sit somewhere. No bleachers, because parents can bring their own blankets and lawn chairs. Bases, home *plate*, some sort of backstop." She looked at Cherise. "You know what that is?"

Cherise nodded. "I have a vague idea. Go on. I'm typing this all into my organizer. What else?"

Larry started counting out items on his fingers. "A line-marking machine to put down the baselines and batting box every game. Bats, mitts, balls. A pitching rubber. Protective gear for the catcher. Shirts and caps, because we don't need actual uniforms if we get everyone matching T-shirts and caps."

"A hot dog, soda and candy stand," Jayne Ann said, then shrugged her shoulders. "Hey, a girl can dream."

"So," Cherise said, closing the organizer, "what we're actually saying here is money. We need money. Who's up for robbing a bank? I'm in for driving the getaway car. I just got a tune-up and a new muffler."

Larry was wearing the rather stunned expression common in men who suddenly realized they were badly outnumbered by females and couldn't begin to understand their language. "We, um, we need a sponsor. Maybe more than one. Probably more than one."

"A sponsor? Oh, wait," Jayne Ann said. "You mean like we used to have for my bowling league? Although I have to tell you, I think the real reason we disbanded is because nobody could face another year of hot-pink shirts with Sam's Exotic Delights stamped on the back."

"You're making that up," Laura said, turning around as she heard a pickup truck pulling onto the edge of the field.

"Oh, come on, Laura, who could make that up?" Jayne Ann placed her hands on her hips. "And, far be it from me to be a wet blanket here, but we have only five kids for this team— these teams. Charlie, Jacob, Duane, Bruce Lee Pak and my Bobby. Until and unless we get a field, get *something,* how are we going to attract more players? Who's that?"

Cherise was waving at the tall man walking toward them. Tall, and fairly close to immense, actually. "That, my friends, is my baby brother. Did I happen to mention that he owns a construction company? You know, a *construction company?* One of those companies that owns bulldozers and backhoes and all those good things? So you can stop worrying about the field. I called him a few minutes ago and he said he'd be right over. He's so obedient, but that's probably because I used to babysit him and he's still afraid of me."

Laura looked at her new friend in amazement. "Cherise Johnson, have I told you lately that I love you? Now," she said, rubbing her palms together, "who else has a friend or relative we can use—that is, ask to volunteer?"

An hour later, after a quick lunch at a fast-food restaurant, the four split up, each with their own assignment except for Jayne Ann, who had just gotten her Realtor's license and had a showing for a customer on the other side of town. Cherise went off to see her sister, who worked for the township (bless the woman, she had eight siblings!), to find out what the chances were that the recreation department had some old baseball equipment lying around that nobody was using anymore. Larry had to go back to work at the bank, but he'd promised to print up some flyers they could deliver to the pediatric departments in all three of the area's hospitals and to several pediatricians' offices.

Once those flyers were out, there'd be no turning back!

And that left Laura the job she hated most but felt she had to tackle since it had been her idea—finding sponsors for the teams. When it came to being a salesperson, she'd always thought of herself as the kind who would knock on a stranger's door, then say, "You don't want to buy a set of encyclopedias, do you?" Jake could sell sand in a desert, but she'd rather eat that sand than try to do the same thing.

But this time she had a mission, and it wasn't calendars for the high-school band, or candy bars for their church group, or even Girl Scout cookies (one of the worst failures of her youth). This time she was raising money for the Heroes. That was the one thing they'd all agreed upon at lunch, the name for their league. The Heroes. Jayne Ann had thought the letters could stand for something and had even come up with Helping Everyone Rise Over...but then they'd all drawn a blank on the ES, so they gave up that idea as a bad job and just stuck with Heroes.

Larry's "Egregious Stuff" hadn't been all that bad, really. And definitely much better than Jayne Ann's pithy suggestion for the S-word.

Laura also had what she believed to be two aces in her pocket—Charlie and Sarah—and she wasn't above using them, either. Charlie was so damn cute with his shock of red hair and his big smile, and if that didn't work, Sarah, who had begged to stay home with Brenda, would wear any prospective donor down with her "my dog just died" expression.

Yes, Laura knew, she was shameless. But it was for a good cause, and that's what she'd keep telling herself.

"So, how much do we need?" Charlie asked as Laura drove along what was known locally as the Golden Strip, home of the two large and four smaller shopping malls in the township. This street had it all—clothing stores, restaurants, automobile dealerships, movie theaters, mattress stores, tanning salons. Laura looked at all the signs, considering which places she could hit up for money. *Hit up.* Yes, she was feeling rather ruthless.

"I don't know," Laura said as she eased up to a red light. "Do you?"

Charlie rolled his eyes. "Mom, I'm fourteen. But a good mitt is over a hundred bucks, easy, and aluminum bats aren't much cheaper, although we'll only need about five or six of those and everyone can share. I've got my own mitt and bat, and so does Bobby, but most of the kids won't, right? And the moms and dads might not be able to afford them, either."

Laura had a quick mental flash of the parking lot at the dialysis center, the one filled with run-down cars. You could pick out the patients' cars by their age and condition. It was the first rule of having a chronically ill or disabled child, or adult, for that matter—go quietly broke, no matter how well cushioned you might have been when the Egregious Stuff first hit the fan. She tapped her fingertips against the steering wheel. "Right. Okay, first stop, a sporting-goods store. We'll price things, and then we'll go asking for money."

Their investigation at the sporting-goods store took another hour and added more items to their "we have to have this" list. Laura was beginning to feel the butterflies back in her stomach when she totaled up the figures in her head and decided they needed over a thousand dollars—and that was if everyone on the team chipped in a sign-up fee, which she didn't want to ask for. She'd been at the bottom of the well herself and knew that even twenty-five or thirty dollars could sometimes seem like a million. The Heroes were supposed to be an opportunity, not yet another problem, so they'd all decided that the fee would be happily accepted but not mandatory.

With Jake leaving in the morning (and her nervousness threatening to get the better of her), Laura decided they'd had enough for one day, so they stopped at the local grocery store for three freshly cut T-bone steaks for dinner—Jake's favorite. After all, once he was off to Boston they could eat more hamburgers and pizza, which the kids liked better anyway.

Laura stood in front of the glassed-in meat counter while Sarah scoped out the homemade cupcakes and Charlie opened a bottle of a sports drink and chugged down half of it. For over two years the amount of fluid he could drink a day was severely restricted, so now he was always drinking something.

"Jerry?" she asked as the butcher loaded three steaks onto a piece of brown paper and tossed them on the scale. "Have you ever thought about sponsoring a baseball team?"

Then she smiled, because she hadn't realized she was going to ask the question until she heard it coming out of her mouth. And, hey, it hadn't been so bad. All Jerry could do was say no, right?

"Sure," Jerry said, eyeballing the scale. "I already do. You know, the township youth league?"

"Oh," Laura said, her shoulders sagging in spite of her best efforts to keep smiling. "Then you wouldn't want to help sponsor another one, would you?"

You don't want to buy a set of encyclopedias, do you...?

"Sure, why not? For Sarah, right?"

"Uh, no. Not Sarah. Charlie."

Jerry hesitated as he reached for the steaks. "Charlie? But Jake was in here last night, and he said Charlie just got cut. I'm sorry about that, Laura. That really stinks."

"I know." Laura stepped to the end of the meat cooler and Jerry joined her there. "We're putting together a new team, actually. One where anyone can play. We..." Suddenly she was speaking quickly, her enthusiasm overcoming her nervousness. "We're gathering up kids who normally couldn't play on a regular team and giving them the chance to learn about baseball. Teamwork. And anything else good about team sports. Charlie's friend Bobby has a seizure disorder, and Duane Johnson has spina bifida, so he wears leg braces—but he's doing great, he really is. Jacob Cohen—"

"I know Jacob," Jerry said. "He and his grandmother come in here a lot." He leaned a hip against the meat case. "How about Toni D'Amato? Antoinette, I mean. She's ten, I think. Cute kid. She comes in here for sour balls all the time. But deaf, you know?" He shook his head. "No, she couldn't play. What if she had her back turned and the ball was coming at her? Nobody could warn her and she could get hurt."

"Then…then she'd have her mom or dad or somebody else in the field with her to make sure she pays attention. That would work, wouldn't it? We're making up our own rules, Jerry. If Toni wants to play, she plays. That's what the Heroes is all about."

"The Heroes, huh?" Jerry walked back behind the counter and pulled out a long pack of solid American cheese, then sheared off a few slices and laid them on a small square of waxed paper. "Here you go—Sarah likes cheese."

"Thank you, Jerry," Laura said, handing the cheese to Sarah, and then picking up the wrapped steaks.

"Put me down for two hundred, okay? Oh, and let me look up Toni's mom's number in the phone book for you before you go. Name's Lucie. Lucie D'Amato. And I'll ask around, see if anyone else wants to chip in. The Heroes, huh? I like that."

"Yeah, I do, too," Laura said, grinning. "Thanks, Jerry."

"Hey, for Charlie? For Jacob and Toni? How could I say no? You're doing a good thing here, Laura. A good thing."

"We're doing a good thing, Jake," Laura told her husband five hours later, once Charlie and Sarah had gone to bed and she was watching Jake pack his suitcase.

He stopped halfway to the bed, where Laura was refolding each piece immediately after he tossed it in the suitcase. "I know that, Laura. You mean well. But Gary—"

"I talked to Gary. He says there's a way around all that liability mumbo jumbo, and he's offered to do any legal work, gratis. Besides, we're not going to use a township field. What else is bothering you?"

Jake's jaw tightened. "You talked to Gary? On your own?"

Laura rolled her eyes even as she rolled up a pair of Jake's black socks. "Yes, *on my own.* They do let me out of the Helpless Females Club once in a while, you know. Why shouldn't I have talked to Gary?"

"Because..." Jake let his arms fall to his sides. "I don't know why, sweetheart. Of course you could talk to Gary. But this is all happening pretty fast, don't you think? And Charlie's all charged up, talking about how he wants to help coach the team, and Sarah was on the phone with one of her friends earlier, rounding up a cheerleading squad, for crying out loud. It's just moving too fast. I don't think you and your friends have really thought this thing out."

"It's already the end of May, Jake. If we're going to float a team, we have to move quickly."

"*Field* a team, Laura, not *float* a team," Jake said, grinning over his shoulder at her even while searching in a drawer for his toiletries bag, the one she'd given him when they were newlyweds. He unzipped it and headed into the bathroom, calling back over his shoulder, "Tell me more about this field you found."

Laura punched her palm with her fist. She wasn't going to get away with it, she would have to tell him about the field. "I thought you didn't care," she said as he came back into the bedroom, trying to zip the stuffed bag shut again.

Jake stopped in front of her, his shoulders sagging. "Charlie cares, Laura. You care. Sarah cares, bless her heart. I'm sort of stuck with having to care. Now, tell me about the field."

Maybe she could sell sand in the desert. Or at least she could give it the old college try. "Well, the land belongs to Cherise Johnson's father-in-law, and he's delighted to let us use part of it for the kids. It's about five miles north of town—plenty of room for parking right in the field. When I was out there today the birds were singing and the sun was shining, and I could just close my eyes and imagine how it's all going to look once we do a little work. Just what these kids need, you know? Fresh air, sunshine, exercise. The camaraderie..."

"Yeah, I get that part. Now maybe you'd like to enlarge on what you mean by a *little work?*"

"Well, you know, Jake. It's a field. But it's flat, and once the weeds are gone there should be no problems. And Cherise's brother is going to use some of his big machinery, so that will get rid of the weeds." *And the rocks. And the beer bottles. And the dog poop...at least, let's hope it's dog poop and there aren't any wild animals out there...* "So, can I sign you up?"

"To rake the field? Sure, why not. You've got to get all the stones out of the infield, Laura, and with these kids, the infield and a little bit of outfield is all you're probably going to need. So you don't have to worry about planting grass—just putting down a layer of good rolled clay. And that's expensive, by the way."

Laura mentally added *good rolled clay* to her list. "Where do we get that?"

Jake closed the suitcase and zipped it shut. "I have absolutely no idea, sorry. But, then, it's not my project, is it?"

"You're still angry," Laura said, following him downstairs as he put the suitcase in the foyer, then headed for the kitchen and a bottle of soda from the refrigerator. "You still think we're going to fall flat on our faces and Charlie and the other kids are the ones who will be hurt."

Jake closed the refrigerator door and turned on her, so that she involuntarily stepped back. "Look, Laura, don't make me into the bad guy here. I'm thinking about our son."

"Then *do* that, Jake, think about Charlie. He's over the moon with this idea."

"Idea? More like a pipe dream. I guess we have different names for it. I said I'd help, Laura, and I will, when I get home from Boston. But I'm not going to pretend to be happy about any of this. Charlie isn't going to enjoy himself, and you know why?"

"No, Jake, but why don't you tell me why."

"Oh, *that* tone. Don't patronize me, Laura, because I'm not being unreasonable here. All right, I'll tell you anyway. Charlie's not going to like it because it isn't going to be *real* baseball. It can't be."

"Half a loaf is better than none," Laura said, and then winced at the old saying.

Jake pushed his fingers through his hair. "Half a loaf? Is that what Charlie fought for all these years? Half a loaf? Is that all he gets? All he deserves? It's not fair, Laura. It's just not *fair*."

"We have to accept that, honey. Sooner or later, we have to accept that. Life isn't fair. If it were, kids like Charlie and Bobby and the rest would be just like all the other healthy kids on the planet. And, by the way, our idea isn't all that far out. I was looking around on the Internet, and——"

"Oh, boy, this ought to be good."

"Well, it is, Jake. I found this great site for an organization in Saint Louis. They call themselves TASK—that stands for Team Activities for Special Kids. We tried that with the Heroes, but we couldn't come up with words that fit—well, that's another story. Anyway, this group started about ten years ago, pretty much the way we're starting, with just a little over two dozen kids and a T-ball baseball team. Now, ten years later? Jake, they've got over eight hundred kids involved, and not just in baseball. It's big—a year-round deal."

"And parents started this TASK deal?"

"It wasn't their idea originally, no, but that of a woman who worked with special kids. I talked to her by the way, when I called down there. She was a *huge* help. Parents are a big, big part of everything, along with community volunteers. These kids play tennis, golf, softball. Twelve different sports in all, I think. They have their own social club and hold three dances a year."

"And you think that's what you're going to do here?"

"Of course not! Well, not at first. But others have done it for their kids. Why shouldn't we try it for our kids? Face it, honey, if anyone can find a way to make this work around all the possible pitfalls, it's parents like us, who've had to learn how to fight for their kids."

"Golf, huh? I've been thinking about golf for Charlie. He wouldn't have to make a team, you know? It would be just Charlie against the golf course, with nobody saying he's too small." He shook his head. "I don't know, Laura. You're biting off an awful lot, don't you think? We've barely got our own lives back on track without trying to fix the world."

"Just our part of it, Jake. I think we need to fix just our small part of it—you and me and our kids. I hate to say this as much as I know you hate to hear it, but we've been handed some lemons. Maybe it's time to make some lemonade. We can't get back what we lost, Jake, that's impossible. But we can't stay like this, either, in this limbo we're living in now. We have to accept that we can't get our old lives back just because Charlie finally has his new kidney. We have to find a way to move on, and this idea might just be what we need. Please, Jake."

Laura reached out a hand to him but he waved her away, heading into the family room. "I need to think about this some more. I don't know that I'm ready to give up yet, Laura, throw in the towel on what we had, what we thought we were fighting so hard to get back. I...I'm going to try to catch the travel forecast on cable, then watch the sports report for the line scores. Don't wait up."

Laura threw up her hands, both literally and figuratively, and went back upstairs, because a long bubble bath was the most polite way she could think of to keep a closed door between herself and her husband. "*Another* closed door," she muttered. "We've already got one."

CHAPTER
~FIVE~

"**M**om?"

Laura had been staring out the kitchen window at nothing in particular, her chin in her hand. Jake had been up and gone before the alarm went off at six, but he'd left her a note on his pillow: *Kissed you goodbye, Sleeping Beauty. I'm sorry—again—and I love you.* So she guessed they were all right, which was what most marriages were most of the time—all right, or not all right.

Without looking around, she said, "Yes, Charlie? What's up? Your math homework is on the dining-room table."

"Yeah, I've got it, Mom, thanks," Charlie said, slipping into a chair on the other side of the table. "I've been thinking about something we should do."

Laura sat back against the chair and gave an exaggerated sigh. "That's usually dangerous. How much will it cost?"

"Not a lot," Charlie said, his expression serious. "But that's not why we should do this."

Laura watched as Sarah reached into the pantry closet and came out with an icing-covered cherry toaster tart. "Ahem, *madam*," she said, and smiled as Sarah returned the box to the shelf in exchange for a box of cereal. "You're learning," she told her daughter. Laura got up and headed to the refrigerator for a carton of milk. "Why we should do what, Charlie?"

"Not play hardball."

The milk carton almost hit the floor, but Laura recovered in time. "What? You don't want to play?"

"Relax, Mom, I said hardball, not baseball." Charlie opened his social studies textbook and pulled out a sheet of paper, which he laid on the tabletop. "I've been thinking about this. Aluminum bats, regulation balls? I don't think the Heroes are going to be up to that. I think we need to play rubber ball, like I used to play. And maybe even use Ts for some of the kids. You know, like I did when I was a kid?"

Laura closed her eyes against the pain. *When he was a kid. Before the kidney disease. Before he had to grow up years before his time. God bless the boy.*

"I remember, Charlie. That tall black rubber stand, or

whatever it was, with the baseball perched on top so you could hit it. But…aren't you a little beyond that?"

"Well, yeah," he said, taking the cereal box Sarah had just put down and pouring a liberal amount into the bowl in front of him. He still ate his cereal dry because he hadn't been allowed enough liquid to have milk on it. Now he liked it dry. "But I'm not going to play much, you know. If it's all right with everybody, I'm going to coach."

His words skittered through Laura's brain and she pretty much had to totter back to her chair and sit down. "Coach," she repeated. "Not play? I know you said that, but I didn't really think—Charlie, you love baseball."

"I still love baseball, Mom, but what I like best is being on a team. Practicing. I can still do that. I'm not good enough for the township team, but I'm probably a little too good for the Heroes. What Dad said the other night? He was right. You don't have to play baseball on a team to be a part of the game. I think I'll be a pretty decent coach, too." He grinned. "All I have to do is remember not to do anything Coach Billig does."

Laura rested her chin on her hand once more as she grinned back at her son. "I love you to pieces, Charlie Finnegan."

"Oh, gross!" Sarah said, picking up her empty cereal bowl and heading for the sink. "I can still be a cheerleader, can't I? Brenda says we can get matching outfits and her mom will buy us pom-poms when you choose the team colors."

"How about red and blue, like my favorite superhero?" Charlie suggested, peeking up at the wall clock. "Come on, Sarah, or we'll miss the bus."

"Okay," his younger sister said, grabbing her lunch bucket from the counter. "Oh, Mom? Do we have any Popsicle sticks anywhere? I have a diorama of an African hut to do for geography class."

Laura narrowed her eyes, remembering a scene very much like this a few years ago, except that Charlie had waited until the night before the project was due to tell her about it. She'd ended up using toothpicks for the hut and nearly a full jar of oregano for the landscape around it. Charlie had only gotten a C+, but his project had smelled good. "Due when, little girl?" she asked, dreading the answer.

"Tomorrow," Sarah said, already halfway out the door so that her mother's groan barely reached her.

The phone rang just as Laura had her hand deep in the freezer in search of Popsicles, then decided it would be better to make a run to the local hobby store than to have the three of them go on a marathon Popsicle-eating binge.

"Hello?"

"Back at you. I'll be by to pick you up in twenty minutes. No, make that a half hour. I still have to walk the dog, and he's looking faintly constipated."

"Jayne Ann?"

"Who else do you know who'd admit to a constipated beagle? Cherise just called, and we're all meeting for breakfast at that little place at the other end of the strip mall from Riley's. She says Larry has all kinds of good news for us. I knew I liked that man."

Laura looked down at her pajamas, which consisted of a pair of pink, pull-on knit shorts and one of Jake's old navy blue Penn State T-shirts. "How about I meet you there?"

When Laura found the others at a large round table at the back of the small restaurant, the first thing she noticed was that there were three people she hadn't met yet.

Larry Cohen did the honors. "Laura, I'd like to introduce you to my boss, Harry Walters, who is going to hand over a check for five hundred dollars as well as help us to set up a free checking account and anything else we need. And this is my son's pediatrician, John Ryan, who's agreed to act as official team doctor. His son Johnny hopes to play with the Heroes. And last but certainly not least is Arthur Brightstone, who has generously offered to provide us with all the hats and shirts and whatever other gear we need. Gentlemen, genius and founder of the Heroes—Laura Finnegan."

Laura looked at her friends, who were grinning from ear to ear, and then numbly held out her hand to each of the three men.

She simply let the conversation wash over her for a few minutes. She thought it was nice of Larry to call her the founder of the Heroes, but everything would still be just one big daydream, wishful thinking, if it weren't for Jayne Ann, and Cherise, and Larry, and... "Volunteers!"

"What, Laura?" Jayne Ann asked around a bite of toast.

"Oh, I'm sorry. I said, 'Volunteers.' We're going to need a bunch of them." She smiled at Harry Walters. "Please forgive me. I have this tendency to think out loud, and usually at inappropriate times."

"Geniuses do that, Mrs. Finnegan," he told her. "You know, Larry here was rather vague—not that I wasn't immediately intrigued and knew the Heroes is something the bank very much wants to be involved in. Perhaps you'd like to tell me more about the program?"

The program. Well, that was terrifyingly formal, wasn't it? It seemed that the moaning about the lack of a team for Charlie and Bobby to play on had turned into a program. A program with a team physician and free checking, no less.

Laura didn't know if it was her lost expression that brought Cherise to the rescue, but she was soon sipping her coffee and making polite comments while her friend talked about the "field of dreams" that was even now taking shape five miles out of town.

By the time the check came and Mr. Brightstone graciously picked it up, no one could have been faulted for thinking the Heroes was all but a done deal, with their first practice only days away.

Once the men, including Larry Cohen, had gone, the women pulled their chairs closer together and looked at each other. Just looked at each other.

And then Jayne Ann began to giggle, rapidly joined by Cherise and Laura, until all of them were in gales of laughter. Their waitress, a woman who looked as if she'd been born harried, plunked down a fresh coffeepot and commented that she wouldn't mind a sip of whatever "hard stuff" they were slipping into their cups.

"It's not that funny!" Jayne Ann gasped as she held on to Laura and tried to catch her breath.

"Yes, it is," Cherise told her sternly, then laughed and snorted at the same time…and set all three of them off again.

"We're really doing this," Laura said. "We may not know *what* we're doing, but we're definitely doing it." She wiped her streaming eyes. "God, I haven't laughed this hard in…I don't even remember, to tell you the truth."

"Well, maybe we all needed a good laugh," Cherise said, pulling out her electronic organizer yet again. "Beats crying all to hell, girlfriends, doesn't it?"

CHAPTER
~ SIX ~

Laura dug into her shorts pocket for her cell phone, then collapsed onto her backside in the dirt, hoping whoever was calling wanted to recite the entirety of the Declaration of Independence in her ear, because then she'd have a good excuse to rest for at least ten minutes.

She had muscles today she hadn't known she owned three days ago, and all of them ached. She'd broken three fingernails and finally given in and cut the rest of them down last night after soaking in the bathtub until both her fingers and toes were pruney. She had a bandage on her left knee, a blister at the base of her right thumb, and she was pretty sure that she'd be tasting dirt in her mouth whenever she chewed for at least the next year.

"Hello—*ouch*," she said into the phone, reaching beneath herself to pull out a fairly sharp rock and toss it into the basket beside her. "Hello?"

"Laura, honey?"

She covered her other ear with her hand because several eighteen-wheelers were passing by on the highway. "Jake? Is that you?"

"You keep a list of men who call you *Laura, honey?*" she heard him ask, and she smiled in the general direction of the entire world.

"I do, I do. But it's a short list, with only one name on it. Where are you?"

"Back in Boston after a four-day tour of the suburbs. But that's the thing, honey. I'm going to have to stay a couple of extra days."

"What's a couple of extra days? You won't be home until Sunday?"

"Try next Wednesday. But there's a good chance we'll see a nice bonus out of this, so I said yes to the plan—think how happy all our creditors will be. I found a Laundromat a few blocks from the hotel, and I'm going to head there now, so you don't have to worry that I'll get hit by a truck and the doctors and nurses will find me in dirty underwear."

"Ha-ha," Laura said, wincing at Jake's joke. "Not until next Wednesday?" she asked, trying to keep a Sarah-whine out of her voice. "But the Heroes start practice on Monday night. Their first *game* is that Saturday."

"I know, and I want to be there. I *will* be there, Laura, I promise. What's that noise in the background? Where are you?"

"I'm at the ball field," Laura said, looking around at the bald, scraped earth that stretched out around her. "I think I'm pretty close to third base, as a matter of fact. It's really coming along, Jake. There are only three parents who haven't been able to volunteer, and that's because they've got new babies at home, or they already work three jobs. But everyone else has been out here as much as possible. We've got twenty-six kids now—can you believe that? All it took was those flyers, and the phones started ringing off the hook. Maybe next year we'll—"

"I miss you, Laura."

She sighed, her muscles relaxing as she crossed her legs and put her other hand on the small phone—physically drawing herself away from the noise and dust of the ball field and into that small, cozy cocoon that was Jake and Laura's World. "I miss you, too, sweetheart. Are you eating enough? Sleeping enough?"

"I'm on an expense account in a four-star hotel, and I feel guilty as hell about that lobster I enjoyed last night while you guys were probably eating macaroni and cheese, but I'll get over it."

"Hot dogs and hamburgers."

"What? Hon, you'll have to talk louder. You've got a lot of noise around you."

"I said, we had hot dogs and hamburgers—and lots of other great picnic food. Sharon Baxter, one of the moms, had us all over to her backyard for dinner after we got done here. I wish you could have been there, Jake, to meet some of the other parents, some of the other kids. Did I tell you we've got twenty-six kids now?"

She could hear Jake's frustrated sigh all the way from Boston even as she winced, realizing her mistake. God, she was nervous. Nervous, speaking to her own husband! "Yes, Laura, you already told me. You have quite the social life all of a sudden, don't you? I thought you didn't like being around other mothers of sick kids. I thought all the depressing *sick talk* upset you."

Laura stood up, began walking into the outfield, away from anyone who might overhear her. "But, Jake, this isn't sick talk. This is something *positive* we're all doing for our kids. Nobody's having a pity party here. We're having fun! The kids are having fun. We're climbing mountains, Jake. And if those mountains are things like making sure the baselines are wide enough for a wheelchair or walker, or making up flash cards so that Johnny Ryan can, hopefully, memorize the bases and where to run to first after he hits the ball—

well, we're climbing them. One by one. Even Kenny Baxter is going to play, and that's fantastic."

Jake's voice sounded more resigned now than angry as he asked, "What's so special about Kenny Baxter?"

"He's blind, that's what's so special about him."

"Blind? You're kidding, right? What the hell position do you have him playing?"

Laura took the phone from her ear and looked at it for a moment—glared at it—before putting it to her ear once more. "That should be obvious, Jake...he *pitches*," she all but growled.

And then she snapped the phone shut and waited to see if it would ring again, which it did, five seconds later.

"*What?*"

"You hung up on me."

"I know that."

"And you should have yelled at me more before you hung up on me. You should have called me a few choice names, too."

Laura smiled as she gripped the phone, one of Sarah's expressions coming to mind. "All right. You're a dumb bunny. Oh, and your mother wears combat boots, whatever that means."

"I never did figure that one out, either," Jake said, and even though the connection was good, he had never sounded so far away, or quite so tired. "Oh, cripes, hon, I'm sorry. I just wanted Charlie away from all that. I wanted him to get his transplant and get back into *life*. I thought we both wanted that, Laura—that we all just wanted to be normal again. I mean, I *heard* you the other night, and I think I understand. Hell, I know I understand. I just have to get from understanding to *accepting*. And it isn't easy, Laura. It just isn't."

Laura looked back toward home plate to see Charlie standing behind young Toni D'Amato, positioning her hands on a bat and helping her swing at the ball on the rubber T. He'd been working with the girl for over an hour, his expression one of almost angelic patience. "Charlie's doing what he wants to do. If you were here, you'd see that."

"I'm trying, Laura. I'm really trying. But this is all happening so fast."

"It's all right—we'll all be all right," Laura said, heading into the outfield once more. "And I'm as guilty as you are. We spent so much time in the hospital, watched so many kids suffer, so many kids die—there were times I thought we'd never recognize normal again when we saw it. I agree, we need to remember what normal life is, what it's like to just be two people trying to raise our kids. But there's a *need* here, Jake. I didn't really see it, I just wanted Charlie to play ball because he wanted to play ball. But Charlie saw the need, and he's really happy. Please be happy for him."

There was another long pause before Jake said, "What would I do without you? I want to be home with you. I want to hold you, just hold on to you."

Laura blinked back tears. For a woman who had willed herself not to cry for more than two years, she certainly was making up for lost time lately. "I want to hold you, too. We're going to be all right, Jake. It's only been six months since the transplant. We're still learning how to live again, that's all. And I think Charlie's showing us how."

CHAPTER
∽ SEVEN ∽

C lay was a great thing. And it was even greater when it came free, courtesy of three separate landscaping companies in the area. Clay wasn't full of sharp stones that could prove to be a problem for the kids. Clay looked really terrific when neat white chalk lines were drawn on its reddish surface. Clay, in short, made Hero Field appear, if not professional, then at least pretty damn good.

Clay did not, however, look good on people, clothing or bathtubs, all of which Laura and the other volunteers found out as thirty extremely filthy adults and several children, armed with rakes, spread, rolled and variously stamped down the clay over the course of three long, hot, sweaty days.

But the worst was over, another mountain had been climbed—and if anyone knew how to climb or even move mountains, it was the parents of very special kids—and now it was time to play ball.

"I think I'm developing some definition in my biceps," Jayne Ann said, flexing her muscle in Laura's face as the two of them loaded canvas bags full of used baseball equipment into the back of Jayne Ann's van. Cherise's sister who worked at the township had come through with bats, mitts and even a dozen batting helmets. "Larry says he can already feel the difference."

"Larry does, does he?" Laura teased, grinning. "And how was the lasagna last night? And no, that's not a euphemism for anything else."

"Bobby was home, and Larry brought Jacob with him," Jayne Ann said, slamming the van door. "Believe me, it was strictly a G-rated evening. We're doing it again tomorrow night, after our first real game. So, do you think Sarah would want to be a flower girl or a junior bridesmaid? I'm open to either."

The two women slid onto the cracked-leather front seat and Laura shook her head at her friend. "One plate of lasagna, and you're hearing wedding bells?"

Jayne Ann turned the key in the ignition and Laura winced as the gears made a grinding sound before the engine reluctantly came to life. Jayne Ann had told Laura that her ex had a BMW and his new wife had a minivan that did everything except steer itself, but that was all right, because "Old Bessie still has a couple thousand miles left in her."

Jayne Ann winked at her. "Never underestimate the power of my lasagna, Mrs. Finnegan. Besides, Larry's lonely, Laura. *I'm* lonely. His mom is getting older and is making noises about moving to Florida to live with her sister. Shared loads are easier to carry. He can't be put off about Bobby's problems and I can't moan about Jacob's problems. We understand problems, and we know how to deal with them. Besides," she said, grinning rather lasciviously, "he's hot."

"He's short, skinny, and when he gives up on those few long strands he combs over the top of his head, he's going to be bald. Cute maybe, but not hot."

"Eye of the beholder, Laura, eye of the beholder. And relax, I didn't mean it about the flower-girl thing. We're friends, Larry and me, that's all. If there's one thing I've learned, it's not to immediately fall for the first guy I think is cute—I mean, look what I ended up with the first time. Where to now?"

"Home, please," Laura told her, quickly buckling her seat belt as Jayne Ann threw the van in Reverse and all but did a wheelie out of the township parking lot…and directly past the police station. "Jake will be home in about an hour and I want to have dinner ready for him before I leave again to pick up Charlie at the field."

"Jake won't come along?"

Laura shrugged. "I don't know. I don't want to push him."

"Have you considered simply bopping him over the head with a heavy object?"

"Funny. He's promised to come to our first game tomorrow, and maybe that's when he should see the Heroes for the first time. You know, with their shirts and caps and everything. Hey, do you think Toni D'Amato is going to be there? She really took a hit yesterday when Johnny Ryan ran over her."

"Yeah. Poor kid. We forgot she couldn't hear us yelling *get out of the way*—she was too busy watching Sarah and Brenda practice their cheers. And Johnny was so happy to get a chance to show he knows where third base is that he plowed right through our shortstop. Lucie sure picked a heck of a time to visit the Porta Potti, didn't she? But Toni's fine, I'm sure she is. She was laughing when she got up, wasn't she?"

"We need another rule." Laura had said that a lot lately as their dream rapidly evolved into a reality. Only two weeks ago, Hero Field had been nothing but a dream. "One volunteer on the field at all times for each two players on the field, not three players. How does that sound?"

"Crowded," Jayne Ann said with a grin. "Relax, Laura. They're kids. They bounce." She pulled up in front of the Finnegan household. "Uh-oh, look who beat you home."

"Jake," Laura said, struggling with the door handle of the van. "Not until eight o'clock, right?"

"Right. Now go—and wipe that goofy smile off your face. Some of us are still at the lasagna stage."

Laura ran into the house, stopping in the foyer to call Jake's name, then racing upstairs when she heard his voice. She trotted into the bedroom and barreled into Jake's open arms with at least as much happy abandon as Johnny Ryan had shown rounding second, and the two of them fell back onto the bed.

"I've got to go away more often," Jake said into her hair as he held her close after they'd kissed. He ran his palms up and down her back. "Have you lost a little weight?"

"You try pushing fifty wheelbarrows full of clay, Jake Finnegan. I may even be developing biceps," she added, stealing a line from Jayne Ann. "Are you impressed?"

"That's one thing I am," he teased, cupping her bottom with both hands. "Where are the kids?"

Laura propped herself up on her elbows and grinned down at her husband. "Charlie stayed at the field—I'm picking him up at eight o'clock—and Sarah is at a sleepover at Brenda's, so we're alone. Why? Did you have something particular in mind?"

"I'll assume that was a rhetorical question," Jake said, rolling her over onto her back as she laughed and held on tight.

Ninety minutes later, freshly showered and munching on the last of the cold chicken sandwiches Laura had thrown together in lieu of the supper she'd planned, they were on their way to Hero Field, and Laura's nervousness was back.

"It's not perfect," she told him as he drove along what, to her, had become very familiar country roads. "The backstop is in pretty bad shape, and Cherise's brother still has to level more weeds for a parking area. Oh, and Miranda Gilbert's father still hasn't quite mastered the line-marking machine, so the third-base line is a little crooked today."

"Miranda? Which one is she?"

"She plays right field for Heroes Two. Oh, you mean what's her problem? We really don't think about that much, except when we're planning how to help the kids play better, but Miranda has cerebral palsy. Duane says he's jealous because she only has a brace on one leg, so Cherise told him she could arrange for a brace on his *head*. You're going to love Cherise. To her, kids are kids, and she doesn't tiptoe around their problems, not one bit. Everyone adores her."

"Just one big happy family, huh?"

Laura snuggled deeper into the leather seat of Jake's sedan. "Yes, we are. John Ryan—the pediatrician, remember? Anyway, John got serious the other night and talked about what we're doing. How we're building confidence and self-esteem, instilling sportsmanship, improving social skills, teaching the kids how to work together, cooperate with each other the way you have to do in team sports. He talked about helping to increase their physical coordination, showing them how to interact with their peers—all those really good things."

"And?" Jake asked, turning onto the road that led to the ball field.

"And Cherise told him, heck, don't scare us with all this technical talk—we just thought we were showing the kids a good time."

"You're right, I'm going to like Cherise. The last thing those kids need is to be told this is *good* for them. Keep the technical jargon out of it, and play ball."

"I knew you'd be okay with this."

"It took me awhile, and I'm sorry for that. But yeah, I finally get it. What's in the bag?"

Laura reached down to pick up the plastic bag she'd brought with her at the last moment, and pulled out a blue shirt with white lettering on the back.

Jake nearly ran the car into a ditch. "Brightstone's Funeral Home?"

"These are for Heroes Two. Heroes One wears red. Look." She shoved the shirt back into the bag and pulled out a red baseball cap with the same logo sewn on the front and stuck it on her head. "Mr. Brightstone's our main sponsor. Bless him, his grandson died last year. Brain tumor. He told us Stevie loved baseball."

"Poor guy, and that's a damn nice gesture. But, Laura, don't you see anything a little strange about plastering the name of a funeral home on shirts for these particular kids?"

"We talked about that, but when Charlie and Bobby told us they thought it was sort of funny, we realized we were over-reacting. Kind of. Sort of." Laura smiled. "I guess it is sort of funny, if you just don't think about it too hard. There's the field—on your left."

There were at least twenty other cars pulled into the mowed weeds, and Laura saw that Jayne Ann and Cherise had made it there ahead of her. With her hand on the door handle, Laura turned to Jake. "Now remember. This is not your ordinary baseball team. Some of them hit from the T-stand, some of them swing on their own. One of the volunteers pitches, not one of the kids, because that's sort of difficult for a lot of them, although Jayne Ann's Bobby pitches for Heroes One. Patty Gerbach runs the bases in her wheelchair, and that takes awhile because she has to blow in a straw to get the thing to move—it's a pretty neat chair, actually—so she gets more time to reach first base. Oh, and Nick O'Brien still uses his walker, but his hip replacement was only last month, so he's really coming along, and—"

"Laura, honey, stop trying to convince me, okay? It's going to be fine. You said Charlie's okay with all this, and if he's okay with it, I'm going to learn to be okay with it. I had a lot of time in Boston to think about everything, and the Heroes aren't a half loaf. They're just a different loaf." He grinned at her as he took her hand. "I'm thinking maybe pumpernickel."

"Are we pumpernickel, too? Not a half loaf, just a new loaf."

"Yeah, I guess so. We're still here, we're still whole. We're just a little different now."

"Okay," Laura said as they walked toward the ball field. "But I want to be raisin bread. With white icing."

Jake squeezed her hand. "It's a deal," he said, then sighed. "We almost lost it, didn't we, hon?"

Laura pretended not to understand, hoping to find time to come to grips with what her husband had just said. "It? What it?"

"Us. That it. It's funny, really. We made it through the bad times, only to start to self-destruct once Charlie got better. But we're going to make it now, right? We're going to talk, and not be afraid to yell when we feel the need. We're allowed to fight. Married people fight sometimes. We've just got to realize that not everything is a life-and-death decision anymore, thank God, and that sometimes that other shoe just isn't going to drop. We're a team, and we'll always be a team. We're going to be…we're going to be—"

"New-loaf normal," Laura said, squeezing his hand. "I love you, Jake Finnegan. Even when I don't."

He grinned at her, then looked out over the field. "Hey, there's Charlie. What's he—oh, God..."

Laura watched as Charlie stood behind Kenny Baxter, who was taller than Charlie by at least eight inches. Kenny Baxter, who had been blind since birth. Charlie had his arms wrapped around Kenny, his hands gripping the bat over Kenny's hands. "Come on, Mr. Johnson, give us your best stuff," he called out to Cherise's "little" brother. "You ready to run, Kenny? We're gonna nail this one."

Walter Johnson leaned forward and tossed the ball in a soft underhand.

"Now!" Charlie yelled, and he and Kenny swung the bat.

"He hit it!" Jake said as he stood behind Laura, his hands on her shoulders.

They both watched as the bat fell to the ground and Charlie grabbed Kenny's hand and ran with him to first base, talking to him, encouraging him all the way.

When they reached the bag it was hard to tell whose smile was the widest, Kenny, who had run through the darkness, his trust in Charlie complete, his excitement overcoming his natural fear of the unknown, or Charlie, who had helped make it all happen.

Laura turned to see Jake's reaction, only to watch him rub at the tears running down his cheeks. "Look at him. That's our son, Laura." His voice broke as he pulled her into his arms. "Thank you," he said, holding her tight. "Thank you..."

"Dad! *Dad!*"

"Charlie's calling you, honey," Laura said, disengaging herself and wiping at her own eyes.

"Hey, Dad! Mr. Johnson has to leave. You wanna pitch for a while?"

Laura took the cap from her head and reached up to put it on Jake's. "Go get 'em, slugger. And remember, the object of this game is to *let* them hit the ball."

Then she watched, hugging herself, as Jake trotted onto the field.

"Everything okay?" Jayne Ann asked, stepping up beside her.

"Everything is fine, better than fine," Laura answered, watching her two boys on the field. "Jayne Ann, you know what I've finally figured out? Life *is* a carnival—you just have to learn how to hang on and do your best to enjoy the ride."

Dear Reader,

The story you just read is fiction, but sometimes authors take bits and pieces from their own experiences and weave them into their stories. At age nine, our son had his first kidney transplant; at fourteen, his second. The "Come back when you grow" line was said to our son when he so desperately wanted to play for the local baseball team. And yes, his heart was broken.

There was no Deb Fruend in our area, no organization like TASK. And we, I'm sorry to say, didn't think to start an organization like TASK—for our son, for other children who had to fight so hard, who just wanted to be children.

Now you've read this story…this fiction. Now you know that when people care, when people get involved, a child's world can be changed for the better. That's *not* fiction.

Please go to www.tasksports.org and read the story of TASK. And when you do, remember, there are children out there, parents out there, who would give anything to have an organization like TASK in their own community.

Maybe you can do something. Maybe you can help. Because children need more than words….

Thank you,

Kasey Michaels

DEBRA BONDE

W ho could have imagined back in 1984 that a small seed of an idea would eventually grow to become one of the world's foremost supportive organizations of literacy for visually impaired children and their families? Debra Bonde, founder and executive director of Seedlings Braille Books for Children in Livonia, Michigan, can scarcely believe it herself—and it was her brainchild.

It was 1978 when Debra began wondering what she could do to make a difference in the world.

"Our job on earth is to help other people, but I was so incredibly shy that it made it very difficult. I needed to come up with a vocation where I could help other people—without talking to other people," she says with a laugh.

She stumbled into braille transcription almost by accident

after speaking with a transcriber. She soon signed up for a community-based class and immediately fell in love with the detailed work. But it wasn't until she spoke to another student in the class—a mother with a visually impaired daughter—that she realized how few books for children were ever produced in braille. The young girl owned only two books, despite the fact that she lived in an affluent suburb.

"It tugged at my heartstrings because it was appalling that there were so few braille books available, and those that existed were generally very expensive—like a hundred dollars for a Hardy Boys book," Debra says.

Joy and wonder

After volunteering as a transcriber and giving birth to her daughters, Anna and Megan, Debra turned her attention to transcribing books for children exclusively. She cherished the time spent reading to her daughters, who had perfect sight, as they shared the gift of literacy through their growing collection of books. Why couldn't blind and visually impaired children experience the same joy and wonderment as her own kids? Debra vowed to find a way to erase the inexcusable disparity between blind and sighted children, to make children's books in braille more accessible and affordable.

In 1983, Debra acquired one of the first computer braille

transcribing programs. Her father, Ray Stewart, stepped in and modified her antiquated Perkins Brailler from manual to electric, and Debra began printing the books from her basement. In the first year, Seedlings developed twelve books for the catalog. The project was on its way.

Despite her extreme shyness, Debra mustered the courage to solicit donations to subsidize book production. Between running her house and taking care of her kids, she also burned the midnight oil, arranging for grants.

And the hard work paid off. In 1985, Debra produced 221 books in her basement office. By 1990, Seedlings was producing five thousand books per year. At last count Seedlings, which employs nine people and uses dozens of volunteers, has produced more than 300,000 braille books for blind children all over the U.S., Canada and over fifty countries around the world.

A vision grows

Although Seedlings created strictly "braille only" books in the beginning, parents and teachers approached Debra with requests for other options. Now Seedlings also offers print-braille-and-picture books for toddlers and preschoolers, board books with braille superimposed over the pictures using clear plastic strips with an adhesive backing. The organization also moved into fiction and nonfiction for older children. Then there are the Seedlings books that run printed text above the braille so sighted children can read along with a blind parent or vice versa. *Goodnight Moon* remains Seedlings' all-time bestseller.

Not surprisingly, Seedlings has moved out of Debra's basement and into an office not far away. But despite the increased cost in keeping Seedlings afloat, Debra does everything she can—from using volunteer labor to recycling—to ensure the books sell for an average of only ten dollars.

"Most companies will make something for ten dollars and sell it for twenty. We make these books for twenty dollars and sell them for ten. I would lower the prices even more if I could," she says.

Despite the long hours and low pay, Debra stays driven because she knows her books have a huge impact on young children who might not ever have become literate in braille without access to books they love at the beginning of their reading career.

Take one young woman, Heather, for example, once one of Debra's most voracious readers and supporters. When Heather was ten, she asked friends coming to her birthday party to give donations to Seedlings in lieu of presents. Today Heather is a university graduate currently attending law school in Ottawa, Ontario.

"Just knowing that we've had a positive influence on lives like hers makes it all worthwhile," says Debra.

SEEDINGS BRAILLE BOOKS FOR CHILDREN

The freedom to learn

In the past years Seedlings has expanded its scope to offer programs to encourage children to love the written word. The thriving nonprofit organization offers the Rose Project, which provides free encyclopedia articles in braille. Children working on projects contact Seedlings by phone, fax, e-mail or via its Web site and request the information. Seedlings staff pull the articles from the World Book CD into their computers, translate them into braille, print them and send them out by courier or mail—usually the same day. For the first time blind students have access to the same research materials as their sighted friends.

Seedlings also offers "Hooray for Braille" kits, which introduce Michigan families of blind babies and preschoolers to braille literacy. Debra hopes to open the programs to other states if funding increases.

But the project closest to Debra's heart is the Book Angel Project. Eight years ago a drunk driver killed Debra's nineteen-year-old daughter, Anna, as she was on her way to New Orleans to tutor disadvantaged children. Memorial donations immediately flooded in. Today that money is used to send at least ten free books out to children in Anna's name each week.

Despite her grief over Anna's death, Debra never swayed from her dream to give visually impaired kids a chance to foster a love of reading. But even with the incredible successes Seedlings gains every day, Debra says they still have a long way to go.

"Even with all our effort, less than five percent of all books out there in print are transcribed into braille," she maintains. "We still have a ton of work to do."

For more information visit www.seedlings.org or write to Seedlings Braille Books for Children, 14151 Farmington Road, Livonia, MI 48154.

CATHERINE MANN
❧ TOUCHED BY LOVE ❧

∽ CATHERINE MANN ∾

Bestselling author Catherine Mann writes contemporary military romances, a natural fit since she's married to her very own USAF research source. Prior to publication, Catherine graduated with a B.A. in fine arts: theater from the College of Charleston, and received her master's degree in theater from UNC Greensboro. Now a RITA® Award winner, Catherine finds following her aviator husband around the world with four children, a beagle and a tabby in tow offers her endless inspiration for new plots. Learn more about her work, as well as her adventures in military life, by visiting her Web site: http://catherinemann.com.

CHAPTER
~ ONE ~

Librarian Anna Bonneau was well on her way to landing in the pokey. And that's exactly where she wanted to be.

She'd handcuffed herself to a park bench in protest all afternoon, and though she'd spent the time reading—hardly a hardship since books were her life—she was beginning to suffer a real case of fanny fatigue while waiting for the police to take notice.

Finally, a cop cruiser squealed to a stop by the curb.

She should have realized the small-town police wouldn't have a problem with her sit-down protest until closing time—5:00 p.m. The recreation area was empty except for autumn trees awash with colors and swings twisting in the breeze off Lake Huron.

Anna's mother used to bring her to the park for tea parties, but she had died in a car accident when Anna was only twelve. That had been the most difficult time in Anna's life. Her father—a local retired judge—had tried to continue the picnic tradition, but their differences of opinion during her teenage years made things difficult.

All in the past. Right now Anna did her best to focus on her book while making a peripheral check of the police officer stretching out of his cruiser. Finally, progress for her cause.

She'd always wanted to be a librarian, and landing a job in her sleepy hometown of Oscoda, Michigan, was a dream come true. She'd worked for three years in a library in the Detroit area, waiting for this position to come open.

Two weeks from now, she would start her job. And there was no way she was going to let the shortsighted members of the town planning commission rip up this park to plop a "gentlemen's club" restaurant and bar right beside *her* library.

She shifted her numb backside off the metal bench, which was growing cooler by the second in the autumn temperature, all the while keeping her eyes firmly focused on rereading a Suzanne Brockmann reissue. Yes, Anna adored her romance novels as much as the long-ago classics.

A child's scream pierced the air.

Anna jolted up from her seat, only to be yanked back down by the handcuff—*ouch*. Her book fell to the ground as she caught sight of a man with a kid in his arms rapidly gaining ground on the approaching police officer. Howling shrieks echoed in the silence of the park, tugging at her heart until she recognized the man with the child—someone she'd hoped never to lay eyes on again after he'd broken her heart in high school.

Forest Jameson.

As he crossed the lawn toward her, Anna's stomach back-flipped—just as it had when she'd first seen him bat one over the fence at the baseball field. He was a hunk, but too uptight during their teenage years. She'd heard he'd come home about four months ago to set up a legal practice in her father's former office, but she hadn't seen him since her return a week ago.

Why was he at the park, and why was he hauling a child? They could have come here to play—not that the kid sounded happy. Forest was likely here because her father, his long-ago mentor, had called and asked him to save Anne from spending a night in jail.

The cop, old Officer Smitty, stopped short of her bench. Closely following, Forest juggled the boy, a briefcase and a tote bag stuffed with toys.

"Anna." He nodded a greeting. "You still look the same."

She wasn't sure how to take that, but before she could answer, he'd turned back to the child.

Forest jostled the wailing, magenta-faced kid. Tears streamed down his cheeks behind the small sunglasses the boy wore. "Hang on, Joey. Just a few minutes and we'll be through here. I promise, son."

His son? Anna quickly checked out Forest's ring finger. Bare. She didn't want to think about the little zing of relief she felt.

Forest met her gaze. "Divorced and the nanny quit."

His tight-lipped answer engendered sympathy, along with embarrassment at her obvious interest.

Forest strode over to the cop. "I'm here to represent the interests of Ms. Bonneau."

Well, sheesh. Wasn't that convenient? "Uh, hello? Miss Bonneau has something to say about that."

The child—around four, maybe?—arched his back, pumping his feet. "I want to go home!"

"Well, you're not going anywhere if you don't settle down." The calmly stated parental threat was betrayed by Forest's harried expression.

Officer Smitty jumped in with a universal key and unlocked the handcuffs confining her to the bench. "H'lo, Miss Bonneau. How about you take care of this little stinker and I'll have a conversation with the lawyer?"

Click. The handcuffs fell away, ending her latest protest, and there wasn't a thing she could do about it. Maybe she would ride this one out and see what Forest had to say—in the interest of being entertained. Right?

She snagged her book from the ground, placed it on the bench and reached for little Joey. He didn't even loosen his lock hold on his dad's neck. Single-parent Forest was clearly overwhelmed.

Hmm. It seemed he needed her to bail him out more than she did him. She might have wanted her standard quick stop in jail, but her father said Forest never lost his cases, so she would simply stay near enough to listen until she came up with plan B.

And the kid surely was a heart-tugger. "Could I take him for you while you work your attorney magic?"

Forest hesitated, which irked her to no end. Finally, he nodded and eased the boy's arms from around his neck, speaking the whole time. "It's okay, son. This is Miss Anna. She's going to play with you while I talk business. Okay?"

Joey hiccuped. "'Kay." His chocolate-colored curls stuck to his head with tantrum-induced sweat. "Can I go swing?"

"Of course." Forest passed Joey to her. "Anna? You're sure you don't mind?"

If he was surprised that she'd guessed his reason for being here, he sure didn't show it.

"Not at all."

She took the child, a solid weight. The scent of baby shampoo and sweat soothed her with its sweet innocence. The little guy was a cutie in his striped overalls, conductor's cap and Thomas the Train sunglasses.

Forest opened his mouth as if to speak further, but Anna turned away. Her nerves were on edge, and she was having trouble resisting the temptation to stare at the grown-up Forest. She used to watch him volunteering with Little Leaguers back in high school, and his gentleness with his son could well draw her in the same way.

She headed toward the swings, offering soothing words both for herself and Joey.

"Can you sit in the swing and hold me, please?" Joey asked.

"Of course, sweetie."

This was easier than she thought. She could hold the child, keep him happy *and* listen to the two men decide her fate as if she weren't even there. *Grrr.* She tickled Joey's chin with the tail of her braid until he chortled. His sunglasses were the cutest things she'd ever seen.

Unable to resist gloating at her success in calming the little guy, Anna glanced past Joey to his father. Bummer. Forest hadn't even noticed. He was too busy unloading kid gear. As he placed the toy bag and briefcase on the bench, his suit coat gaped open to reveal a broad chest covered by his crisp white shirt. She swallowed hard.

He whipped off his steel-rimmed glasses and snatched a tissue from the briefcase to clean away the evening mist. Anna's breath hitched. Even as she swung with Joey, she could see Forest's blue eyes glittering like a shaken bottle of soda water.

Darn it, she wouldn't let herself forget that he had left town without so much as a farewell.

"Miss Anna, higher!" Joey squealed, yanking her braid. "Miss Anna, let's go higher."

Joey had the strength of a fifth-grader, and Anna welcomed the wake-up call.

Why couldn't her father understand she believed in justice as strongly as he did? She merely approached it from a different angle, organizing protests since her first petition in the second grade for new monkey bars in the playground.

The men finished their discussion and the older cop ambled off to his patrol car. Forest strode toward her with determined steps and held his arms out for his son, tapping the boy on the shoulder. "Time to go, Joey."

The little fella pivoted in her lap and launched himself at his dad with obvious affection. This time, however, he squirmed down to walk, holding his dad's hand.

Anna eased herself up from the swing. "What's the verdict?"

"Since we made it out of here before closing, you got off with a simple ticket, but no jail time."

"I guess that will have to do, but I was hoping we could squeeze in some news coverage."

A tight smile crooked his perfectly sculpted mouth as he

mimicked her voice. "Why, thank you, Forest, for keeping me from paying an expensive fine. And heaven forbid I might have actually had to go to jail and eat their fine cuisine. It's great to see you again."

She slumped back in the swing. He had gone to a lot of trouble for her and she was being ungrateful. "Thank you for your time and help. It's, uh, good to see you, too."

Even if it had cost her the short stint in jail and a much-coveted feature in the weekly local newspaper.

Forest shrugged through the kink in his neck and picked up the pace as he made his way back to his truck in the now-dark park, carefully leading his son around trees and over jutting roots.

Anna had seriously snagged his attention in high school, even if she was more than a little quirky. And yeah, spunky. He'd admired those qualities, even though he'd craved normalcy after a lifetime spent with parents who hip-hopped from one outrageous commune to another. But she sure was pretty and he knew her beauty owed nothing to the pricey spa treatments his ex craved.

His newest client wore her corn-silk blond hair in a single thick braid down her back. Her hair had a bit of spring to it in the curl at the end of the braid and the stray wisps teasing cheeks pink from the cool lake breeze.

Her fresh-scrubbed face glowed with health, even the freckles dotting her nose. The flowing green dress she wore, with its sunflower pattern, and her cheery yellow sweater brightened the drab overcast evening.

But despite her uncomplicated beauty, understanding Anna required more study than the bar exam. Forest had given up second-guessing her when she'd staged a protest outside his high-school baseball game. She and a group of her friends had handcuffed themselves to bike racks in a protest against budget cuts that cost the chorus teacher his job, while leaving the sports budget intact.

"Where's your car?" he asked.

She strolled past him to the bicycle stand. "I rode my mountain bike."

Anna worked the lock that secured her bike to the metal rack while Officer Smitty fired up his cruiser over by the curb. Forest sighed at the inevitable.

"Let me give you a ride. We can store your bike in the back of my truck."

Still she didn't face him, just stowed her lock and wheeled her bike backward. Was that a yes or no?

He couldn't let her pedal off in the dark. Even in this sleepy little town, with Officer Smitty readying to cruise the streets, it wasn't all that safe for an attractive woman to be out alone on the backwoods roads that ran along the lake. Shoot, he was here in the first place to watch over her because of the debt he owed Judge Bonneau for mentoring him during the year his parents spent in Oscoda—their longest stint anywhere in his entire life.

The cop rolled down his car window and nodded to Forest. "Good evening, Counselor. Quite a change from your regular stuff, with, uh—"

"Insurance litigation." Forest smiled tightly as the wind wafted the scent of vanilla. He was mighty sure that didn't come from Smitty or Joey. "Every client's important."

Anna waved to the cop. "Hi, Officer Smitty. Hope to see you at the recycling drive this coming weekend. Make it a family day. There'll be treats for the kids."

"Thanks for the tip. I'm always looking for things to occupy the girls on my weekend with them." He nodded sympathetically to Forest, another single father.

Anna pulled a flyer from her oversize backpack and passed it to the cop. "Always happy to help out. About my handcuffs—"

Smitty had begun to roll his window up again. "Oh, right. Here ya go."

Forest waited while Anna chatted with Smitty about his kids. Joey ran circles around him, trailing his hand around his father's knees as he wore himself out. Anna flung her braid over her shoulder, her face animated and her eyes sparkling as she spoke to the police officer.

Beautiful eyes.

Forest almost dropped the tote bag full of toys.

Maybe he should start dating again. He'd been celibate since his divorce three years ago, but he didn't trust his judgment in women. He and Paula had seemed a perfect match with shared dreams, but it hadn't worked. He definitely wasn't ready for a relationship, especially not with a woman who was trouble incarnate.

Besides, his son needed him as he grew up without the love and care of a mother to help him through the tough times ahead.

Forest snagged Anna's helmet from her handlebars to impede any thoughts of escape. Her tantalizing vanilla fragrance teased his nose. "Anna, can we speed this along? I need to get Joey fed and tucked into bed."

He could almost feel the wind whipping over him. Countless summers, he'd tooled around the country in his parents' motorcycle sidecar. Other children, kids blessed with family trips in the comfort of a station wagon, had giggled and pointed. Forest's grip tightened on the helmet buckle.

He would take her home to her little cottage on the water and then his debt to the judge would be canceled.

So why did that vanilla scent seem to taunt him, making him believe that Anna was back in his life for a reason?

* * *

Anna knew when to fight and when to surrender with grace.

Insisting on biking home in the dark would sound petty. And while she considered herself independent, that didn't give her the right to be rude. Inside the extended-cab truck, she reached into the backseat to stroke Joey's chocolate-brown curls and savor the feeling of peace that stole over her as the child tipped his face into the chilly night breeze drifting through the open windows.

Forest leaned toward her as Anna grappled with her own seat belt. Her arm brushed his chest.

"Uh, Anna—"

"I don't know what's wrong with this seat belt." She wrestled with the buckle. "I can't seem to get it clicked."

Forest shifted in his seat. "Do you, uh, need some help?"

Heavens, she hoped not. She straightened, her palm extended. "Gummi Worm!"

"What?"

"There was a Gummi Worm stuck in it."

"Joey's snack. A token of single fatherhood. Bribes." He passed the half-full bag of Gummies to Joey. "Here ya go, son."

"Well, I didn't think it was yours." She flicked the biodegradable candy out the window. "Actually, I'm starving. I ran out of snacks around three."

She'd sneaked off for bathroom breaks when the place looked deserted, but there weren't any vending machines, and going into a restaurant to grab a hamburger seemed like cheating.

Oaks and pines whizzed past as they drove along the deserted roads. Forest was quiet, and so was Joey, happy with his treat. But Anna was still geared up.

Five minutes passed before she finally exploded, "They want to build a—" she glanced back at Joey then over at Forest "—S-T-R-I-P club there. Oh sure, they're calling it a 'gentleman's club,' but we all know what that really means. It's bad enough to have an establishment like that in our town, but especially awful right next to the library." She shook her head. "I can't stand silently by."

"I'm frustrated, too, Anna, but it sounds like a done deal." The dashboard light illuminated his strong square jaw.

"It's not over until they roll in the bulldozers. I couldn't stay quiet while there's time to make a difference."

"I hear you and I understand. But there are better ways." Forest turned into Anna's driveway, gravel crunching as he drove toward the brick cottage she'd rented last week.

Headlights swept across the dormant garden and highlighted the man rocking on the front porch. Judge Edward Bonneau sat bathed in the hazy glow. Her father.

No doubt he'd received his courtesy call from the police station on how things had shaken down. Politics and protocol were more than a little loose in small-town Oscoda. Of course. Why else would Forest have shown up in the first place?

Could the night get any worse?

Anna eased her achy body out of the vehicle, stiff from sitting so long. She really could have benefited from a bike ride home. Her father pushed to his feet, short and wiry, but imposing nonetheless. The porch light cast a friendly glow over the paver stones she'd crafted with inset marbles. She'd carted those hefty steppers from home to home—treasures she'd made with her mother as a child.

Her father snapped his suspenders over his seersucker pajama top. "Sugar, you've come to the end of the line. I hear my old rival Judge Randall's gonna crack down next time you get a ticket, and throw the book at you. We're talking serious jail time, daughter dear."

Sugar? Daughter dear? She was twenty-five years old, for Pete's sake. Why couldn't they communicate as adults?

Uh, wait. Her feet stalled. *Serious* jail time? She was cool with being booked for a few hours or even a night, as had happened in the past. But nothing more, especially if it interfered with her new job. "I'll be working at the library before he can make a big stink."

Her father ambled down three of the five steps, stopping eye level with Forest. "Well, boy, what's your plan?"

"Pop, calm down." She breezed over and kissed his leathery

cheek. She missed the simpler days of their attempted picnics and homework review. "Forest will take care of everything. You can go home."

"Not a chance. I need to hear his plan of action."

Of course he would. She knew this battle wasn't worth fighting. Her father showed his love through trying to micro-manage her life. She'd learned to basically keep her silence and go her own way.

She might as well play with Joey, who was squirming to get out of his booster seat. Anna turned to the two men on the porch.

The sooner Forest could talk to her dad, the sooner both men would head home. "Fine. I'll just let Joey out to play."

"Anna," Forest called out. "About Joey—"

She waved over her shoulder. "Don't worry. I may not be a parent, but I can handle one little boy."

The dome light illuminated Joey's frustration as he strained against the confines of his booster seat. He continued to thrash until his precious little sunglasses flew off to one side—

Revealing wide, unseeing blue eyes.

CHAPTER
~TWO~

"Forest?" She turned to look at him for affirmation of what she couldn't deny but didn't want to voice out loud in case she upset the child.

Little Joey was blind. Only now did she see the white stick at his feet on the floorboard. Forest had been carrying him earlier or holding his hand. She thought of all his sentences, which she'd interrupted, and now—

Forest simply nodded his head, his expression fiercely protective. Of course. Any normal parent would be, because she'd learned long ago that people could be cruelly imperceptive at times.

Her heart ached for the little guy and the extra challenges

he would face. As if life wasn't already tough enough. But she refused to make Joey feel self-conscious. He was an active young boy, just like the students she'd worked with in her reading groups—special needs or not—during her previous library position.

The minute they cleared up things with her father, she would go online to the Seedlings Braille Books for Children Web site to place her order for some preschool books with Braille added.

"Hi, Joey. It's Miss Anna." She announced herself so he wouldn't be surprised. "I'll let you out now so you can play while we talk. If you're hungry, how about graham crackers?"

"I'm full of Gummies now. I just wanna play."

"Fair enough, big guy."

She unstrapped him and helped him out of the seat, then slipped her hand into his. She leaned into the truck for his white cane and passed it to him. In her work at the library, she'd learned that small children needed a cane that reached shoulder level rather than sternum level. The smaller canes caused too many injuries if a child stumbled forward. At four, Joey would still be acclimating to the cane, so she called out potential hazards and kept hold of his hand.

"Big tree root ahead," she announced, lifting him over it with a squeal of "Whee!"

His giggle swept away all the frustrations of a long day. She glanced up to the porch. The gratitude on Forest's face stirred an entirely different sort of excitement in her.

Swallowing hard, she returned her attention to Joey. She needed to think of something to keep him occupied in this unfamiliar environment while the adults spoke. Her eyes lit on the wheelbarrow. "Would you like a ride in my magic wagon?"

"Magic?" His face tipped up to hers, his sightless gaze slightly left of her.

"Magic and super speedy." Most little boys enjoyed fast-moving toys, and bottom line, he was like any other child.

She slid her hands under his armpits, plopped him in the wheelbarrow and started steering him along the bumpy yard. He clutched the sides and squealed, apparently content with the magic chariot for the moment at least.

Her father made his way down the steps of her two-bedroom cottage so they could converse while she jostled around the yard with Joey.

"Anna," Pop said, "word around the courthouse has it Judge Randall wants to get back at me for all the years I beat him out for a position on the bench. We all know he's a vindictive old cuss. You're playing right into his hands with your protesting." His expression of concern mirrored Forest's for his child a few minutes earlier. "I'm worried about you."

That small show of affection from her father almost crumbled her defenses. *Almost.* But she'd stopped looking for his approval long ago. They just didn't connect. "Pop, I'm an adult. What I do doesn't reflect on you. Disown me. I officially absolve you of responsibility."

Gasping for breath, she turned and jabbed her finger toward Forest, quickly grabbing the wheelbarrow handle again. "And you—there won't be any need for you to defend me, because I will simply lie low as Dad suggests."

Her father fished out a handkerchief from his pocket. "Now, sugar, don't get all fired up. You look just like your mama when you do that. You're gonna make me get all maudlin, and that's not good for the old ticker."

Sometimes, Anna thought, listening to her father, it was hard to believe he was a respected judge. She steered a cheering Joey toward her father. "Pop, you have the heart of a sixteen-year-old."

"Please, Anna." He raked a hand through his rusty-red hair. "Listen and pretend to care about my opinion."

Anna reminded herself that her father didn't pay her bills, hadn't since she'd graduated from high school and landed her first scholarship. So why should she care about his opinion?

Because he was still her father and she was a natural-born caregiver. She sighed. "Five minutes, tops."

"Five it is then. Come on over here and have a seat, you two. Pass that little fella to me."

A possessive feeling stirred within her. "I've got Joey."

"Joey," her father called. "Wanna come sit with me?"

"Papa Bonneau! You have any candy?" The boy turned his head, a huge smile creasing his precious chubby cheeks.

He scrambled out of the wheelbarrow, but Anna caught him a split second before he hit the ground. She took his hand and led him to her father, which was apparently where he wanted to be.

Her father scooped up the little guy and pulled out a roll of Lifesavers. "Forest?"

Anna wilted onto the porch swing. "We might as well hear Pop out," she said to Forest. "He'll only track us down later."

"Fine." Forest scrubbed a hand over his face, shaking his head as if to clear his thoughts.

He climbed the steps slowly, like a man marching toward the gallows. His eyes narrowed as he joined Anna on the swing, the only seat left on the porch. Had the swing shrunk with the last rain?

She breathed in the calming, earthy scents from the vegetable garden. "Okay, Pop. I'm listening."

Her father thumbed another piece of candy for Joey, tapping his shoes as he rocked. "You've done well for Anna today, Forest. I always knew you'd make a levelheaded attorney. But daughter dear, I'm afraid even Forest can't save your hide if you land in Randall's court."

Anna drummed her fingers along the armrest and studied

a water bug scuttling across the planked porch. Forest shifted, crossing his long legs at the ankles as he set the swing into motion. How much had he grown since high school?

"I appreciate your, uh, concern, Pop, but I'm not giving up my protests for anyone." She'd seen in college how effective a simple sit-in could be to protest a book banning at the library. "If Judge Randall wants to turn tough next time, I'll be the one stuck with the consequences."

Her father shot a pleading look at Forest. "Got any thoughts on this in your bag of summation tricks?"

Forest hooked his arm along the back of the porch swing and faced Anna. "Do you realize how lucky you are to have grown up in a town like this? An established good name isn't something to throw away."

She hesitated. Of course she had considered that aspect, not that she would acknowledge it to the pair of controlling males on her porch. The answer flowered in her mind like the blossoming buds on her tomato plants in season.

"You're both right."

Their slack jaws could have trapped a healthy supply of flies.

She continued while she had them off balance. "I know the best way to keep me out of Judge Randall's radar. Poor Forest is in a real pickle with no nanny. How can he work with his son underfoot all day?"

Forest stared at her with a deep intensity until she couldn't

255

resist the gravitational pull. He had such beautiful eyes, baby blues, now filled with a concern that caressed her like a refreshing spring shower.

"Okay, Anna, what's your idea?"

She inhaled deeply, afraid if she actually considered this scheme any longer than a few seconds, she'd back out before telling them. "While you're looking for a permanent nanny, I'll be Joey's sitter for the next two weeks. It's a way to help you and at the same time will keep me out of the judge's radar."

And quite frankly, it was something she *wanted* to do, to help that precious little boy.

She looked up for their reaction.

Forest jerked and attempted to stand up, launching the swing forward. Anna grabbed his arm just as the chain closest to the edge of the porch snapped, tipping the swing seat sideways.

They slid off the swing and the porch, tumbling into the tomato and cucumber patch. And the only thing that surprised Anna was why she was still holding on to Forest's arm.

"Forest? Forest? Are you okay?"

Soft hands patted his cheeks. His head throbbed. The aroma of mashed vegetation hovered around him. How many veggies could be left in the garden this late in the season?

He struggled to pull himself out of this dazed fog. He couldn't move yet, so he just lay sprawled on his back.

"Wake up. Come on, Forest. You're scaring Joey."

At the mention of his son, Forest forced his eyes open. He had to be okay for his son. There was no one else to take care of Joey with his mother in the Riviera and the nanny out the door. But there was something soft pressing down on him, preventing him from moving.

Anna. She lay atop Forest without room for a summons to slide between them.

"Forest? Forest!"

Forest. He cringed at the constant repetition of his name. What had possessed his parents to name him for the place where they'd conceived him? He should probably be grateful they hadn't opted to name him after the stars or something. Betelgeuse would have been beyond bearing.

He winced, and it wasn't from the lump on the back of his head or the lovely woman on top of him. Hadn't he suffered enough from his unconventional family life? His biker parents turned commune teachers had served up plenty of embarrassment.

"Forest?" Anna rested her elbows on his chest, her face less than an inch away. "Are you awake?"

"Barely."

"Thank goodness."

Forest could feel her relax against him. "Anna? It's time for me to—"

"Why didn't you tell me about Joey?" she whispered.

"I tried. There wasn't a chance."

She nodded and stayed politely quiet while he formed his explanation.

Forest stared up at her, a fierce protectiveness surging through him. "Joey was a preemie, two and a half months early. He has retinopathy of prematurity—ROP. He can see light and dark, but that's it."

He didn't want pity for his son, simply acceptance, and thank heavens, that's exactly what he saw in Anna's beautiful green eyes...

The porch floor creaked. Judge Bonneau peered over the broken swing. Joey was cradled to his chest, drooling a green Lifesaver. "Are you two all right?"

"I think so." Anna's breath puffed over Forest. "And you?"

"Just fi—"

"Daughter dear," the judge said, grinning, "you'll make a wonderful nanny for little Joey."

Nanny? Nanny! Forest's hands fell away from Anna as if he were scalded. How could he have forgotten her proposition? He jackknifed up, and Anna rolled to the side in a flurry of arms and legs.

"It's perfect." Her father nodded in agreement. "You could use the money to tide you over, and you have the time free before you start to work at the library. Forest needs the help since his ex is away."

Forest scrambled for words in his definitely scrambled brain. "I've had some women in town offer to help out."

The judge shook his head, jowls jiggling. "Those aren't the kind of women to look out for Joey. They're not interested in the child, just the father. Not like you, daughter dear."

Forest wasn't sure whether to be relieved or insulted.

Anna shoved to her feet. "So, Forest? What's your verdict on me as a sitter? Yes or no?"

As if on cue, Joey started to cry. Before Forest could even think to move, Anna had rushed to her father's side and scooped up the child from his lap.

"Would you like some chocolate milk?" she whispered. "Hmm?"

The judge tapped Forest on the arm. "Watch."

Anna swayed gently, running her hand over Joey's curls until he sagged against her and buried his face in her neck. With his fingers, he traced her features, learning her face.

He wanted to know her.

"I like chocolate milk." His soft voice carried on the wind.

Forest didn't consider himself a man stirred by strong emotions, but his heart gave an extra *ka-thump*, like an engine turning over. He wanted a normal life for himself, and the same for his son. Yet, he couldn't even manage to keep a nanny for Joey, much less a mother.

"Sir, no disrespect meant, but I'm fairly certain your daughter and I would find it hard to get along even for that short a time."

"It's only a couple of weeks, until her job starts and your ex is back in the country to pitch in. You'll be at work during the day." The older man leaned in for the kill. "Forest, my boy, think of your son. We fathers have to put our children's interests first."

Joey snuggled closer to Anna. A hiccuping sigh shuddered through his solid body as she headed inside for the promised treat. Forest had always prided himself on his control, but Anna had a way of breaking down barriers.

It was only for a couple of weeks.

He could feel himself caving. He had to do the right thing for Joey. The kid rarely had his mother around. How could Forest deny him the closest thing to maternal affection in town?

He couldn't, no matter what the cost to his personal sanity.

CHAPTER
~THREE~

"**A**re you sure you'll be all right?" Forest stood in the middle of the kitchen in his newly constructed track home, shuffling his briefcase from one hand to the other.

"Stop worrying. I have a bachelor's degree in early childhood education as well as library studies. I had reading groups for special-needs children at my old library job. I can care for one small boy."

Anna settled into the breakfast nook, planting herself in a seat beside Joey's booster chair to keep from shaking the kid's overprotective father. If he gave her one more list of ways to pacify a four-year-old…

"We're going to have a great time. Aren't we, sweetie?"

Joey slapped his spoon against the bowl of oatmeal and grinned. "I don't wanna eat this. Bleck!"

Forest slammed his briefcase on the oak table. "That's it. I'll cancel—"

"Don't even think about it. He's only testing me." Geez, no wonder the other nanny had quit. Somebody needed to lighten up. "I'll keep him so busy he won't have time to act out. Go."

"If you're sure." He still didn't leave, but let his hand rest on the baseball mitt hanging on the post of his kitchen chair, rubbing the leather like a talisman.

"I'm positive. You've left a pageful of phone numbers."

Anna tucked aside her resentment. Forest was only displaying textbook signs of an overanxious parent and yes, there were special concerns for Joey, but the best thing Forest could do for his son was treat him as normally as possible.

Still, his concern was rather sweet. She gentled her scowl into a smile. "He'll be okay once you leave. If I have a question, I'll call. I promise."

He glanced at his watch. "You're right, and court starts in less than an hour." He ruffled his son's hair. "Be good for Anna."

"Scoot." Anna waved her hand to shoo him away.

"All right, I'll get out of your hair, braid, whatever. Don't worry about supper. I'll grill something for us all when I get home since you'll probably be worn out from the full day."

She froze. Was that a dinner-date invitation?

Forest grabbed his briefcase from the table and scooped his jacket from the chair, slinging it over one deliciously broad shoulder. "Anna?"

She was startled out of her daze. "Yes?"

"Thanks." The screen door swooshed closed behind him.

She twisted her braid through her fingers as she stared out the bay window. Elbow on the table, she watched him saunter along the walk toward his truck. Such a bold, confident stride.

Pivoting away, Anna focused on the son instead of the father. "Well, sweetie, how about we clean up the breakfast dishes. You can help."

He scrunched his nose but didn't argue.

"After lunch, we'll walk to the park and feed the ducks."

"Ducks? Yay!" Joey catapulted out of his seat and into her arms with such trust her heart twisted.

"That's right. We'll take some bread along."

Anna passed him a damp cloth while grabbing one for herself, and the two of them cleared the dishes and wiped the table.

"Good job, Joey," she said when they'd finished.

She tossed their cloths into the overflowing laundry basket on top of the washer. She would show her father *and* Forest Jameson. She'd aced her way through a degree in early childhood education as well as library studies, unable to tell which she enjoyed more, until a wise college counselor advised her to apply that love of children to her library positions.

She was a well-educated, seasoned pro now.

How much trouble could one kid be?

One well-behaved, chipper child would have been simple.

The tiny tyrant looking too cute in his overalls and train-conductor cap wasn't chipper, sweet or even remotely well behaved. Why was he so cranky?

Anna had tried everything to keep him entertained at home for the morning. They'd hung out in his amazing backyard, full of playground equipment specifically designed for Joey. But he hadn't wanted any part of it today. She'd moved on to story time, singing and dancing.

After lunch, they'd walked to the duck pond as promised. The edge of the pond had a brick border where they could sit and let the ducks come right up to them without getting their feet wet.

"Yuckie!" Joey flung the bag of bread into the pond. "The bread smells gross."

"Oh, sweetie." Anna sighed as the bag floated away. She couldn't leave it behind and risk a duck choking on the plastic, but she couldn't leave Joey unattended either.

"Come on, Joey. We're going in." She hitched him onto her hip and waded into the pond. Her muslin dress soaked up the cold water as she grabbed the bag.

Joey smacked the water, cheerful for the first time in an hour. "This is fun!"

"Yes, it is, sugar." And *sooo* chilly.

Still, she considered hanging out in the muddy pond all afternoon. She would gladly sacrifice her favorite dress, patterned with Shakespearean verses and flowers, if it would keep Joey from fussing and testing her further.

Anna glanced down at her wet dress and read, *What fools these mortals be...* No kidding. She'd topped that list of foolish mortals by wading into a duck pond to scoop out a bag of bloated bread.

"The fishes are tickling my ankles!" Joey squealed.

"Cool, kiddo!" Maybe she could work in a quick science lesson. The plan seemed sound and the kid definitely needed to be kept active, but he also needed a nap, and she did *not* want Forest to hear about their impromptu swim.

His next instruction list would rival the Magna Carta.

Anna scanned the clusters of mothers and children scattered around the playground, having picnics and making memories under leafy bowers.

She recognized some of the families, but no one seemed to have noticed her and Joey. She should be able to make a clean getaway.

Her gaze snagged on Mrs. LaRoche. Joey's ex-nanny had brought her granddaughter to the park. The blue-haired bat waved to Anna. She stifled a groan and waved back. The know-it-all would probably turn cartwheels at Anna's lack of success with Joey and report it to Forest.

Anna hugged him closer. "We need to go home now——"

His face scrunched. "I don't wanna——"

"To get a treat!"

"A treat? Graham crackers?"

"Two of them." She reminded herself it wasn't a bribe, merely positive reinforcement.

A rose by any other name... Shakespeare's words mocked her.

Anna trudged forward, her clothes sponging up the water. Joey hadn't fared much better.

By the time Anna rounded the last corner on their way home, she was truly worried about Joey. Something wasn't right. She pressed her wrist to his forehead, then against his warm stomach. He wasn't just irritable. He was sick.

Guilt chugged through her. He must have been coming down with something, and dragging him through a chilly pond hadn't helped. "Do you feel bad, sweetie?"

Joey wriggled against her. "I'm sleepy. I wanna nap."

The kid *wanted* to go to sleep? It must be serious.

"Poor fella. No wonder you've been grumpy." She cuddled him closer, his damp body shivering against her. Anna walked faster up the driveway toward the one-story ranch-style house. "We're almost there. You can curl up in your own bed."

"Thank you, Anna." His chubby arms clutched tighter.

An odd ache squeezed her chest. He *needed* her. Her world consisted of books, think tanks and causes. No one had ever needed her before. That hug meant more to her than a dean's list semester.

She pressed a kiss to Joey's forehead. He really was feverish. Logic told her it probably wasn't anything more serious than a common virus. That didn't make her feel one darned bit better.

Joey opened his mouth. She tensed, preparing herself for more whining or worse yet, an ear-popping tantrum.

He spewed his lunch all over her.

Joey crinkled up his nose. "Yuckie!"

"Yeah, sweetie," Anna agreed. "Defintely yuckie."

Several hours and countless loads of laundry later, she surrendered to fate. She'd tried to call Forest, but he was in court, and then when he'd called to check in, she'd told him she'd finally gotten things under control. Sort of. The pediatrician's nurse had thought that as long as Joey was keeping down liquids, there was no need to worry. Even so, Anna felt out of her league.

She cradled Joey, who was now asleep, wrapped in a blanket with just his tiny boxer shorts on. There wasn't a clean T-shirt or a pair of jeans left in the house, since he'd thrown up on everything in sight. She'd had such great plans for starting their reading tomorrow with the Seedlings print-and-Braille books she'd ordered express mail off the Internet last night. With luck Joey would be feeling better then. Funny how plans for this child were already filling her life.

She pushed back a hank of sweaty hair from her brow, picked up the kitchen phone and dialed from memory. "Dad, could you bring me a change of clothes, please?"

Forest whipped into the driveway with uncharacteristic haste just as a car pulled away from the curb. He slid the truck into Park and looked at his house, his haven.

It was still standing. Anna and Joey must have survived their first day together.

Working without the stress of worrying about his son had lightened his mood. A call home during a court recess had re-assured him that Anna seemed to have everything under control, even though Joey was not feeling well.

She'd been right. Hiring her as a temporary sitter was the perfect solution for everyone. Meanwhile, Forest told himself, he'd exaggerated his response to Anna the night before.

He stepped into the spotless kitchen. The humming washer and dryer greeted him in the otherwise silent house. The nursery monitor was on the table, light glowing, but no grumbling from his son filtered through.

Peace? Or the calm before the storm?

"Anna? Joey?" Forest called over his shoulder while reaching into the refrigerator. He dodged the pitcher of tea with mint leaves, Anna's no doubt, and grabbed a soda. "Hello?"

"Hold on a second! Joey's asleep." Her voice wafted from behind the laundry-closet doors. "I'll be right out."

"No need to hurry. I'm going to check on Joey." He tossed his briefcase on the table, kicking the refrigerator shut as he guzzled his cola on his way down the hall. After brushing a hand over his son's cool forehead and tucking the baseball mitt back under the covers, Forest breathed a sigh of relief and returned to the kitchen.

Anna shoved the louvered doors closed. She brushed aside a stray lock of hair with a harried sweep of her hand. "You're home early."

Wow, she looked good. Her face was flushed and her eyes wide, and that green dress hugged her curves like a wet leaf. "I brought paperwork with me so I could check on Joey. How's he feeling?"

"Better," she told him. "I called his pediatrician's office again. Joey's keeping liquids and Tylenol down, so there's no need to worry for now. He wanted to take your mitt to bed with him. He seems to take comfort from the smell of the oils."

Her insightfulness caught him square in the midsection and squeezed hard.

Being around Anna so much wasn't going to work. He needed to feed her the grilled steak as promised, then take her home.

"I guess there's nothing left for me to do but crank up the grill."

"Good idea." She lounged against the doors, arms behind her.

There was something very different about her. Her hair had been braided when he'd left, and now it was in a ponytail. And she'd been wearing some kind of sack dress with weeds and quotations all over it, but now was in a formfitting silk dress.

The door behind her moved. Her eyes widened. "Maybe you should check on Joey again?"

Her high-pitched voice grated along Forest's heightened nerve endings. A first-year law student could note the body language red flags. She was concealing something.

Why would a woman shower and change into a slinky little number in the middle of the day? And what was she hiding in the laundry closet?

Or rather, *who?*

Forest saw red, and it wasn't a flag. Could Anna have put his son down for a nap while she "entertained" a guy?

He told himself that the pounding in his ears was merely the thumping of the off-balance washing machine. If not that, then it stemmed from anger because she'd abused his trust. It was *not* jealousy. She was simply an old high-school girlfriend. That relationship had no bearing on their present.

He mustered a cool voice. "Joey was fine when I looked in on him."

"Oh, all right then."

The door bucked behind her. She flattened both hands against it and smiled, a tight, overbright grimace that told Forest too much. She had some boy toy hidden behind that door.

Time's up. Forest pinned her with his best witness-breaking stare. "Anna, please, step away."

"I, uh, I can't."

"Why?"

Her full bottom lip quivered. "It's too embarrassing."

"Embarrassing?" He hadn't considered there might be a *half-dressed* sap in the closet.

The washer clicked, then hit the spin cycle. *Ker-thunk. Ker-thunk.*

Forest almost felt sorry for the guy. He knew what a wallop Anna delivered to an unsuspecting male. He'd wanted a reason to get over his absurd attraction to her, and now he had it. Why wasn't he happy?

He closed the last three steps between them. Anger and disappointment warred within him. He stuffed his hands in his pockets so he wouldn't shake her by the shoulders. "Anna, step aside so we can get this over with."

Ker-thunk. The washer spun and rattled. *Ker-thunk. Ker-thunk.*

Anna sniffled. "Do you ever get tired of being right?"

"No more procrastinating."

She eased forward. The louvered doors inched open as if nudged, then burst free. Anna stumbled into Forest's arms.

Baskets tipped. Loose laundry overflowed around them. Forest clutched Anna's soft body while clothes tangled around their ankles.

Not a cowering male in sight. "Anna?"

"I'm just so mortified!" She sniffled. "Only one day alone with Joey and I took him into the chilly pond. Now he's sick. The laundry is out of control. I've been through three outfits of my own—although why my dad would send *this* for me to wear while watching a kid is beyond me. And you so don't want to see where Joey upchucked on the comforter in your bedroom."

She collapsed against Forest's chest, bursting into shuddering sobs. He didn't want to feel the incredible relief that surged through him as she leaned into him.

In a flash, he lost his battle with suppressing the desire to kiss the freckles on the bridge of her nose. He tried to remind himself that he wanted a peaceful, normal life—something a woman like Anna was incapable of.

Forest looked into her mossy green, heartbroken eyes, and knew he'd not only forsaken peace, but plunged headfirst into a hurricane.

CHAPTER
~❦~ FOUR ~❦~

Anna stood wrapped in Forest's arms and blinked back tears. She'd never failed at anything. She'd studied her way into A-plus achievements. Why then couldn't she manage one tiny child? And why couldn't she stop this attraction to that same boy's totally uptight father?

Forest's arms locked around her waist, anchoring her to him. His solid muscles beneath her palms turned her legs to half-set Jell-O. His head dipped toward her and she couldn't resist the temptation to stretch up on her toes. His pupils widened, darkening his blue eyes to a murky sea.

Anna plunged in headfirst.

She slid her hands up his chest and around his neck. Shouldn't she be pulling away? She'd barely formed the thought when his mouth skimmed along hers. How could she have forgotten the lovely sensation of Forest Jameson's kiss?

He inched away. "Anna? What are we doing?"

"I don't know. But I want to do it again."

A low growl rumbled in his chest.

He nuzzled her neck, inhaling. "Why do you have to be so appealing?"

Anna resisted the urge to laugh. She'd never considered herself much of a femme fatale. Heaven knew, Forest could have his pick of the multitude of big-haired women with perfect makeup who strutted themselves through her father's office begging for advice on their overdue parking tickets in hopes of snagging a lawyer husband. Were those same sorts of women trailing through Forest's office? A chill settled over her.

"Forest." She stepped back. "I think I hear Joey."

"Joey. Right." Exhaling long and hard, Forest glanced over at the silent nursery monitor.

She wrapped her arms around herself. "One of us really should check on him."

The quiet house mocked her.

"Uh-huh." Forest stuffed his hands in his pockets, his breathing ragged. "Give me five seconds to remember how to breathe and I'll apologize."

"I don't want an apology."

"I owe you one anyway."

"Don't be silly. We're both adults. It was only a kiss." A kiss guaranteed to peel the paint off the walls. "It's not as if either of us is interested in a relationship. Right?"

Forest looked up fast. "No!"

"You don't have to be quite so emphatic."

"Sorry." He gripped her wrist, sliding his hand along the length of her hair. "No offense meant."

"None taken. Not much anyway." Did he have to look so nice, so genuinely concerned that he might have hurt her feelings? "You were only being honest. We're too different."

Anna felt as if she'd swallowed a dryer sheet. Forest all moody and brooding was easier to resist. This man with twinkling eyes, mussed hair and a five o'clock shadow was dangerous. She canted toward him anyway. "Forest—"

"Of course you're right, though. It didn't work in high school. There's no reason to believe it will be any different now." The sparkle faded from his baby blues.

Anna hugged herself again, a poor shield against the emotions chugging through her. She should be long over the sting of insecurity caused by years of censure from her dad, but for some reason, hearing Forest question her judgment really stung. "It's okay. I know we have to think of Joey. He and I formed a bond today. Besides, those big-haired bimbos would toss me into Lake Huron if they saw me as competition."

Forest leaned back against the counter. "Big-haired bimbos?"

"You mean you haven't noticed an increase in unpaid parking tickets lately? My dad always rolled his eyes over the phenomenon. It seemed as if every single female in town landed herself in trouble to garner his attention."

He cocked his head to the side. "Is that what you're doing with me?"

"No!" She blinked fast, banishing memories of the times she'd peeked through the stadium fence as a teen to watch him practice baseball. "I was talking about those spike-heeled jaywalkers who apply their makeup with a spatula before wobbling into your office."

"Oh, them. Yes, I've noticed one or two. Only an idiot would be attracted to women like that. They don't really want me, just a husband. Any guy would do."

"Whatever." Didn't he ever look in the mirror?

"I doubt I'll get married again, anyway. I can't afford another mistake. Joey doesn't need more upheaval in his life."

Anna got the message. He might as well have shouted it over a megaphone. She was fine as a temp sitter, maybe even a candidate for a tumble in the towels, but that was it.

She should have been mad. Instead, she was hurt. "I really should check on Joey. And don't worry, Forest. I won't throw myself at you again."

Anna raced into the hall, wondering, wanting. *Why not?*

Too bad she didn't have a textbook answer.

* * *

Forest stuffed laundry into the baskets, cursing with each fistful of socks and towels. Kissing Anna had been beyond stupid. She'd spent only one day in his house and already he'd stepped over the line. If he'd kept his hands off her, he could have deluded himself that the attraction was all in his imagination.

Now he knew better. He wanted her, and nothing he could do would change that fact. All his life he'd tried to exert a strong control over his actions to overcome what he'd learned to think of as his irresponsible genes. But one simple, relatively tame kiss from Anna had made him want to do something really crazy. He had to consider his son and rely on willpower to get himself in control of his life once more.

Silence echoed from down the hall, broken only by the creak of an opening door. Forest couldn't stop himself from listening, absorbing Anna's husky voice.

"Joey?" she whispered softly. "Still sleepy? Enjoy your nap, precious boy. You can play ball with your daddy later."

One of those Madonna images rose in Forest's mind. He could imagine too well the way she would stroke her hand over Joey's curls, drape the blanket over him, being careful to leave his feet uncovered the way he preferred.

Paula had struggled with motherhood right from the start because of Joey's blindness. She'd traded Forest in for another model, a high-powered international attorney. She'd never even asked for custody of Joey, and now her weekend visits had dwindled to accommodate those European jaunts. After the divorce, Joey's pleas for his mama had just about torn Forest's heart to bits. Now Joey never asked for her. Somehow that hurt more.

Anna's voice continued to drift down the hall, "Sweet dreams. You're going to feel better in the morning."

Forest feared his world wouldn't settle quite so quickly. He glanced up to find Anna standing in the doorway, quietly, so somehow he must have sensed her presence.

She tilted her head toward Mt. Washmore. "What did you think I was hiding in the laundry closet?"

He tugged his ear. "Nobody."

"Nobody? *Nobody!*" She headed for the kitchen, indignation sparking from her. "You actually thought I would bring a man over while I was watching Joey? You should remember enough about me from that year we dated to know I'm not like that. Just because I don't live by your uptight rules doesn't mean I don't have my own moral code."

She dashed out the door.

Forest panicked. He sprinted after her, bounding down the steps. "Anna, I was just jeal—" No way would he admit that to her. *Swap tactics, Counselor.* "You can't quit."

She yanked her helmet off the handlebars. "I didn't say that. I finish what I start. But I have a problem coming here if you think I'm not trustworthy enough to watch your son."

"Don't be ridiculous. I know how much you care about kids." If he kept her talking, she wouldn't take off and he could sort things out.

"How big of you to concede that." She spun to face him, helmet clutched to her like a shield. "Did you or did you not think I had a paramour perched on top of your perfectly matching washer-dryer set?"

"Well—"

"Quit tugging your ear." She crinkled her nose. "It gives you away every time."

Damn. He hadn't even realized he was doing it. His hand fell to his side. "The thought may have crossed my mind."

"Apparently we don't know each other at all anymore."

With that, she launched her bicycle into motion, her hair sailing behind her as she made her way down the street. She pedaled slower than in the morning, her energy obviously depleted from taking care of Joey.

Forest kicked himself for not offering her a ride—not that she would have accepted it. But seeing her weary pace reminded him of how much she'd already given to his son.

And if for no other reason than that, he would keep his libido zipped up tight so she would stay.

* * *

On Friday evening, Anna stood by her front door and watched Forest park her bike beside the vegetable patch. Since he'd had to work late, past dark, he'd given her a ride home.

What a week they'd had. She'd gotten a Braille label maker and labeled everything in the house. After all, sighted children were exposed to words right away even if they couldn't yet read them. Why shouldn't children who were blind have the same experience?

The labels were clear, with Braille bumps, like the see-through sheets Seedlings used in their toddler books. When Anna read to Joey, she was still able to see the words, but Joey could run his fingers along the raised bumps, working to heighten his touch sensitivity.

Forest had been surprised at first, then embarrassed not to have started to do this himself. She'd reassured him it was easy for her to step in and point things out when he'd been mired in the day-to-day routine of raising a special needs child alone.

Any young child was tough work.

Mostly she'd done her best to keep up with a very active little boy who wasn't being challenged enough intellectually. She couldn't fault Forest as a father. He'd arranged his whole house and yard so Joey could run off all that energy.

But their house was sadly devoid of a variety of children's books. She'd found some fuzzy-textures board books for preschoolers. Most of the time Forest made up stories to tell his son. That was wonderful, too. Joey could create images in his mind. He didn't "see" the world the way his father or Anna did, but he had a vision all his own.

What was missing was reading. Forest hadn't been doing much with Joey, and Anna hoped that would change now.

Sheesh, the little stinker surely was working his way into her heart. The father wasn't too far behind.

Maybe she was coming down with Joey's virus.

She needed to get inside fast before she did something reckless like ask Forest to come in for a while. "Thanks for driving me home. That really wasn't necessary. I ride around at night all the time."

Leaving Joey snoozing in the truck, Forest ambled up the steps and leaned on the porch post with a weary sigh. "You've had a long day. We both have. It was the least I could do."

Anna fidgeted with her key ring. "You're such a nice man. You would probably rather be anywhere than here with me, yet here you are, doing the polite thing. When are you going to do something *you* want?"

Forest gave a half smile. "I already did that once earlier this week, and we almost ended up making out on a pile of laundry."

Anna gulped. Having the kiss hang between them all week had been tough enough. Flinging it out in the open sent her stomach into a somersault.

And they were alone. "Uh, Forest—"

"Don't worry." He grinned. "I've used up my supply of impulsive moves for the year."

She relaxed. A little. "It would be nice, wouldn't it, if we were the types who could do that."

"Do what?"

"Roll around in the laundry, get it all out of our system and move on with life."

His blue eyes swept over her. "Yes, it would."

"But we're not that way, are we?"

"Afraid not."

"Can we be friends?" she asked.

"I think we already are."

"Then why didn't you write me after you moved away from Oscoda all those years ago?" The words tumbled out of her mouth without her permission, but she couldn't bring herself to call them back.

His eyes turned sad even as he reached out to tuck a stray lock of hair behind her ear. "Because I was certain back then I wasn't good enough for you. When I left town, I figured a clean break would be best. It was better to let you lead your own life than string things out."

He'd broken her heart because he'd decided he wasn't good enough? Hadn't he seen how special he was then? Even her father thought he'd hung the moon. She'd even been a little jealous, feeling as if Forest was the son her father had always wanted.

"And now?" There she went again, blurting out words without thinking.

"Now? We're too different, and I have Joey to think of."

"Right. So we're friends." She stuck out her hand.

"Friends," he agreed, clasping her hand in his.

Why couldn't he have argued with her? And why couldn't she let go of him? "Then it's all settled."

Forest leaned toward her until Anna could feel the whisper of his breath against her skin, see every sweep of his long, black lashes.

Closing that last inch between them, he gripped her shoulders and pressed his lips to her forehead. Anna didn't move, merely held herself still just as he did, and breathed in the delicious, tangy scent of him, Forest, her high-school ex, who was fast becoming her grown-up friend.

He stepped back. "See you tomorrow at the recycling drive."

Forest pivoted away and loped back down the stairs to his truck. She watched him leave and wanted to cry with frustration. After this weekend to regroup her defenses, she still had one week left to fill out her contract.

Why did that scare her more than any extended stint in jail?

The next morning, Forest stared out over the library's parking lot. Suburbans, minivans and trucks were parked at odd angles while people unloaded bags and boxes full of recycling. Brown bins were parked near the tables for a recycling drive to earn money for the library—in particular, the children's section. Anna's doing, no doubt, after less than a month in town. He wove around the clusters of people. Smitty the cop held one of his daughters and a clear, blue plastic bag full of cans.

Forest tugged Joey forward, his gaze darting from group to group. Geez, was he really scouring the area for a simple glimpse of Anna?

Yep. He sure was.

Then he found her. She stood behind a table, clipboard in hand, directing the flow of activity. The sun glinting off her hair and the pencil tucked behind her ear. Forest's grip tightened around the twine binding his stack of newspapers.

They'd made it through their first week together with ease. Anna fit into his life so well it scared him. But people in town reminded him of the intense passion she'd shown for her various causes over the years—a passion that sometimes landed her on the wrong side of the law.

He welcomed the reminder. These people had known Anna longer than he had. It was tough seeing her smile when Joey brought her a flower. Hearing her laugh as they watched Joey soar down a slide.

Feeling the air crackle when they accidentally brushed against each other.

But right now, he needed to turn in his contribution to the recycling drive. Glancing down at his son, Forest straightened Joey's train conductor cap. "How about a treat? They've got cookies and juice."

"Cookies?"

"You bet. A whole tableful." Right next to Anna.

There wasn't any need to beat himself up about joining in the recycling effort. He had just as much right to be at the drive as anyone else. Like a good friend, he was supporting Anna's pet project. Why then did he feel like a teenager changing his route between classes so he could catch a glimpse of the new girl in school?

Joey tipped his ear to listen more closely, then a smile illuminated his round face. "Anna!"

He yanked his father's hand, pulling him toward the sound of her chiming laugh. With his other hand he waved the piece of newspaper he held. "Anna! I brought a 'cycling for you!"

Anna looked up from her clipboard. A grin spread over her face, brighter than the sun glistening off the asphalt as she took his lone flyer. "Hey there, Joey. What's this?"

"A recycling paper." He stuffed his hand in his pocket and pulled out a mangled dandelion. He lifted it toward her the way Forest had seen her do when Joey and Anna were playing

"Name That Flower." Except Joey waggled it closer to her chin than her nose. "And a flower!" he announced.

"Oh, what a charmer you are!" Anna knelt eye level and received her presents as if they were bounty from a knight. She pressed a kiss to his cheek. "Thank you, sweetie, these are absolutely the best gifts ever."

Forest lifted his neatly bundled stack. If Joey got a kiss for a scrap of paper, how would she react to a week's worth of *The New York Times?* "Joey and I wanted to do our part."

Joey gripped the edge of the table, stretching up on tiptoe. "Where's the cookies?"

Anna looped an arm around his waist and hoisted him level with the table so he could smell the cookies while she patiently identified each one. Finally, he settled on peanut oatmeal raisin. "Help yourself. There're plenty more."

Forest lifted his bundle of papers. "Where should I put these?"

She glanced over, her smile widening. "Toss them into the marked bin. We'll get a total weight at the end of the day."

If he got such a pulse-kicking smile for a measly week's worth of *The New York Times* and some old issues of *Sports Illustrated,* he could hardly wait to see her reaction to his bag of milk jugs.

Geez, he was worse now than during his teenage year when he'd tried to win her over with candy and meals out. "How much do you expect to raise today?"

"Not a whole lot. But that's not the point. If we earn enough to add a few books to the library while doing our bit for the environment and strengthening the community bond, then it's worth the effort."

"Well put." Forest untied the twine and pitched his offering in with ease. Ready to receive more praise for doing his part in saving natural resources, he pivoted to Anna. "I've got some free time this afternoon. As long as Joey cooperates, I'd be happy to help out, if you need an extra pair—"

He stared at the back of her head.

She was already preoccupied answering questions, offering directions to a group of people. He shuffled from one foot to the other, waiting for his turn.

It was an odd thing, being low on her list of priorities. And Forest was seeing a very different side of Anna. She was in her element, the undisputed queen of the day.

Accustomed to thinking of Anna as quirky and unconventional, he was startled to glimpse this smoothly efficient woman. Not even Judge Randall could accuse her of being disruptive today. She directed the whole event, armed only with a pencil and clipboard.

She didn't need him at all. Here, Anna was the cool, efficient professional, and he was just another guy with a pile of garbage.

CHAPTER
❧ FIVE ❧

Monday morning, Anna pedaled up Forest's driveway and parked her bike where he wouldn't see it when he left. She had a surprise for him, and she didn't want him spotting it on his way out to work. They both deserved a reward for surviving the past week together.

And he had contributed to her recycling drive.

The image of him striding across the parking lot with his neatly bundled newspapers still warmed her. His offer to help had come as a shock, probably to him as well. He really could be sweet when he dropped the uptight act.

She rapped on the door, shrugging her backpack off her shoulders. No one answered, so she knocked again, harder.

After another minute passed, she stepped halfway inside. "Good morning! Forest? Joey? It's just me."

"Hang on, Anna!" Forest shouted. "We're running late."

Late? Forest? She breezed into the house, through the masculine living room with its big brown corduroy sofas and chairs, but little else for Joey to trip over. His toys all stayed piled in the same corners so he could find them. A few more steps took her to the breakfast nook.

Forest plowed into the kitchen, briefcase in hand. He scooped Joey up, gripping him by the back of his overalls and carrying him like a lunch box.

Joey squealed, "I'm an airplane! Flying high!"

"In for a carrier landing!" Forest skimmed his son to a stop on the tabletop. "Okay, kiddo. I have to get moving."

He plopped Joey into his booster chair and glanced over his shoulder at Anna. "Hope you don't mind feeding him breakfast. We lost track of time playing this morning."

A single lock of hair brushed his brow, just tapping the top of his glasses.

"Anna?"

"Huh?" She'd been totally focused on those baby blues. "Breakfast! Sure, I'd be happy to feed him. Cheese toast, right? No oatmeal."

"Are you all right?"

"I'm fine. Just thinking about all the money we raised at the recycling drive."

Anna had to make herself remember why she should keep her distance. Forest was too much like her conservative father. She was a free spirit. She would drive him nuts, and she truly believed this wonderful guy deserved happiness.

Bottom line, she'd had a lifetime of gentle censure from her father. She didn't want to deal with it in any of her other relationships. Anna blinked back tears. *Think of your plans for Joey today, not Forest.*

She had dominoes in her backpack to help Joey work on numbers. He would be able to feel the indentions—almost like reverse Braille. She'd also ordered a few more Seedlings print-and-Braille books, even though he always wanted to end every reading session with *Seymour the Sea Turtle Snaps Up Lunch.* Good thing these books were so affordable because her budget was tight and she hated to ask Forest for money. Whenever she mentioned trying new things with Joey, a look of guilt crossed Forest's face as he blamed himself for not doing more for his son.

Forest knotted his tie. "I've never been to a recycling drive before. You really did a bang-up job organizing it."

"Thanks." Why did he have to be so nice?

"Okay. I really do need to go." He launched into motion again, snapping his briefcase open and dropping files inside. "I caught up with laundry over the weekend. That isn't in your job description here and I apologize for taking advantage. There's plenty of Joey's favorite juice in the fridge. And he has a new train set he really likes if you want to pull it out. Careful, though, because those pieces hurt like crazy if you step on them barefooted."

He grabbed the briefcase and his coat.

"Bye, son." He dropped a kiss on Joey's forehead, then turned to Anna.

Ohmigosh! Was he going to kiss her, too? He stood so close, and Anna held her breath. She wanted to kiss him more than she wanted air.

He stepped back.

She must have imagined the whole thing. Good thing he couldn't see what was inside her head?

"Bye, Anna."

"Goodbye." It took every ounce of restraint she had not to smooth that lock of hair back from his forehead. She bit her lip, mumbling, "Nothing in common, nothing in common…"

Forest stopped at the door. "Did you say something?"

"Nothing important."

Friday couldn't come fast enough.

"Hold still, sweetie!" Anna struggled with the chin strap of the helmet. She hoped she'd bought the right size. The box had said it would fit a four-year-old. The buckle clicked into place. "There! Ohhh, you look so cute!"

Joey stood in the middle of the kitchen, a neon-blue bicycle helmet in place. His head looked twice the size of his body, kind of like an alien child. He was all set for his first ride in her newly installed kiddy bicycle seat, complete with all the latest safety features.

She'd bought it over the weekend as a gift to herself after learning that hours alone in a house with a four-year-old could give a person an incredible case of cabin fever. Joey could only walk so far. The last thing she needed was more time to sit around and moon over Forest Jameson.

So why was she going to see him for lunch? *Just for Joey.* The little guy would enjoy seeing his daddy. She latched on to the logical explanation with desperation.

"We're going to have such fun cycling around town today." She tucked the rest of their lunch in her backpack. "Ready to go? Do you need a potty break first?"

Much as Anna loved the kid, if she didn't get some adult conversation soon, she'd be a prime candidate for a strait-jacket.

"Let's go see Daddy." Joey waddled around the kitchen with a wide-legged cowboy swagger.

"Balancing that head must be quite a challenge, huh?" Anna knocked on his helmet. "Time to roll if we want to get that picnic lunch to your dad before noon. Daddy's going to be so proud to see his little boy in his very first helmet."

Twenty minutes later, Anna stowed the bike behind a row of bushes outside Forest's office and clasped Joey's hand in hers. "Ready to kidnap your dad, sweetie?"

Her heart beat faster with every step she took toward Forest's office door. She forced herself to walk slower along the cracked sidewalk, keeping more in step with the leisurely pace of her hometown.

The park loomed at the end of the street. At least she had memories of the time spent there. She was happy in her hometown, and if she wanted to continue to live here, she had to keep her job at the library. That meant no more protests, even if her park became a strip club. She shuddered. There had to be something she could do before time ran out.

Sighing, she pushed through the front door into the reception area of her father's old office, still featuring the same old-time trio of leather, mahogany and wainscoting.

And the Big-Hair Brigade.

Of course, these weren't the same women she'd seen in her father's office over the years, but they were carbon copies, and no fewer than five of them were wedged into the burgundy leather sofa and chairs. Ceiling fans clicked overhead, stirring the scent of furniture polish and hair product. All that gel

· should be considered a fire hazard. If anyone lit a cigarette, the whole place could go up in flames.

Anna strolled toward one of the women, an old classmate of hers. "Hi, Shirley."

Shirley Rhodes stuffed a tube of bubblegum-pink lipstick in her purse. "Good afternoon, Anna." She glided to her feet and pinched Joey's cheeks. "You are just the cutest little thing! You look just like your daddy-waddy."

Joey squirmed away, clinging to Anna.

"Sorry, he's just shy around strangers." Anna made a mental note to give Joey three treats later for his loyalty. She turned to the grandmotherly receptionist who used to work for her father before he retired. "Kay, is Forest free?"

Leather crackled as four women scooted to the edge of their seats.

The receptionist glared at them, then gave Anna a genuine smile. "He's tied up at the moment. But I'll let him know you and Joey are waiting."

"Thanks." Anna set Joey down and watched him scamper over to the receptionist's desk. He felt his way down the drawers as if counting, until he pulled open the bottom one, where Kay apparently kept toys for him. Once he was settled with a pile of race cars, Anna turned her attention to Shirley. "What brings you here?"

"Another one of those blasted unpaid parking tickets. I don't know why I keep forgetting to mail the money. So here I am back in Forest's, I mean, Counselor Jameson's office." Shirley arched her back, making the very most of her chest. "Aren't we lucky to have such a smart young lawyer in Oscoda?"

"Hmm."

"Why are you here? Did you handcuff yourself to something else?" Shirley glanced back at her cohorts. Four compacts snapped closed, in synch.

"You heard about that?" A tic started right in the corner of Anna's eye.

"We're a small town of caring people," Shirley answered with ill-disguised insincerity.

Anna knew she should turn and walk away. A mature woman would smile politely and leave. She should ignore the spiteful bimbos and take Joey back to see his daddy-waddy.

Revenge was petty.

Joey tipped his face up from his Tonkas, grinning. She would have sworn his sightless expression said, *Go get 'em, Anna!*

If Joey insisted, who was she to argue? A wicked and wonderful plan took shape in her mind. She could help Forest *and* her park without whipping out cuffs.

"Well, Shirley, actually, it's a rather sensitive matter." She paused for effect. "It's about Forest."

"Forest?"

"Oh, never mind." Anna pressed a hand to her cheek. "You're probably not interested in all this."

She didn't have a chance to pivot more than halfway around before Shirley grabbed her arm in a death grip.

"Spill it!" Shirley cleared her throat. "I mean, I would love to hear. Poor Forest may need a sympathetic shoulder."

He would probably asphyxiate on her perfume. "I'm sure he could use some friendly support."

"Well?"

Anna noticed that she had the attention of all five women and moved in for the kill. "It's about his park."

"His park?" Shirley arched a penciled brow.

This was too easy. "Remember the old park by the library?"

They frowned. Okay, maybe not as easy as Anna had thought.

"By the lake."

The women nodded in unison.

"It's slated to be a strip club."

Shirley shrugged. "So?"

Anna exhaled. They must be too busy time-sharing a brain cell—or maybe they actually cared what happened in this town after all. "That's where Forest's parents got engaged."

"Oh!" Shirley's hand fluttered to her chest. "How romantic."

"If it weren't for those oaks, Forest wouldn't be alive today." Anna shook her head slowly. The women were hooked. Now to reel them in. "He told me it's his fondest wish to find the woman of his dreams and propose beneath those branches."

"Oh, wow!" Shirley glanced back at her wide-eyed friends.

Anna sighed. "Too bad nobody's willing to help out with, maybe, marching in a picket line."

Shirley was first to the door.

Her cohorts weren't more than two steps behind her. The five frantic women pushed through the entranceway.

The door banged shut behind them.

Anna smirked, dusting her hands. She turned to the receptionist and shrugged. "Well, Kay, I had to clear them out so Joey could have some time with his daddy-waddy."

Kay winked. "Nice work, kiddo."

"Is he free yet?"

"He was hiding from the vultures, but I buzzed him when you arrived. He should be out in a minute." Kay winked. "I'll have to call you when the next batch flocks in."

Her stomach constricted. "Next batch?"

"There are plenty more where they came from." She shrugged. "Word gets around. At least he doesn't have to worry about ulterior motives with you."

"Of course not." She wasn't like *them*. She'd merely helped Forest, with the side benefit of offering her park another shot at life. She couldn't have acted out of… jealousy?

Horror-struck, she gulped. "Uh, Kay. I just remembered

something back at home I need to check on." She reached for Joey. "Come on, sweetie. We've got—"

"Kay, are they gone yet?" Forest asked as he stepped from his office. "Hi, Anna. I'm glad you're still here." He knelt and ruffled his son's hair.

He was? Anna stopped breathing. Their faces weren't more than six inches apart. If she breathed in even a hint of the spicy aftershave he wore, she might very well find herself staking out a spot for herself on the sofa.

She smiled weakly. "We stopped in to take you on a picnic."

"A picnic?" He looked wary. Was he remembering that almost kiss? With any luck, it would be the fastest lunch hour in history.

More importantly, they needed to finish before Shirley organized her troops.

"I loooove going to Anna's park," Joey squealed from atop his father's shoulders. He grabbed fistfuls of dried leaves from swaying branches while Anna and Forest strolled down Main Street.

Forest clutched Joey's feet to steady him as they walked past the row of lampposts. What a great small town. He'd have given anything to grow up in a place like this. Of course, that was why he'd chosen it for his son.

He'd almost kissed Anna again this morning at the house. Not some impulsive, hormonal kiss, but one of those "see you later" kisses. Those were the dangerous sort. They implied an ease with each other that went beyond just attraction.

After this week with Anna, he knew he respected her too much for a fling and he'd vowed he didn't want to get married again. What a mess.

Still, he owed her so much for all she'd done for him and his son. "Thanks for bringing lunch over."

"No problem." She clutched her sweater to her chest, the insulated food sack dangling from her elbow.

"It's nice to see Joey in the middle of the day."

"You can come home, you know. You don't have to hide from me in your office like you do from those other women. I'm not out to cuff you to the altar or anything."

The determined thrust of her jaw shouldn't have stung his pride, but it did. "I lose track of time at the computer."

"Then it's good we made you take a break." She hip bumped him. "You need to lighten up a little bit. Relax."

"I'm not that uptight." He felt relaxed—perhaps too relaxed. Maybe he should rile her a little and put some much-needed distance between them. "What's on today's menu? Any tofu in that sack? Nothing like a big slice of bran cake to stick to a man's ribs."

When she didn't answer, Forest glanced down at her. He couldn't have hurt her feelings, could he? He sometimes forgot how tenderhearted she was. She had one of those personalities that filled a room, even knocked down a few walls. "Anna?"

She nibbled her lip, staring straight ahead. The park loomed ahead, complete with her favorite bench. If he wasn't careful, Anna would have him cuffed to a parking meter while she sprinted over for an impromptu protest.

He needed to get her talking, fast. "You could have called me to come get you. It's a long way for you and Joey to walk."

"Oh, we didn't wa—"

"What the—?" Forest squinted, tipped his head to the side, then squinted again. Sure enough, a small crowd had gathered around an old oak, chanting and marching.

It was his waiting-room regulars, Shirley Rhodes and her pals. "It's our park! It's our pride! Those bulldozers better run and hide! It's our park..."

He turned to the woman beside him. "Anna!"

She blinked up at him with overly innocent eyes. "What? I'm not protesting. I'm having a picnic. I even brought Joey's jingle ball for you two to play catch."

Forest looked from her to the bizarre march. He knew she must have orchestrated it, but damned if he could figure out how. Which made him nervous. There wasn't a chance he could let her out of his sight now.

Worse yet, he didn't want to.

Grinning, Anna tugged him by the elbow, walking backward. "Come on. Don't let *them* ruin this for Joey."

Lord help him, she was beautiful. Radiant. The sun glinted

off her hair like fire. She had just the kind of body he liked, with soft, womanly curves.

Why was he supposed to resist her?

Oh yeah, their differences and his determination not to marry again. Funny how often he forgot about all that lately. "Okay. Whatever you did, I don't think I want to know. At least you're not dancing with that cheering squad."

She gazed longingly at the picketing bunch. "They're cheerleaders. Apparently they knew how to organize that sort of rhyming demonstration with a speed and ease I could learn from."

Shirley waggled a wave at Forest before resuming her hip-twitching strut and upping the volume. "Take your saw! Take your chain! Take them and go home again! Take your saw…"

The whole town had gone nuts.

Forest looked away from Shirley and her pals, not a difficult task, and focused on Anna. Her wide eyes blinked up at him. Tears glinted. Ah man, he was a sucker for tears.

He stroked a knuckle along her jaw. "Why is the park so important to you?"

Her eyes widened. She blinked faster. Anna dodged his touch and walked ahead.

He caught up, ducking to look at her. "Anna?"

She took her time answering as they padded across the park lawn. "You're the first person to ever ask me why."

"Huh?"

"No one ever wants to know *why* I protest. Not even my father. I always thought that even if he didn't agree with me, maybe he would want to know why." She slumped back against a tree. "It hurts to think he doesn't care enough."

"Anna, of course he cares." Forest stopped in front of her and hefted Joey from his shoulders to the ground. "Your dad worries himself crazy about you."

"That's the whole point. He worries because he doesn't trust me. Strange, huh? I'm twenty-five years old, self-supporting, and he doesn't trust me to have enough sense to manage my life."

His heart thumped, and it had nothing to do with Joey's tennis shoes drumming against his chest. "Tell me, why is the park so important? I want to understand."

He really did want to know. A good attorney would have dug for the reasons the first night. An honorable man would have had the patience to listen. He'd let her down on both counts.

She traced her toe through the dirt. "My mother and I spent so many hours here. After she died, Dad packed picnics and brought me here so we could feel close to her. We'd sit under that tree with our PB&Js and root beer. He would ask me about my day and help with my homework. Silly memories, huh?"

"Not at all." Forest looked at the crown of her bowed head and wanted to hug her.

His throat closed. There was his reason for never asking. A vulnerable Anna was impossible to resist.

She flicked her braid over her shoulder, the old spunky Anna seeming to have returned. Maybe it was just a woman thing, attaching so much sentimental value to a park. Women kept scrapbooks and pressed flowers. Definitely a woman thing. Even Shirley Rhodes and her pals had joined in the effort.

The former cheerleaders broke from a huddle and stood in a chorus line. "It's no joke. Save our oaks. It's no joke…"

Anna's shoulders slumped. The old Anna would have been joining in the march and scripting better lyrics.

Had he and her father done this to her? Dimmed the spark that made her so special?

Forest knew he was in deep trouble. With half a nudge, he could find himself painting signs and joining the march to save a bunch of trees with root rot.

CHAPTER
∽ SIX ∽

H eart lighter than she could ever remember, Anna skipped over a root jutting from the sidewalk while Forest carried a sleepy Joey back to the office.

It meant so much to her that Forest had asked her about the park, and in talking, she had come to realize part of her reason for hanging on so tight. As long as the park was here she had hopes of healing the distance between her and her father. Odd how acknowledging a problem somehow eased its weight. Forest's logic had helped her with that.

"Be honest, now," Forest said. "You set up Shirley."

Anna enjoyed a much-needed grin. "I'm not admitting anything until I speak with my attorney."

"Your attorney needs the truth to properly represent you." He lifted a brow. "The truth?"

"They were driving Kay crazy. I told them how your mom proposed to your dad under the old oak tree and that you'd always wanted to propose to your bride beneath it." She shrugged. "And voilà, they called up their old cheerleading skills in a heartbeat for an instant big-haired riot."

"You did it because Kay wanted them gone?"

Anna tugged at her turtleneck. "Maybe they were bugging me a little, too."

He grinned. "You were jealous."

Why lie? "A smidge."

Forest reached across to stroke a windswept strand of hair behind her ear.

Grinning back, Anna kicked a rock along the sidewalk as they walked to Forest's office. Lunch had been nice, but it would have been so much better without Shirley and Company. If Shirley Rhodes had thrust her chest under Forest's nose one more time, Anna would have gagged.

Then there was her own attraction to Forest mucking up everything. They couldn't keep jumping ten feet every time they accidentally rubbed against each other.

Accidentally? Or were those toe-curling moments intentional? At least she would have the bike ride home to clear her head.

Once outside the office, Anna reached to take the droopy Joey from Forest's arms. "Okay, kiddo, nap time."

Forest passed his son over. His broad hand skimmed her neck. Anna forced herself not to jerk away. If she moved, that would only make matters worse, because then they would look at each other. Aware.

She swallowed the lump in her throat. "Uh, thanks."

His brow furrowed, then smoothed. "Do you have a minute? We could set Joey down on the bench while we talk."

Talk? Oh Lord. He was going to harp on the Shirley debacle again.

"Sure," she said with little enthusiasm, gently settling a snoozing Joey on the bench. She shrugged out of her sweater and draped it over him. Bracing herself, she turned. "What do we need to discuss?"

"This." He dipped his head and brushed his mouth over hers, once, twice, before pulling away.

Breathless, she flattened her hands to his chest, grateful for the privacy of the overgrown hedges. "I thought you said we were going to talk."

"I lied. Do you have a problem with that?"

She couldn't deny the obvious. "No problem at all."

He took off his glasses and lifted her against him. Anna could only hang on, her toes off the ground, the delicious rasp of his afternoon beard against her skin reminding her they weren't in high school any longer.

She stroked the hair at the base of his head. How odd that she'd always preferred longer hair on a man. Not now.

Easing back, Anna looked up at him. "Wow."

"Ditto. Lady, you pack quite a wallop."

He set her on her feet again, not that it eased the feeling of floating.

She gulped. "I should take Joey home now."

Slowly he nodded. "Hang on a second." He wouldn't meet her gaze. "I'll check in with Kay, then drive you home. It's too far for you to carry Joey while he's sleeping."

"Oh, uh, I didn't walk. I started to tell you before we got sidetracked with my park. I have a little surprise."

"Surprise?" he said, voice tight.

"A kiddie bike seat." She slipped behind the row of bushes and returned with her bike. Joey stirred when she set him in the seat and adjusted his helmet, then settled back into slumber as she buckled him in.

"Cool, huh?" she said. "We had a nice little ride over."

Anna turned to look at Forest. He stood as still as the biblical Lot's wife when she'd taken that fatal peek over her shoulder.

Wow! She'd rendered Counselor Jameson speechless for once. Of course, Joey was mighty cute. "Maybe you could look into buying one for yourself, take father-son weekend trail rides. Oh, and I bet he would enjoy camping trips when he's a little older."

Why couldn't she stop babbling? So he'd shown an interest in her feelings, her concerns. That didn't mean anything. But Anna didn't even wait for his reply. She needed to get home before Forest did something sweet again. She did not need to have her heart trounced.

She swung her leg over the bike, ready to forget all about the man with the tender blue eyes. The first man to care enough to ask about her day since she'd gobbled PB&Js under the oaks twenty years ago. With a quick wave goodbye, Anna pedaled off, Shirley's taunting chants drifting on the breeze.

"We'll keep the park! We'll keep the land! We don't need no strip-club band!"

Standing outside his office, Forest watched Anna cycle away, his son's helmeted head bobbing from side to side.

And he just couldn't stop thinking about all those years riding in the side car of his parents' motorcycle, helmet in place. He winced at the memory of other kids in station wagons pointing and making faces, while he'd clutched his baseball and mitt. After graduating from law school, he'd bought the biggest truck he could afford.

He realized his knee-jerk reaction to seeing Joey in a helmet was silly. His adventurous son would enjoy the free-flying sensation and Forest wanted him to live life to the fullest.

For someone who'd known Joey only a week, Anna was doing an amazing job of introducing him to new experiences. After he'd finished reading the judge's proposal for his old congressman friend last night, Forest had spent hours on the Web site for Seedlings Braille Books for Children.

He'd been so focused on making sure Joey's physical life was unhampered, he'd missed other needs, assuming they would be addressed at school. Anna had simply smiled and said the two of them had everything covered now. That he was a loving, proactive father and Joey would have a rich life because of it.

Her praise meant a lot to him when every day he questioned whether he'd done enough for his son.

He was starting to care about Anna, too much, and that was dangerous. He just wasn't ready to think about relationships, especially marriage.

A long shadow stretched on the sidewalk in front of him, and someone tapped him on the shoulder. Just to be safe, Forest checked the shadow for big hair, then turned to find the judge. The father of the very woman Forest was all but panting after.

Forest swallowed heavily. It didn't help. "Hello, sir."

"Good afternoon, boy!" The judge snapped his plaid suspenders. "I hear you've been out for a little picnic."

"Word sure travels fast."

"I stopped in at the office and Kay told me."

Forest gestured up the steps toward the office door. "Why don't we head inside, where it's warmer."

The judge shook his head. "I only wanted to congratulate you on making it through the first week without any hardships."

Friday seemed five years away, rather than five days. "We're…managing."

"Thank you for keeping her out of trouble."

Forest bristled. An image of Anna's sad eyes as she stared at *her* park stabbed him. For the first time, he looked at the judge and found himself questioning his mentor's judgment. Were they right to keep their proposal to the congressman a secret from her? Her father swore it was best not to get her hopes up. "Actually, she's been a real godsend."

"Sure, she's good with kids. But those meals of hers." Judge Bonneau shuddered, a hint of a grin peeking through.

Forest resented the way the judge seemed to put down Anna. She was an amazing woman. Sure, her style was different, but different could be good. Exciting. Fun. "Her spinach lasagna's actually not half-bad. It's the first time Joey ate vegetables without flinging them across the room—"

Had the judge actually chortled? Forest frowned, certain he must be mistaken.

Judge Bonneau cleared his throat. "That's quite gentlemanly of you, son. But you don't have to defend her to me. I understand my daughter, faults and all, and she's going to need extra watching until I can persuade my friend in the House to get behind an injunction."

She needed watching? Damn it. There the judge went again, treating Anna like a child. "Sir, with all due respect, I think you need to spend some time with Anna and get to know your *adult* daughter. She's a bright, funny woman."

Also a beautiful woman who turned him inside out with her unreserved smiles.

The judge's bushy brows rose up to his receding hairline. "You can't actually be having, uh, feelings for my Anna?"

"Of course not." Maybe. A distinct possibility. Most likely.

"Now, don't get me wrong, I love that daughter of mine, but you two are oil and water and I really want you both to be happy."

Forest studied the judge, then realized that he himself might have spouted the same pompous-sounding bull a week ago.

Forest climbed the first step toward his office. "Think about what I said. Consider it the student passing along advice to the teacher for a change. Stop in and talk to your daughter sometime when you haven't been called by the police station."

"Sure, boy." The judge thumped Forest on the shoulder.

Forest felt oddly lighthearted as the wind spiraled autumn leaves down the sidewalk. But one fact clanged loud and clear in his mind. He could lighten up on his uptight ways, but he couldn't change who he was, and didn't really want to. Anna was special. He'd only just begun to realize how special. A man like him would take all that spark from her, just like her father was trying to do. That would be a real crime.

She needed someone with an adventurous spirit to match her own. He wanted peace and his *Sports Illustrated* subscription, for himself and Joey. Forest didn't like surprises, and Anna was like a magician's sack full of them. He never knew if he might get a cute rabbit, or if she would saw him in half.

Where did they go from here? Friendship?

At least it was something, a relationship of sorts, because he couldn't bring himself to tell her goodbye altogether. But he needed to make their friendship work.

If he'd learned nothing else from his debacle of a marriage, it was that relationships required compromise. He almost shuddered at the thought of more scenes like the one they'd just endured at the park. Protests and sit-ins and handcuffings. Somehow, he would have to convince her to compromise, as well, starting with throwing out those cuffs.

Forest stared at his mentor and resisted the urge to snap at him. The judge hadn't made his life one bit easier by throwing Anna and him together. He might as well have tossed a match onto a puddle of gasoline.

Anyone with sense could have seen how attracted Forest was to Anna back in high school. And the judge was too smart of a man to have missed that.

Forest thunked himself on his dense, hormone-fogged forehead and sank down onto the step. "You set us up."

The judge raised a bushy, red brow.

It suddenly made sense. "You orchestrated all of this. You knew full well that tenderhearted Anna wouldn't be able to keep herself from offering to help with Joey."

Forest sifted through the obvious, all the while kicking himself that he'd missed the signs earlier, including his nanny's abrupt departure. "Mrs. LaRoche's resignation seemed to come out of the blue. You sent me to help Anna with the handcuff deal and brought her those clingy clothes the day Joey was sick."

"Guilty as charged." The judge smirked, apparently not ashamed of being caught in his cupid antics. "You two were both so stubborn back in high school, too prideful to write to each other over the years. Trudy LaRoche and I decided to give you a little help this time."

Forest had a clear image of the judge and Mrs. LaRoche plotting his downfall. Who else was in on their scheme? "Judge Randall?"

"That part's real, and convenient timing."

"Why should I believe you now?"

"You should be complimented! I'm offering you my greatest treasure, my daughter."

"Sir, she's not yours to give." And perhaps not Forest's to have. The thought wasn't as comforting as a confirmed bachelor should have wanted. "Anna has a mind of her own, and a lot more sense than you give her credit for."

Wasn't the irate father supposed to be coming after him with a double-barrel shotgun? This kind of endorsement was too weird, and distinctly uncomfortable. Worst of all, he hated the sense that he'd been played, Anna, too, for that matter.

The judge chuckled. "I do so enjoy being right. This is perfect for everybody. You get a new wife, a keeper this time, because I didn't raise a quitter. Even that cute little boy of yours comes out a winner with a full-time mama."

Wife? Mama? The judge had blindsided him with the shotgun after all.

Forest gasped for breath. Of course the judge was thinking rings and weddings. Anna was his daughter.

But Forest had screwed up his first marriage, and he hated making mistakes. He wouldn't make the same one twice. He loved his son too much to put him through that again. He lov—

He *liked* and respected Anna too much to offer her anything but honesty. For now, he wanted picnics and friendship. They could continue or call it quits anytime. It wasn't as if he couldn't live without her.

Why then did he know without question that he planned to let Mrs. LaRoche finish her "vacation" just so he could have a few more days to play house with Anna?

* * *

Anna turned the last page on the Seedlings Braille book she'd been reading to Joey. "The end."

"Again! Again! Again!" He bounced on the sofa.

"You've already memorized the words to this one." As well as the feel of the bumps, she hoped. "How about we try a new one. It's about a fire truck."

"A fire truck?" He tipped his head in concentration. "I like trucks."

She heard the rumble of Forest's truck outside. "Oops. Daddy's home. Maybe he can read this one to you."

The front door creaked open.

Joey's face lit up. "Daddy!"

He catapulted off the sofa and ran across the room, his tiny boot catching on a wrinkle in the rug. But Forest hefted him up just in time. What an amazing man. He'd been there in so many ways for Joey. Her heart ached a little more.

Joey plastered a big wet kiss on his father's cheek, then pulled back. "Guess what, guess what, guess what?"

"What, big guy?" Forest gave him a bear hug hello before letting him slide back to the ground. The two held hands as they made their way toward the recliner chair where they always sat to share reviews of their day.

"Anna is teaching me to read."

Forest settled, half in, half out of his chair. "Could you explain that to me again?"

Joey squiggled and squirmed to get more comfortable in his father's lap. "Anna's teaching me to read bumpy books. I don't got it all right yet, but I like feeling the words while she tells me the story."

Forest's eyebrows met in the middle of his forehead.

Anna rose, raced over and knelt in front of him, giving him the small stack of books from her most recent Seedlings order. She placed them in his hands. "You have to let go and enjoy the books the same way you enjoy Joey's baseball-beeper." Her hands fluttered to rest on his knees. "Besides, you can't expect to think of everything yourself."

He covered her hands with his. "Thank you."

The connection crackled between them, until she wanted to crawl up in his lap and kiss him until they both couldn't think, much less talk, but Joey was in the room. And yeah, when it came to her shifting feelings for this man, she was a bit of a coward.

Anna slid her hands free, standing. "Well then, I guess I'll leave you two to your supper."

"Anna, do you want to—"

"I'll see you tomorrow." She cut short his invitation to join them before she caved and accepted. It would be too easy to let herself become a part of their evening routine and then be crushed when he found her unconventional ways unsuitable for a lawyer's wife—much less the mother of his child.

Unwilling to end this time with Anna and not sure why, Forest slid Joey off his lap and picked up her backpack for her. "Don't forget your bag."

He tried to close the bag, but the zipper kept hitching on something. By the time he caught up to her on the porch, he had figured out the problem. He pulled out a crumpled piece of paper that was part of a stack of letters held by a clip. He took them out to straighten the top paper.

Across from him, Anna froze.

It was a letter to the editor about saving the park, with copies to be sent to everyone from the governor to the garden committee. The letter bordered on libel, and violated their agreement for Anna to lie low.

How odd that he felt more betrayed than mad, Forest thought.

He passed her the backpack and her letters. "What an interesting definition you have of lying low."

She took the items solemnly. "People in this town express their displeasure about the part right and left, but no one else seems interested in doing anything about the situation."

Forest cocked his head. "How can you be so sure?"

"I watch. I listen."

"But you don't know all that's going on. Your father has a pal in the House of Representatives who owes him a favor. We've been working toward an injunction for over a week now."

Her features froze. "It would have been nice if you'd told me."

"The last thing your father wanted was you handcuffing yourself to the man's waiting-room sofa."

Her fists were clenched, her eyes wounded. "That's not only unfair, it's hurtful. I may not do things your way, but I am an intelligent adult."

She was right, and just like her father with Mrs. LaRoche and the congressman, he'd gone behind her back without asking for her input. He was just as guilty as her old man, whom he'd condemned a few hours earlier. "Wait, Anna, I'm sorry."

She backed away down the steps, toward her bike. "Sorry may not be enough if that's really how you feel about me."

He didn't want to let her go, ever. But what about her penchant for protesting? Would it increase over the years? Aside from giving him an ulcer, what kind of example would it set for Joey and any other children he and Anna might have together?

Other children. An impish little girl with freckles, red pigtails and stars in her innocent green eyes. The image was so distracting he almost walked into a ditch.

Not that Anna would agree to make babies with him anyway. She was looking at him as if he'd locked up Santa Claus on Christmas Eve.

Damn. There had to be some way to convince her to lighten up on the protesting, because he couldn't imagine letting her walk away from him. Or rather pedal away.

She climbed onto her bike and raced down the sidewalk before he could blink. Even if her views differed from his, he'd always loved the way she—

Loved? Hell, yes! He loved *her.*

Forest rested his forehead against a porch post. How was he ever going to win her back now? She would probably slam the door in his face.

Turning to go inside, he noticed she'd left some of her books behind, which gave him a perfect excuse to show up on her doorstep.

Somehow that seemed a little too obvious, and she had said the books were for Joey. Forest needed something big to snag her attention. His hand gripped her purse, the spare set of handcuffs poking the canvas.

Inspiration hit. He had a pretty good idea how to make sure she listened. "Hang on, Joey. We've got a few errands to run."

And he knew exactly where to go for mentorship.

CHAPTER
∘⌐ SEVEN ⌐∘

T he next morning, Anna stuffed her backpack full of
the supplies she needed for the nature-walk activities
she had planned for Joey—presuming Forest still let
her in the house after their argument.

After stomping around her cottage for an hour, then tossing
and turning half the night, she'd finally called her father. He'd
surprised her by simply including her in the endeavor to appeal
to his congressman friend. Pop asked her to stop by the park
on her way to Forest's home this morning and snap some
photos to go along with the paperwork he would be sending
up to his friend in the House.

She tucked her digital camera into her backpack and zipped

it closed before heading out. Pedaling over, she envisioned the different angles that would best show off the park's beauty and community appeal. She even considered moving benches around. Or what if she had time to add some of the equipment Forest had in his backyard?

Forest's backyard.

A vision began to form in her mind of a whole different park altogether——or rather a section of the park devoted to children with special needs.

Her excitement level rose as she envisioned a summer camp run in partnership with the library. It would offer activities for special-needs children that would give them the opportunity to stretch their legs, minds and emotional wings. Now, wouldn't that put little Oscoda on the map faster than any strip club?

Of course, the cool, collected Forest would be the best front man for her plan. They would be working together, combining their individual strengths. Just as they'd worked together to give Joey everything he needed. Why couldn't she have thought of that before?

Partnership. Passion. And love. The perfect blend.

After the way she'd dashed out yesterday, she had some apologizing to do. She thought about the photos she was going to take for her dad.

Working with Forest and her father. How funny. It was something she would never have considered less that two weeks ago. But then without Forest's influence, she would never have been open-minded enough to envision this park idea at all. What an amazing man.

Her heart filled with a love for him bigger than Lake Huron. So why had she run from him last night? Time to start taking some risks in her personal life as well as her professional life. Starting today—after she finished these photos for Pop.

Anna fished around inside her backpack and pulled out the digital. She aimed, focused, took one shot after another, figuring she could weed through the pictures and choose the best later. She would definitely have to stop by again this afternoon with Joey and snap more photos when the park was full of people. She wondered why Pop had insisted she come now, when it was so darn chilly the mist hadn't even burned off the lake yet. A couple of joggers circled the perimeter. A lone man sat parked on the bench reading his newspaper.

Well, she could at least take some pictures of him to show the diversity of people who enjoyed the park. And it did make a romantic tableau—a handsome man, the Great Lake stretching out beyond him.

Handsome?

Her mind snagged on the shape of his head, the color and texture of his hair. It couldn't be. She moved closer.

It was.

Deep breath. She inched nearer as the park slowly came alive with morning activity. A dog walker headed for the lake. Three mothers appeared, pushing strollers. Anna stopped in front of the man just as he folded his paper and draped it over his arm.

"Hi, Forest," she said, her voice a breathless whisper. She glanced around. People were out for a stroll or a bike ride. "Where's Joey?"

"I have a friend watching him while I came looking for you." His wary blue eyes glittered behind his glasses.

She'd do anything to erase that wariness. "You were? I was just about to come over to your place so we could talk."

"Good." A lock of hair slid free and brushed the top of his glasses. "What did you want to tell me?"

"Not here," Anna said. "Too many people, and this is kind of private."

He clasped her hand in his and tugged her over beside him. "What's wrong with a little audience now and then?"

Could that really be her reserved attorney talking?

Snap. Forest clicked a handcuff around her wrist.

Anna stood frozen with shock.

Snap. He closed the other around his wrist until they sat side by side, the chain looped through a bar on the same park bench where she'd staged her protest.

"Forest!" Had he gone nuts? She tugged. "Forest! Unlock us. Stand up!"

"Nope."

"Have you lost your mind?"

"Nope." Her uptight lawyer had never looked more at ease. He was even grinning.

What did he find so amusing?

Clusters of people gathered around them. Forest's secretary, Kay, wandered over with a few of her friends from the garden club, and Shirley Rhodes and her friends waved from the beauty salon across the street, clutching their morning lattes from a nearby coffeehouse.

"Forest, you're really causing a scene here." Frantically, Anna looked left and right, expecting a police officer to appear. "Quit this! Now, before somebody calls the cops. You're a lawyer. You can't afford to be arrested."

He didn't budge.

"Be reasonable! What do you think you're doing?"

Forest gripped her hand in his. "I'm protesting the way you walked away from me without giving us a fighting chance at working things out."

His words sunk in, and her knees folded. She wilted down beside him. "Oh!"

From behind a dilapidated visitors' center, her father stepped out with Trudy LaRoche, who held Joey by the hand. Edward Bonneau winked at Anna as he slung an arm around Trudy's shoulders. "Hello, Anna."

"Pop?"

"I love you, daughter dear." He smiled at her with an openness she hadn't seen since her mother was alive. "I just want you to be happy."

Anna smiled back, but she was beginning to understand how Alice had felt in Wonderland. Just what was going on here?

She looked around at the familiar faces and realized their presence here couldn't be simply coincidence. Had her father and Trudy been matchmaking?

Anna turned to Forest. "You planned this, for me?"

He nudged his glasses. "You of all people should know you can't have a protest without an audience. So I'm making my statement."

Something warm and wonderful unfurled inside her, a renewed flicker of hope. "You are?"

"You bet."

While she told herself it shouldn't matter after he'd made such a grand gesture, she couldn't help asking, "What about last night and your disapproval of my protest methods?"

His thumb caressed the inside of her wrist. "I started thinking about that after you left, and letters are a perfectly acceptable means of protest. You were right. I was just... uh..."

"Hurt?" she dared ask.

"I thought you would have come to me for help with something like that. But then I realized your father and I should have trusted you as well with our congressional plans. My only excuse is that I can't think when you're around."

She understood completely, since she couldn't form coherent thoughts around him most of the time either. "You do say the sweetest things, Counselor."

"No, I don't, but I'm going to try, because I happen to think we've got something pretty special going between us."

Could this be real? "I agree. I want to work with you, and today I had a great idea for this special park. I want us to work *with* each other."

"You do?"

She gestured to the crowd and tapped the cuffs. "You sure know how to get your point across."

He smiled that wonderful lopsided grin. "All in the name of love."

Anna sure hoped she'd heard right. Just in case, she needed to hear him say it again. "For love?"

"For love. Isn't that what it's all about?" Forest linked hands with her. "Anna, marry me. Not because you're great with Joey or because we're attracted to each..." He paused, glancing at the crowd gathering around them. "Marry me because I love you."

Anna cupped his face with her free hand. "Those words beat a bouquet of flowers hands down, Counselor."

"Wait, I'm not finished yet." Forest stood, dragging Anna up with him. He turned to Trudy LaRoche and the judge. "Did you hear that? I love her! Did everyone hear me? I love this incredible woman. And if she'll have me, I'll even buy a tandem bike—with helmets."

Applause broke out, echoing up through the trees speckled with autumn leaves.

Forest rested his forehead against Anna's, creating a bubble of privacy in the overpopulated park. "Let's plant our own seedlings to grow into trees that we can sit under for picnics with our children and grandchildren. What do you say? Will you marry me?"

"Yes." She whispered the word, hearing it echo in her heart. "Yes to you, Forest, and yes to Joey."

She extended her arms for Joey, the precious child who'd really brought them together. "Joey?"

"Anna!" he shouted, arms outstretched as he launched himself toward Forest and her.

"She said yes!" Mrs. LaRoche squealed.

A rousing cheer filled the park. Anna eased away with a laugh just in time to see her father kiss Trudy LaRoche. She hoped he was feeling as happy as she was.

Shifting her attention back to Forest, Anna caressed his face. "I love you so much."

He gave an exaggerated sigh. "Thank heaven. Now I can cancel the circus that was going to perform on your lawn if you'd said no."

"Well, in case you're in doubt, my answer is yes! Forever." What a perfect team they would make.

Forest nuzzled her ear. "Are you ready for a family breakfast picnic? I've packed all your favorites."

She rattled the cuffs. "Shouldn't we ditch these first?"

"Good idea," Forest agreed. "Hey, Judge, pass me the keys."

Anna's father searched one pocket, then another. "Uh, hold on, son. I'm sure they're here somewhere."

No keys?

Forest cradled Anna against him. "No rush." He gazed down into her eyes. "This is exactly where I'd like to be for the rest of my life."

Dear Reader,

I am honored to have had the chance to work with Harlequin's More Than Words program, and I appreciate the serendipity to have been paired with the Seedlings Braille Books for Children project in particular, as it's a subject very near to my heart. My youngest sister, Beth, suffered an accident at the age of six that left her partially blind. Due to therapy in conjunction with one of her many surgeries, she spent a summer completely blind. I was her "seeing-eye sister," helping her find her way around the world, reading to her for hours on end.

So you can imagine my heart swelled all the more when I heard from Seedlings founder Debra Bonde about the amazing tribute she has built in honor of her daughter Anna. After Anna died in an accident on her way to New Orleans to tutor disadvantaged children, Debra began the Book Angel Project, which donates at least ten free Seedlings books a week. I knew right away I would want to name the heroine in my story after this awesome young woman.

To learn more about Seedlings Braille Books for Children, check out their fabulous Web site, www.seedlings.org. I hope you will consider purchasing a book to donate to your local library or making a donation directly to Seedlings to help fund their efforts to bring the gift of words to all. The quote on their Web site says it best: "By the touch of a finger behold the world."

Many thanks,

[signature]

http://catherinemann.com/